PORTNOY'S COMPLAINT

PORTNOY'S COMPLAINT

PHILIP ROTH

RANDOM HOUSE · NEW YORK

Portnoy's Complaint (pôrt′-noiz kəm-plänt′) *n.* [after Alexander Portnoy (1933-   )] A disorder in which strongly-felt ethical and altruistic impulses are perpetually warring with extreme sexual longings, often of a perverse nature. Spielvogel says: 'Acts of exhibitionism, voyeurism, fetishism, autoeroticism and oral coitus are plentiful; as a consequence of the patient's "morality," however, neither fantasy nor act issues in genuine sexual gratification, but rather in overriding feelings of shame and the dread of retribution, particularly in the form of castration.' (Spielvogel, O. "The Puzzled Penis," *Internationale Zeitschrift für Psychoanalyse*, Vol. XXIV p. 909.) It is believed by Spielvogel that many of the symptoms can be traced to the bonds obtaining in the mother-child relationship.

PORTNOY'S COMPLAINT

THE MOST UNFORGETTABLE
CHARACTER I'VE MET

She was so deeply imbedded in my consciousness that
for the first year of school I seem to have believed that
each of my teachers was my mother in disguise. As soon
as the last bell had sounded, I would rush off for home,
wondering as I ran if I could possibly make it to our
apartment before she had succeeded in transforming herself. Invariably she was already in the kitchen by the time
I arrived, and setting out my milk and cookies. Instead
of causing me to give up my delusions, however, the feat
merely intensified my respect for her powers. And then it
was always a relief not to have caught her between in-

carnations anyway—even if I never stopped trying; I knew that my father and sister were innocent of my mother's real nature, and the burden of betrayal that I imagined would fall to me if I ever came upon her unawares was more than I wanted to bear at the age of five. I think I even feared that I might have to be done away with were I to catch sight of her flying in from school through the bedroom window, or making herself emerge, limb by limb, out of an invisible state and into her apron.

Of course, when she asked me to tell her all about my day at kindergarten, I did so scrupulously. I didn't pretend to understand all the implications of her ubiquity, but that it had to do with finding out the kind of little boy I was when I thought she wasn't around—that was indisputable. One consequence of this fantasy, which survived (in this particular form) into the first grade, was that seeing as I had no choice, I became honest.

Ah, and brilliant. Of my sallow, overweight older sister, my mother would say (in Hannah's presence, of course: honesty was her policy too), "The child is no genius, but then we don't ask the impossible. God bless her, she works hard, she applies herself to her limits, and so whatever she gets is all right." Of me, the heir to her long Egyptian nose and clever babbling mouth, of me my mother would say, with characteristic restraint, "This *bonditt?* He doesn't even have to open a book—'A' in everything. Albert Einstein the Second!"

And how did my father take all this? He drank—of course, not whiskey like a *goy,* but mineral oil and milk of magnesia; and chewed on Ex-Lax; and ate All-Bran morning and night; and downed mixed dried fruits by the pound bag. He suffered—did he suffer!—from constipation. Her ubiquity and his constipation, my mother flying in through the bedroom window, my father reading the evening paper with a suppository up his ass . . . these, Doctor, are the earliest impressions I have of my parents, of their attributes and secrets. He used to brew dried senna leaves in a saucepan, and that, along with the suppository melting invisibly in his rectum, comprised *his* witchcraft: brewing those veiny green leaves, stirring with a spoon the evil-smelling liquid, then carefully pouring it into a strainer, and hence into his blockaded body, through that weary and afflicted expression on his face. And then hunched silently above the empty glass, as though listening for distant thunder, he awaits the miracle . . . As a little boy I sometimes sat in the kitchen and waited with him. But the miracle never came, not at least as we imagined and prayed it would, as a lifting of the sentence, a total deliverance from the plague. I remember that when they announced over the radio the explosion of the first atom bomb, he said aloud, "Maybe that would do the job." But all catharses were in vain for that man: his *kishkas* were gripped by the iron hand of outrage and frustration. Among his other misfortunes, I was his wife's favorite.

To make life harder, he loved me himself. He too saw in me the family's opportunity to be "as good as anybody," our chance to win honor and respect—though when I was small the way he chose to talk of his ambitions for me was mostly in terms of money. "Don't be dumb like your father," he would say, joking with the little boy on his lap, "don't marry beautiful, don't marry love—marry rich." No, no, he didn't like being looked down upon one bit. Like a dog he worked—only for a future that he wasn't slated to have. Nobody ever really gave him satisfaction, return commensurate with goods delivered—not my mother, not me, not even my loving sister, whose husband he still considers a Communist (though he is a partner today in a profitable soft-drink business, and owns his own home in West Orange). And surely not that billion-dollar Protestant outfit (or "institution," as they prefer to think of themselves) by whom he was exploited to the full. "The Most Benevolent Financial Institution in America" I remember my father announcing, when he took me for the first time to see his little square area of desk and chair in the vast offices of Boston & Northeastern Life. Yes, before his son he spoke with pride of "The Company"; no sense demeaning himself by knocking them in public—after all, they had paid him a wage during the Depression; they gave him stationery with his own name printed beneath a picture of the *Mayflower*, their insignia (and by extension his, ha ha); and every spring, in the fullness of their benevolence, they sent him and my mother for a hotsy-totsy free weekend in Atlantic City, to a fancy *goyische* hotel no less, there (along with all the other insurance agents in the Middle Atlantic states who had exceeded the A.E.S., their annual expectation of sales) to be intimidated by the desk clerk, the waiter, the bellboy, not to mention the puzzled paying guests.

Also, he believed passionately in what he was selling,

yet another source of anguish and drain upon his energies. He wasn't just saving his own soul when he donned his coat and hat after dinner and went out again to resume his work—no, it was also to save some poor son of a bitch on the brink of letting his insurance policy lapse, and thus endangering his family's security "in the event of a rainy day." "Alex," he used to explain to me, "a man has got to have an umbrella for a rainy day. You don't leave a wife and a child out in the rain without an umbrella!" And though to me, at five and six years of age, what he said made perfect, even moving, sense, that apparently was not always the reception his rainy-day speech received from the callow Poles, and violent Irishmen, and illiterate Negroes who lived in the impoverished districts that had been given him to canvass by The Most Benevolent Financial Institution in America.

They laughed at him, down in the slums. They didn't listen. They heard him knock, and throwing their empties against the door, called out, "Go away, nobody home." They set their dogs to sink their teeth into his persistent Jewish ass. And still, over the years, he managed to accumulate from The Company enough plaques and scrolls and medals honoring his salesmanship to cover an entire wall of the long windowless hallway where our Passover dishes were stored in cartons and our "Oriental" rugs lay mummified in their thick wrappings of tar paper over the summer. If he squeezed blood from a stone, wouldn't The Company reward him with a miracle of its own? Might not "The President" up in "The Home Office" get wind of his accomplishment and turn him overnight from an agent at five thousand a year to a district manager at fifteen? But where they had him they kept him. Who else would work such barren territory with such incredible results? Moreover, there had not been a Jewish manager in the entire history of Boston & Northeastern (Not Quite Our Class, Dear, as they used to say on the *Mayflower*), and my father, with his eighth-grade education, wasn't exactly suited to be the Jackie Robinson of the insurance business.

N. Everett Lindabury, Boston & Northeastern's president, had his picture hanging in our hallway. The framed photograph had been awarded to my father after he had sold his first million dollars' worth of insurance, or maybe that's what came after you hit the ten-million mark. "Mr. Lindabury," "The Home Office" . . . my father made it sound to me like Roosevelt in the White House in Washington . . . and all the while how he hated their guts, Lindabury's particularly, with his corn-silk hair and his crisp New England speech, the sons in Harvard College and the daughters in finishing school, oh the whole pack of them up there in Massachusetts, *shkotzim* fox-hunting! playing polo! (so I heard him one night, bellowing behind his bedroom door)—and thus keeping him, you see, from being a hero in the eyes of his wife and children. What wrath! What fury! And there was really no one to unleash it on—except himself. "Why can't I move my bowels—I'm up to my ass in prunes! Why do I have these headaches! Where are my glasses! Who took my hat!"

In that ferocious and self-annihilating way in which

so many Jewish men of his generation served their families, my father served my mother, my sister Hannah, but particularly me. Where he had been imprisoned, I would fly: that was his dream. Mine was its corollary: in my liberation would be his—from ignorance, from exploitation, from anonymity. To this day our destinies remain scrambled together in my imagination, and there are still too many times when, upon reading in some book a passage that impresses me with its logic or its wisdom, instantly, involuntarily, I think, "If only he could read *this*. Yes! Read, and understand—!" Still hoping, you see, still if-onlying, at the age of thirty-three . . . Back in my freshman year of college, when I was even more the son struggling to make the father understand—back when it seemed that it was either his understanding or his life—I remember that I tore the subscription blank out of one of those intellectual journals I had myself just begun to discover in the college library, filled in his name and our home address, and sent off an anonymous gift subscription. But when I came sullenly home at Christmastime to visit and condemn, the *Partisan Review* was nowhere to be found. *Collier's Hygeia, Look,* but where was his *Partisan Review?* Thrown out unopened—I thought in my arrogance and heartbreak—discarded unread, considered *junk*-mail by this schmuck, this moron, this Philistine father of mine!

I remember—to go back even further in this history of disenchantment—I remember one Sunday morning pitching a baseball at my father, and then waiting in vain to see it go flying off, high above my head. I am eight, and for my birthday have received my first mitt and hardball, and a regulation bat that I haven't even the strength to swing all the way around. My father has been out since early morning in his hat, coat, bow tie, and black shoes, carrying under his arm the massive black collection book that tells who owes Mr. Lindabury how much. He descends into the colored neighborhood each and every Sunday morning because, as he tells me, that is the best time to catch those unwilling to fork over the ten or fifteen measly cents necessary to meet their weekly premium payments. He lurks about where the husbands sit out in the sunshine, trying to extract a few thin dimes from them before they have drunk themselves senseless on their bottles of "Morgan Davis" wine; he emerges from alleyways like a shot to catch between home and church the pious cleaning ladies, who are off in other people's houses during the daylight hours of the week, and in hiding from him on weekday nights. "Uh–oh," someone cries, "Mr. Insurance Man here!" and even the children run for cover—the *children*, he says in disgust, so tell me, what hope is there for these niggers' ever improving their lot? How will they ever lift themselves if they ain't even able to grasp the importance of life insurance? Don't they give a single crap for the loved ones they leave behind? Because "they's all" going to die too, you know—"oh," he says angrily, "'they sho' is!'" Please, what kind of man is it, who can think to leave children out in the rain without even a decent umbrella for protection!

We are on the big dirt field back of my school. He sets

his collection book on the ground, and steps up to the plate in his coat and his brown fedora. He wears square steel-rimmed spectacles, and his hair (which now I wear) is a wild bush the color and texture of steel wool; and those teeth, which sit all night long in a glass in the bathroom smiling at the toilet bowl, now smile out at me, his beloved, his flesh and his blood, the little boy upon whose head no rain shall ever fall. "Okay, Big Shot Ballplayer," he says, and grasps my new regulation bat somewhere near the middle—and to my astonishment, with his left hand where his right hand should be. I am suddenly overcome with such sadness: I want to tell him, *Hey, your hands are wrong,* but am unable to, for fear I might begin to cry—or he might! "Come on, Big Shot, throw the ball," he calls, and so I do—and of course discover that on top of all the other things I am just beginning to suspect about my father, he isn't "King Kong" Charlie Keller either.

Some umbrella.

It was my mother who could accomplish anything, who herself had to admit that it might even be that she was actually too good. And could a small child with my intelligence, with my powers of observation, doubt that this was so? She could make jello, for instance, with sliced peaches *hanging* in it, peaches just *suspended* there, in defiance of the law of gravity. She could bake a cake that tasted like a banana. Weeping, suffering, she grated her own horseradish rather than buy the *pishachs* they sold in a bottle at the delicatessen. She watched the butcher, as

she put it, "like a hawk," to be certain that he did not
forget to put her chopped meat through the kosher
grinder. She would telephone all the other women in the
building drying clothes on the back lines—called even the
divorced *goy* on the top floor one magnanimous day—to
tell them rush, take in the laundry, a drop of rain had
fallen on our windowpane. What radar on that woman!
And this is *before* radar! The energy on her! The thor-
oughness! For mistakes she checked my sums; for holes,
my socks; for dirt, my nails, my neck, every seam and
crease of my body. She even dredges the furthest recesses
of my ears by pouring cold peroxide into my head. It
tingles and pops like an earful of ginger ale, and brings to
the surface, in bits and pieces, the hidden stores of yellow wax, which can apparently endanger a person's hearing. A medical procedure like this (crackpot though it
may be) takes time, of course; it takes effort, to be sure—
but where health and cleanliness are concerned, germs
and bodily secretions, she will not spare herself and sacrifice others. She lights candles for the dead—others invariably forget, she religiously remembers, and without
even the aid of a notation on the calendar. Devotion is
just in her blood. She seems to be the only one, she says,
who when she goes to the cemetery has "the common
sense," "the ordinary common decency," to clear the
weeds from the graves of our relatives. The first bright
day of spring, and she has mothproofed everything wool
in the house, rolled and bound the rugs, and dragged
them off to my father's trophy room. She is never
ashamed of her house: a stranger could walk in and open

any closet, any drawer, and she would have nothing to
be ashamed of. You could even eat off her bathroom floor,
if that should ever become necessary. When she loses at
mah-jongg she takes it like a sport, not-like-the-others-
whose-names-she-could-mention-but-she-won't-not-even-
Tilly-Hochman-it's-too-petty-to-even-talk-about-let's-just-
forget-she-even-brought-it-up. She sews, she knits, she
darns—she irons better even than the *schvartze*, to whom,
of all her friends who each possess a piece of this grin-
ning childish black old lady's hide, she alone is good.
"I'm the only one who's good to her. I'm the only one
who gives her a whole can of tuna for lunch, and I'm
not talking *dreck*, either. I'm talking Chicken of the Sea,
Alex. I'm sorry, I can't be a stingy person. Excuse me,
but I can't live like that, even if it is 2 for 49. Esther
Wasserberg leaves twenty-five cents in nickels around the
house when Dorothy comes, and counts up afterwards to
see it's all there. Maybe I'm too good," she whispers to
me, meanwhile running scalding water over the dish from
which the cleaning lady has just eaten her lunch, alone
like a leper, "but I couldn't do a thing like that." Once
Dorothy chanced to come back into the kitchen while
my mother was still standing over the faucet marked H,
sending torrents down upon the knife and fork that had
passed between the *schvartze's* thick pink lips. "Oh, you
know how hard it is to get mayonnaise off silverware
these days, Dorothy," says my nimble-tongued mother
—and thus, she tells me later, by her quick thinking, has
managed to spare the colored woman's feelings.

When I am bad I am locked out of the apartment. I

stand at the door hammering and hammering until I
swear I will turn over a new leaf. But what is it I have
done? I shine my shoes every evening on a sheet of last
night's newspaper laid carefully over the linoleum; afterward I never fail to turn securely the lid on the tin of
polish, and to return all the equipment to where it belongs. I roll the toothpaste tube from the bottom, I brush
my teeth in circles and never up and down, I say "Thank
you," I say "You're welcome," I say "I beg your pardon,"
and "May I." When Hannah is ill or out before supper
with her blue tin can collecting for the Jewish National
Fund, I voluntarily and out of my turn set the table, remembering always knife and spoon on the right, fork on
the left, and napkin to the left of the fork and folded
into a triangle. I would never eat *milchiks* off a *flaishe-
digeh* dish, never, never, never. Nonetheless, there is a
year or so in my life when not a month goes by that I
don't do something so inexcusable that I am told to pack
a bag and leave. But what could it possibly be? Mother,
it's me, the little boy who spends whole nights before
school begins beautifully lettering in Old English script
the names of his subjects on his colored course dividers,
who patiently fastens reinforcements to a term's worth of
three-ringed paper, lined and unlined both. I carry a
comb and a clean hankie; never do my knicker stockings
drag at my shoes, I see to that; my homework is com-
pleted weeks in advance of the assignment—let's face it,
Ma, I am the smartest and neatest little boy in the history
of my school! Teachers (as you know, as they have *told*
you) go home happy to their husbands because of me.

So what is it I have done? Will someone with the answer to that question please stand up! I am so awful she will not have me in her house *a minute longer*. When I once called my sister a cocky-doody, my mouth was immediately washed with a cake of brown laundry soap; this I understand. But banishment? What can I possibly have done!

Because she is good she will pack a lunch for me to take along, but then out I go, in my coat and my galoshes, and what happens is not her business.

Okay, I say, if that's how you feel! (For I have the taste for melodrama too—I am not in this family for nothing.) I don't need a bag of lunch! I don't need anything!

I don't love you any more, not a little boy who behaves like you do. I'll live alone here with Daddy and Hannah, says my mother (a master really at phrasing things just the right way to kill you). Hannah can set up the mah-jongg tiles for the ladies on Tuesday night. We won't be needing you any more.

Who cares! And out the door I go, into the long dim hallway. Who cares! I will sell newspapers on the streets in my bare feet. I will ride where I want on freight cars and sleep in open fields, I think—and then it is enough for me to see the empty milk bottles standing by our welcome mat, for the immensity of all I have lost to come breaking over my head. "I hate you!" I holler, kicking a galosh at the door; "you stink!" To this filth, to this heresy booming through the corridors of the apartment building where she is vying with twenty other Jewish women to be the patron saint of self-sacrifice, my mother has no choice but to throw the double-lock on our door. This is when I start to hammer to be let in. I drop to the doormat to beg forgiveness for my sin (which is what again?) and promise her nothing but perfection for the rest of our lives, which at that time I believe will be endless.

Then there are the nights I will not eat. My sister, who is four years my senior, assures me that what I remember is fact: I would refuse to eat, and my mother would find herself unable to submit to such willfulness—and such idiocy. And unable to for my own good. She is only asking me to do something *for my own good*—and still I say *no*? Wouldn't she give me the food out of her own mouth, don't I know that by now?

But I don't want the food from her mouth. I don't even want the food from my plate—that's the point.

Please! a child with my potential! my accomplishments! my future!—all the gifts God has lavished upon me, of beauty, of brains, am I to be allowed to think I can just starve myself to death for no good reason in the world?

Do I want people to look down on a skinny little boy all my life, or to look up to a man?

Do I want to be pushed around and made fun of, do I want to be skin and bones that people can knock over with a sneeze, or do I want to command respect?

Which do I want to be when I grow up, weak or strong, a success or a failure, a man or a mouse?

I just don't want to eat, I answer.

So my mother sits down in a chair beside me with a long bread knife in her hand. It is made of stainless steel, and has little sawlike teeth. Which do I want to be, weak or strong, a man or a mouse?

Doctor, *why*, why oh why oh why oh why does a mother pull a knife on her own son? I am six, seven years old, how do I know she really wouldn't use it? What am I supposed to do, try bluffing her out, at seven? I have no complicated sense of strategy, for Christ's sake—I probably don't even weigh sixty pounds yet! Someone waves a knife in my direction, I believe there is an intention lurking somewhere to draw my blood! Only *why?* What can she possibly be thinking *in her brain?* How crazy can she possibly be? Suppose she had let me win—what would have been lost? Why a *knife*, why the threat of *murder*, why is such total and annihilating victory necessary—when only the day before she set down her iron on the ironing board and *applauded* as I stormed around the kitchen rehearsing my role as Christopher Columbus in the third-grade production of *Land Ho!* I am the star actor of my class, they cannot put a play on without me. Oh, once they tried, when I had my bronchitis, but my teacher later confided in my mother that it had been decidedly second-rate. Oh *how*, how can she spend such glorious afternoons in that kitchen, polishing silver, chopping liver, threading new elastic in the waistband of my little jockey shorts—and feeding me all the while my cues from the mimeographed script, playing Queen Isabella to my Columbus, Betsy Ross to my Washington, Mrs. Pasteur to my Louis—how can she rise with me on the crest of my genius during those dusky beautiful hours after school,

and then at night, because I will not eat some string beans
and a baked potato, point a bread knife at my heart?
   And why doesn't my father stop her?

WHACKING OFF

Then came adolescence—half my waking life spent
locked behind the bathroom door, firing my wad down
the toilet bowl, or into the soiled clothes in the laundry
hamper, or *splat,* up against the medicine-chest mirror,
before which I stood in my dropped drawers so I could
see how it looked coming out. Or else I was doubled over
my flying fist, eyes pressed closed but mouth wide open,
to take that sticky sauce of buttermilk and Clorox on my
own tongue and teeth—though not infrequently, in my
blindness and ecstasy, I got it all in the pompadour, like a
blast of Wildroot Cream Oil. Through a world of matted
handkerchiefs and crumpled Kleenex and stained pajamas, I moved my raw and swollen penis, perpetually in
dread that my loathsomeness would be discovered by
someone stealing upon me just as I was in the frenzy of
dropping my load. Nevertheless, I was wholly incapable
of keeping my paws from my dong once it started the
climb up my belly. In the middle of a class I would raise
a hand to be excused, rush down the corridor to the lava-

tory, and with ten or fifteen savage strokes, beat off standing up into a urinal. At the Saturday afternoon movie I would leave my friends to go off to the candy machine—and wind up in a distant balcony seat, squirting my seed into the empty wrapper from a Mounds bar. On an outing of our family association, I once cored an apple, saw to my astonishment (and with the aid of my obsession) what it looked like, and ran off into the woods to fall upon the orifice of the fruit, pretending that the cool and mealy hole was actually between the legs of that mythical being who always called me Big Boy when she pleaded for what no girl in all recorded history had ever had. "Oh shove it in me, Big Boy," cried the cored apple that I banged silly on that picnic. "Big Boy, Big Boy, oh give me all you've got," begged the empty milk bottle that I kept hidden in our storage bin in the basement, to drive wild after school with my vaselined upright. "Come, Big Boy, come," screamed the maddened piece of liver that, in my own insanity, I bought one afternoon at a butcher shop and, believe it or not, violated behind a billboard on the way to a bar mitzvah lesson.

It was at the end of my freshman year of high school—and freshman year of masturbating—that I discovered on the underside of my penis, just where the shaft meets the head, a little discolored dot that has since been diagnosed as a freckle. Cancer. I had given myself *cancer*. All that pulling and tugging at my own flesh, all that friction, had given me an incurable disease. And not yet fourteen! In bed at night the tears rolled from my eyes. "No!" I sobbed. "I don't want to die! Please—no!" But then, because I would very shortly be a corpse anyway, I went ahead as usual and jerked off into my sock. I had taken to carrying the dirty socks into bed with me at night so as to be able to use one as a receptacle upon retiring, and the other upon awakening.

If only I could cut down to one hand-job a day, or hold the line at two, or even three! But with the prospect of oblivion before me, I actually began to set new records for myself. Before meals. After meals. *During* meals. Jumping up from the dinner table, I tragically clutch at my belly—diarrhea! I cry, I have been stricken with diar-rhea!—and once behind the locked bathroom door, slip over my head a pair of underpants that I have stolen from my sister's dresser and carry rolled in a handkerchief in my pocket. So galvanic is the effect of cotton panties against my mouth—so galvanic is the *word* "panties"—that the trajectory of my ejaculation reaches startling new heights: leaving my joint like a rocket it makes right for the light bulb overhead, where to my wonderment and horror, it hits and it hangs. Wildly in the first moment I cover my head, expecting an explosion of glass, a burst of flames—disaster, you see, is never far from my mind. Then quietly as I can I climb the radiator and remove the sizzling gob with a wad of toilet paper. I begin a scrupulous search of the shower curtain, the tub, the tile floor, the four toothbrushes—God forbid!—and just as I am about to unlock the door, imagining I have covered my tracks, my heart lurches at the sight of what is hanging like snot to the toe of my shoe. I am the Raskolnikov of jerking off—the sticky evidence is everywhere! Is it on

my cuffs too? in my *hair?* my *ear?* All this I wonder even
as I come back to the kitchen table, scowling and cranky,
to grumble self-righteously at my father when he opens
his mouth full of red jello and says, "I don't understand
what you have to lock the door about. That to me is beyond comprehension. What is this, a home or a Grand
Central station?" ". . . privacy . . . a human being . . .
around here *never*," I reply, then push aside my dessert
to scream, "I don't feel well—*will everybody leave me
alone?*"

After dessert—which I finish because I happen to like
jello, even if I detest them—after dessert I am back in
the bathroom again. I burrow through the week's laundry
until I uncover one of my sister's soiled brassieres. I string
one shoulder strap over the knob of the bathroom door
and the other on the knob of the linen closet: a scarecrow
to bring on more dreams. "Oh beat it, Big Boy, beat it to
a red-hot pulp—" so I am being urged by the little cups
of Hannah's brassiere, when a rolled-up newspaper smacks
at the door. And sends me and my handful an inch off the
toilet seat. "—Come on, give somebody else a crack at
that bowl, will you?" my father says. "I haven't moved my
bowels in a week."

I recover my equilibrium, as is my talent, with a burst
of hurt feelings. "I have a terrible case of diarrhea!
Doesn't that mean anything to anyone in this house?"—in
the meantime resuming the stroke, indeed quickening the
tempo as my cancerous organ miraculously begins to
quiver again from the inside out.

Then Hannah's brassiere *begins to move.* To swing to

and fro! I veil my eyes, and behold!—Lenore Lapidus! who has the biggest pair in my class, running for the bus after school, her great untouchable load shifting weightily inside her blouse, oh I urge them up from their cups, and over, LENORE LAPIDUS'S ACTUAL TITS, and realize in the same split second that my mother is vigorously shaking the doorknob. Of the door I have finally forgotten to lock! I knew it would happen one day! *Caught!* As good as *dead!*

"Open up, Alex. I want you to open up this instant."

It's locked, I'm *not* caught! And I see from what's alive in my hand that I'm not quite dead yet either. Beat on then! beat on! "Lick me, Big Boy—lick me a good hot lick! I'm Lenore Lapidus's big fat red-hot brassiere!"

"Alex, I want an answer from you. Did you eat French fries after school? Is that why you're sick like this?"

"Nuhhh, nuhhh."

"Alex, are you in pain? Do you want me to call the doctor? Are you in pain, or aren't you? I want to know exactly where it hurts. *Answer me.*"

"Yuhh, yuhhh—"

"Alex, I don't want you to flush the toilet," says my mother sternly. "I want to see what you've done in there. I don't like the sound of this at all."

"And me," says my father, touched as he always was by my accomplishments—as much awe as envy—"I haven't moved my bowels in a week," just as I lurch from my perch on the toilet seat, and with the whimper of a whipped animal, deliver three drops of something barely viscous into the tiny piece of cloth where my flat-chested eighteen-year-old sister has laid her nipples, such as they are. It is my fourth orgasm of the day. When will I begin to come blood?

"Get in here, please, you," says my mother. "Why did you flush the toilet when I told you not to?"

"I forgot."

"What was in there that you were so fast to flush it?"

"Diarrhea."

"Was it mostly liquid or was it mostly poopie?"

"I don't look! I didn't look! Stop saying poopie to me— I'm in high school!"

"Oh, don't you shout at *me*, Alex. I'm not the one who gave you diarrhea, I assure you. If all you ate was what you were fed at home, you wouldn't be running to the bathroom fifty times a day. Hannah tells me what you're doing, so don't think I don't know."

She's missed the underpants! *I've been caught!* Oh, *let* me be dead! I'd just as soon!

"Yeah, what do I do . . . ?"

"You go to Harold's Hot Dog and *Chazerai* Palace after school and you eat French fries with Melvin Weiner. Don't you? Don't lie to me either. Do you or do you not stuff yourself with French fries and ketchup on Hawthorne Avenue after school? Jack, come in here, I want you to hear this," she calls to my father, now occupying the bathroom.

"Look, I'm trying to move my bowels," he replies. "Don't I have enough trouble as it is without people screaming at me when I'm trying to move my bowels?"

"You know what your son does after school, the *A*

student, who his own mother can't say poopie to any more, he's such a *grown-up?* What do you think your grown-up son does when nobody is watching him?"

"Can I please be left alone, please?" cries my father. "Can I have a little peace, please, so I can get something accomplished in here?"

"Just wait till your father hears what you do, in defiance of every health habit there could possibly be. Alex, answer me something. You're so smart, you know all the answers now, answer me this: how do you think Melvin Weiner gave himself colitis? Why has that child spent half his life in hospitals?"

"Because he eats *chazerai.*"

"Don't you dare make fun of me!"

"All right," I scream, "how *did* he get colitis?"

"Because he eats *chazerai!* But it's not a joke! Because to him a meal is an O Henry bar washed down by a bottle of Pepsi. Because his breakfast consists of, do you know what? The most important meal of the day—not according just to your mother, Alex, but according to the highest nutritionists—and do you know what that child eats?"

"A doughnut."

"A doughnut is right, Mr. Smart Guy, Mr. Adult. And *coffee.* Coffee and a doughnut, and on this a thirteen-year-old *pisher* with half a stomach is supposed to start a day. But you, thank God, have been brought up differently. You don't have a mother who gallivants all over town like some names I could name, from Bam's to Hahne's to Kresge's all day long. Alex, tell me, so it's not a mystery, or maybe I'm just stupid—only tell me, what are you trying to do, what are you trying to prove, that you should stuff yourself with such junk when you could come home to a poppyseed cookie and a nice glass of milk? I want the truth from you. I wouldn't tell your father," she says, her voice dropping significantly, "but I *must* have the truth from you." Pause. Also significant. "Is it just French fries, darling, or is it more? . . . Tell me, please, what other kind of garbage you're putting into your mouth so we can get to the bottom of this diarrhea! I want a straight answer from you, Alex. Are you eating hamburgers out? Answer me, please, is that why you flushed the toilet—was there hamburger in it?"

"I told you—I don't look in the bowl when I flush it! I'm not interested like you are in other people's poopie!"

"Oh, oh, oh—thirteen years old and the mouth on him! To someone who is asking a question about *his* health, *his* welfare!" The utter incomprehensibility of the situation causes her eyes to become heavy with tears. "Alex, why are you getting like this, give me some clue? Tell me please what horrible things we have done to you all our lives that this should be our reward?" I believe the question strikes her as original. I believe she considers the question unanswerable. And worse of all, so do I. What *have* they done for me all their lives, but sacrifice? Yet that this is precisely the horrible thing is beyond my understanding—and still, Doctor! To this day!

I brace myself now for the whispering. I can spot the whispering coming a mile away. We are about to discuss my father's headaches.

"Alex, he didn't have a headache on him today that he

could hardly see straight from it?" She checks, is he out of earshot? God forbid he should hear how critical his condition is, he might claim exaggeration. "He's not going next week for a test for a tumor?"

"He is?"

"'Bring him in,' the doctor said, 'I'm going to give him a test for a tumor.'"

Success. I am crying. There is no good reason for me to be crying, but in this household everybody tries to get a good cry in at least once a day. My father, you must understand—as doubtless you do: blackmailers account for a substantial part of the human community, and, I would imagine, of your clientele—my father has been "going" for this tumor test for nearly as long as I can remember. Why his head aches him all the time is, of course, because he is constipated all the time—why he is constipated is because ownership of his intestinal tract is in the hands of the firm of Worry, Fear & Frustration. It is true that a doctor once said to my mother that he would give her husband a test for a tumor—if that would make her happy, is I believe the way that he worded it; he suggested that it would be cheaper, however, and probably more effective for the man to invest in an enema bag. Yet, that I know all this to be so, does not make it any less heartbreaking to imagine my father's skull splitting open from a malignancy.

Yes, she has me where she wants me, and she knows it. I clean forget my own cancer in the grief that comes— comes now as it came then—when I think how much of life has always been (as he himself very accurately puts it) beyond his comprehension. And his grasp. No money, no schooling, no language, no learning, curiosity without culture, drive without opportunity, experience without wisdom . . . How easily his inadequacies can move me to tears. As easily as they move me to anger!

A person my father often held up to me as someone to emulate in life was the theatrical producer Billy Rose. Walter Winchell said that Billy Rose's knowledge of shorthand had led Bernard Baruch to hire him as a secretary—consequently my father plagued me throughout high school to enroll in the shorthand course. "Alex, where would Billy Rose be today without his shorthand? Nowhere! So why do you *fight* me?" Earlier it was the piano we battled over. For a man whose house was without a phonograph or a record, he was passionate on the subject of a musical instrument. "I don't understand why you won't take a musical instrument, this is beyond comprehension. Your little cousin Toby can sit down at the piano and play whatever song you can name. All she has to do is sit at the piano and play 'Tea for Two' and everybody in the room is her friend. She'll never lack for companionship, Alex, she'll never lack for popularity. Only tell me you'll take up the piano, and I'll have one in here tomorrow morning. Alex, are you listening to me? I am offering you something that could change the rest of your life!"

But what he had to offer I didn't want—and what I wanted he didn't have to offer. Yet how unusual is that? Why must it continue to cause such pain? At this late date! Doctor, what should I rid myself of, tell me, the hatred

. . . or the love? Because I haven't even begun to mention everything I remember with pleasure—I mean with a rapturous, biting sense of loss! All those memories that seem somehow to be bound up with the weather and the time of day, and that flash into mind with such poignancy, that momentarily I am not down in the subway, or at my office, or at dinner with a pretty girl, but back in my childhood, *with them*. Memories of practically nothing—and yet they seem moments of history as crucial to my being as the moment of my conception; I might be remembering his sperm nosing into her ovum, so piercing is my gratitude—yes, *my* gratitude!—so sweeping and unqualified is my love. Yes, me, with sweeping and unqualified love! I am standing in the kitchen (standing maybe for the first time in my life), my mother points, "Look outside, baby," and I look; she says, "See? how purple? a real fall sky." The first line of poetry I ever hear! And I remember it! *A real fall sky* . . . It is an iron-cold January day, dusk—oh, these memories of dusk are going to kill me yet, of chicken fat on rye bread to tide me over to dinner, and the moon already outside the kitchen window—I have just come in with hot red cheeks and a dollar I have earned shoveling snow: "You know what you're going to have for dinner," my mother coos so lovingly to me, "for being such a hard-working boy? Your favorite winter meal. Lamb stew." It is night: after a Sunday in New York City, at Radio City and Chinatown, we are driving home across the George Washington Bridge—the Holland Tunnel is the direct route between Pell Street and Jersey City, but I beg for the bridge, and because my mother says it's "educational," my father drives some ten miles out of his way to get us home. Up front my sister counts aloud the number of supports upon which the marvelous educational cables rest, while in the back I fall asleep with my face against my mother's black sealskin coat. At Lakewood, where we go one winter for a weekend vacation with my parents' Sunday night Gin Rummy Club, I sleep in one twin bed with my father, and my mother and Hannah curl up together in the other. At dawn my father awakens me and like convicts escaping, we noiselessly dress and slip out of the room. "Come," he whispers, motioning for me to don my earmuffs and coat, "I want to show you something. Did you know I was a waiter in Lakewood when I was sixteen years old?" Outside the hotel he points across to the beautiful silent woods. "How's that?" he says. We walk together—"at a brisk pace"—around a silver lake. "Take good deep breaths. Take in the piney air all the way. This is the best air in the world, good winter piney air." *Good winter piney air*—another poet for a parent! I couldn't be more thrilled if I were Wordsworth's kid! . . . In summer he remains in the city while the three of us go off to live in a furnished room at the seashore for a month. He will join us for the last two weeks, when he gets his vacation . . . there are times, however, when Jersey City is so thick with humidity, so alive with the mosquitoes that come dive-bombing in from the marshes, that at the end of his day's work he drives sixty-five miles, taking the old Cheesequake Highway—the Cheesequake! My God! the stuff you uncover here!—drives sixty-five miles to spend the night with us in our breezy room at Bradley Beach.

He arrives after we have already eaten, but his own dinner waits while he unpeels the soggy city clothes in which he has been making the rounds of his debit all day, and changes into his swimsuit. I carry his towel for him as he clops down the street to the beach in his unlaced shoes. I am dressed in clean short pants and a spotless polo shirt, the salt is showered off me, and my hair—still my little boy's pre-steel wool hair, soft and combable—is beautifully parted and slicked down. There is a weathered iron rail that runs the length of the boardwalk, and I seat myself upon it; below me, in his shoes, my father crosses the empty beach. I watch him neatly set down his towel near the shore. He places his watch in one shoe, his eye-glasses in the other, and then he is ready to make his entrance into the sea. To this day I go into the water as he advised: plunge the wrists in first, then splash the underarms, then a handful to the temples and the back of the neck . . . ah, but slowly, always slowly. This way you get to refresh yourself, while avoiding a shock to the system. Refreshed, unshocked, he turns to face me, comically waves farewell up to where he thinks I'm standing, and drops backward to float with his arms outstretched. Oh he floats so still—he works, he works so hard, and for whom if not for me?—and then at last, after turning on his belly and making with a few choppy strokes that carry him nowhere, he comes wading back to shore, his stream-ing compact torso glowing from the last pure spikes of light driving in, over my shoulder, out of stifling inland New Jersey, from which I am being spared.

And there are more memories like this one, Doctor. A lot more. This is my mother and father I'm talking about.

But—but—but—let me pull myself together—there is also this vision of him emerging from the bathroom, savagely kneading the back of his neck and sourly swallowing a belch. "All right, what is it that was so urgent you couldn't wait till I came out to tell me?"

"Nothing," says my mother. "It's settled."

He looks at me, so disappointed. I'm what he lives for, and I know it. "What did he do?"

"What he did is over and done with, God willing. You, did you move your bowels?" she asks him.

"Of course I didn't move my bowels."

"Jack, what is it going to be with you, with those bowels?"

"They're turning into concrete, that's what it's going to be."

"Because you eat too fast."

"I don't eat too fast."

"How then, slow?"

"I eat regular."

"You eat like a pig, and somebody should tell you."

"Oh, you got a wonderful way of expressing yourself sometimes, do you know that?"

"I'm only speaking the truth," she says. "I stand on my feet all day in this kitchen, and you eat like there's a fire somewhere, and this one—this one has decided that the food I cook isn't good enough for him. He'd rather be sick and scare the living daylights out of me."

"What did he do?"

"I don't want to upset you," she says. "Let's just forget the whole thing." But she can't, so now *she* begins to cry. Look, she is probably not the happiest person in the world either. She was once a tall stringbean of a girl whom the boys called "Red" in high school. When I was nine and ten years old I had an absolute passion for her high school yearbook. For a while I kept it in the same drawer with that other volume of exotica, my stamp collection.

> *Sophie Ginsky the boys call "Red,"*
> *She'll go far with her big brown eyes and her clever head.*

And that was my mother!

Also, she had been secretary to the soccer coach, an office pretty much without laurels in our own time, but apparently *the* post for a young girl to hold in Jersey City during the First World War. So I thought, at any rate, when I turned the pages of her yearbook, and she pointed out to me her dark-haired beau, who had been captain of the team, and today, to quote Sophie, "the biggest manufacturer of mustard in New York." "And I could have married him instead of your father," she confided in me, and more than once. I used to wonder sometimes what that would have been like for my momma and me, invariably on the occasions when my father took us to dine out at the corner delicatessen. I look around the place and think, "We would have manufactured all this mustard." I suppose she must have had thoughts like that herself.

"He eats French fries," she says, and sinks into a kitchen chair to Weep Her Heart Out once and for all. "He goes after school with Melvin Weiner and stuffs himself with French-fried potatoes. Jack, you tell him, I'm only his mother. Tell him what the end is going to be. Alex," she says passionately, looking to where I am edging out of the room, "*tateleh*, it begins with diarrhea, but do you know how it ends? With a sensitive stomach like yours, do you know how it finally ends? *Wearing a plastic bag to do your business in!*"

Who in the history of the world has been least able to deal with a woman's tears? My father. I am second. He says to me, "You heard your mother. Don't eat French fries with Melvin Weiner after school."

"Or ever," she pleads.

"Or ever," my father says.

"Or hamburgers out," she pleads.

"Or hamburgers out," he says.

"*Hamburgers*," she says bitterly, just as she might say *Hitler*, "where they can put anything in the world in that they want—and *he* eats them. Jack, make him promise, before he gives himself a terrible *tsura*, and it's too late."

"I *promise!*" I scream. "I *promise!*" and race from the kitchen—to where? Where else.

I tear off my pants, furiously I grab that battered battering ram to freedom, my adolescent cock, even as my mother begins to call from the other side of the bathroom door. "Now this time don't flush. Do you hear me, Alex? I have to see what's in that bowl!"

Doctor, do you understand what I was up against? My wang was all I really had that I could call my own. You should have watched her at work during polio season! She should have gotten medals from the March of Dimes! Open your mouth. Why is your throat red? Do you have a headache you're not telling me about? You're not going to any baseball game, Alex, until I see you move your neck. Is your neck stiff? Then why are you moving it that way? You ate like you were nauseous, are you nauseous? Well, you ate like you were nauseous. I don't want you drinking from the drinking fountain in that playground. If you're thirsty wait until you're home. Your throat is sore, isn't it? I can tell how you're swallowing. I think maybe what you are going to do, Mr. Joe Di Maggio, is put that glove away and lie down. I am not going to allow you to go outside in this heat and run around, not with that sore throat, I'm not. I want to take your temperature. I don't like the sound of this throat business one bit. To be very frank, I am actually beside myself that you have been walking around all day with a sore throat and not telling your mother. Why did you keep this a secret? Alex, polio doesn't know from baseball games. It only knows from iron lungs and crippled forever! I don't want you running around, and that's final. Or eating hamburgers out. Or mayonnaise. Or chopped liver. Or tuna. Not everybody is careful the way your mother is about spoilage. You're used to a spotless house, you don't begin to know what goes on in restaurants. Do you know why your mother when we go to the Chink's will never sit facing the kitchen? Because I don't want to see what goes on back there. Alex, you must wash everything, is that clear? Everything! God only knows who touched it before you did.

Look, am I exaggerating to think it's practically miraculous that I'm ambulatory? The hysteria and the superstition! The watch-its and the be-carefuls! You mustn't do this, you can't do that—hold it! don't! you're breaking an important law! *What* law? *Whose* law? They might as well have had plates in their lips and rings through their noses and painted themselves blue for all the human sense they made! Oh, and the *milchiks* and *flaishiks* besides, all those *meshuggeneh* rules and regulations on top of their own private craziness! It's a family joke that when I was a tiny child I turned from the window out of which I was watching a snowstorm, and hopefully asked, "Momma, do we believe in winter?" Do you get what I'm *saying?* I was raised by Hottentots and Zulus! I couldn't even contemplate drinking a glass of milk with my salami sandwich without giving serious offense to God Almighty. Imagine then what my conscience gave me for all that jerking off! The guilt, the fears—the terror bred into my bones! What in their world was not charged with danger, dripping with germs, fraught with peril? Oh, where was the gusto, where was the boldness and courage? Who filled these parents of mine with such fearful sense of life? My father, in his retirement now, has really only one subject into which he can sink his teeth, the New Jersey Turnpike. "I wouldn't go on that thing if you paid me. You have to be out of your mind to travel on that thing—it's Murder Incorporated, it's a legalized way for people to go out and get themselves killed—" Listen, you know what he says to me three times a week on the telephone—and I'm only counting when I pick it up, not the total number of rings I get between six and ten every night. "Sell that car, will you? Will you do me a favor and sell that car so I can get a good night's sleep? Why you have to have a car in that city is beyond my comprehension. Why you want to pay for insurance and garage and upkeep, I don't even begin to understand. But then I don't understand yet why you even want to live by yourself over in that jungle. What do you pay those robbers again for that two-by-four apartment? A penny over fifty dollars a month and you're out of your mind. Why you don't move back to North Jersey is a mystery to me—why you prefer the noise and the crime and the fumes—"

And my mother, she just keeps whispering. *Sophie whispers on!* I go for dinner once a month, it is a struggle requiring all my guile and cunning and strength, but I have been able over all these years, and against imponderable odds, to hold it down to once a month: I ring the bell, she opens the door, the whispering promptly begins! "Don't ask what kind of day I had with him yesterday." So I don't. "Alex," *sotto voce* still, "when he has a day like that you don't know what a difference a call from you would make." I nod. "And, Alex"—and I'm nodding away, you know—it doesn't cost anything, and it may even get me through—"next week is his birthday. That Mother's

Day came and went without a card, *plus* my birthday, those things don't bother me. But he'll be sixty-six, Alex. That's not a baby, Alex—that's a landmark in a life. So you'll send a card. It wouldn't kill you."

Doctor, these people are incredible! These people are unbelievable! These two are the outstanding producers and packagers of guilt in our time! They render it from me like fat from a chicken! "Call, Alex. Visit, Alex. Alex, keep us informed. Don't go away without telling us, please, not again. Last time you went away you didn't tell us, your father was ready to phone the police. You know how many times a day he called and got no answer? Take a guess, how many?" "Mother," I inform her, from between my teeth, "if I'm dead they'll smell the body in seventy-two hours, I assure you!" "Don't *talk* like that! God *forbid!*" she cries. Oh, and now she's got the beauty, the one guaranteed to do the job. Yet how could I expect otherwise? Can I ask the impossible of my own mother? "Alex, to pick up a phone is such a simple thing—how much longer will we be around to bother you anyway?"

Doctor Spielvogel, this is my life, my only life, and I'm living it in the middle of a Jewish joke! I am the son in the Jewish joke—*only it ain't no joke!* Please, who crippled us like this? Who made us so morbid and hysterical and weak? Why, why are they screaming still, "Watch out! Don't do it! Alex—no!" and why, alone on my bed in New York, why am I still hopelessly beating my meat? Doctor, what do you call this sickness I have? Is this the Jewish suffering I used to hear so much about? Is this what has come down to me from the pogroms and the persecution?

from the mockery and abuse bestowed by the *goyim* over
these two thousand lovely years? Oh my secrets, my
shame, my palpitations, my flushes, my sweats! The way
I respond to the simple vicissitudes of human life! Doctor,
I can't stand any more being frightened like this over
nothing! Bless me with manhood! Make me brave! Make
me strong! Make me *whole!* Enough being a nice Jewish
boy, publicly pleasing my parents while privately pulling
my putz! Enough!

THE JEWISH BLUES

Sometime during my ninth year one of my testicles apparently decided it had had enough of life down in the
scrotum and began to make its way north. At the beginning I could feel it bobbing uncertainly just at the rim of
the pelvis—and then, as though its moment of indecision
has passed, entering the cavity of my body, like a surviver
being dragged up out of the sea and over the hull of a
lifeboat. And there it nestled, secure at last behind the
fortress of my bones, leaving its foolhardy mate to chance
it alone in that boy's world of football cleats and picket
fences, sticks and stones and pocketknives, all those dan-
gers that drove my mother wild with foreboding, and

about which I was warned and warned and warned. And warned again. And again.

And again.

So my left testicle took up residence in the vicinity of the inguinal canal. By pressing a finger in the crease between my groin and my thigh, I could still, in the early weeks of its disappearance, feel the curve of its jellied roundness; but then came nights of terror, when I searched my guts in vain, searched all the way up to my rib cage—alas, the voyager had struck off for regions uncharted and unknown. Where was it gone to! How high and how far before the journey would come to an end! Would I one day open my mouth to speak in class, only to discover my left nut out on the end of my tongue? In school we chanted, along with our teacher, *I am the Captain of my fate, I am the Master of my soul,* and meanwhile, within my own body, an anarchic insurrection had been launched by one of my privates—which I was helpless to put down!

For some six months, until its absence was observed by the family doctor during my annual physical examination, I pondered my mystery, more than once wondering—for there was no possibility that did not enter my head, *none* —if the testicle could have taken a dive backwards toward the bowel and there begun to convert itself into just such an egg as I had observed my mother yank in a moist yellow cluster from the dark interior of a chicken whose guts she was emptying into the garbage. What if breasts began to grow on me, too? What if my penis went dry and brittle, and one day, while I was urinating, snapped off in my hand? Was I being transformed into a girl? Or worse, into a boy such as I understood (from the playground grapevine) that Robert Ripley of *Believe It or Not* would pay "a reward" of a hundred thousand dollars for? Believe it or not, there is a nine-year-old boy in New Jersey who is a boy in every way, *except he can have babies*.

Who gets the reward? Me, or the person who turns me in?

Doctor Izzie rolled the scrotal sac between his fingers as though it were the material of a suit he was considering buying, and then told my father that I would have to be given a series of male hormone shots. One of my testicles had never fully descended—unusual, not unheard of . . . But if the shots don't work, asks my father in alarm. What then—! Here I am sent out into the waiting room to look at a magazine.

The shots work. I am spared the knife. (Once again!)

Oh, this father! this kindly, anxious, uncomprehending, constipated father! Doomed to be obstructed by this Holy Protestant Empire! The self-confidence and the cunning, the imperiousness and the contacts, all that enabled the blond and blue-eyed of his generation to lead, to inspire, to command, if need be to oppress—he could not summon a hundredth part of it. How could he oppress?—he *was* the oppressed. How could he wield power?—he *was* the powerless. How could he enjoy triumph, when he so despised the triumphant—and probably the very idea. "They worship a Jew, do you know that, Alex? Their whole big-deal religion is based on worshiping someone who was an established Jew at that time. Now how do you like that for stupidity? How do you like that for pulling the wool over the eyes of the public? Jesus Christ, who they go around telling everybody was God, was actually a Jew! And this fact, that absolutely kills me when I have to think about it, *nobody else pays any attention to*. That he was a Jew, like you and me, and that they took a Jew and turned him into some kind of God after he is already dead, and then—and this is what can make you absolutely crazy—then the dirty bastards turn around afterwards, and who is the first one on their list to persecute? who haven't they left their hands off of to murder and to hate for two thousand years? The Jews! who gave them their beloved Jesus to begin with! I assure you, Alex, you are never going to hear such a *mishegoss* of mixed-up crap and disgusting nonsense as the Christian religion in your entire life. And that's what these big shots, so-called, believe!"

Unfortunately, on the home front contempt for the powerful enemy was not so readily available as a defensive strategy—for as time went on, the enemy was more and more *his* own beloved son. Indeed, during that extended period of rage that goes by the name of my adolescence, what terrified me most about my father was not the violence I expected him momentarily to unleash upon me, but the violence I wished every night at the dinner table to commit upon his ignorant, barbaric carcass. How I wanted to send him howling from the land of the living when he ate from the serving bowl with his own fork, or sucked the soup from his spoon instead of politely waiting for it to cool, or attempted, God forbid, to express an opinion on any subject whatsoever . . . And what was especially terrifying about the murderous wish was this: if I tried, chances were I'd succeed! *Chances were he would help me along!* I would have only to leap across the dinner dishes, my fingers aimed at his windpipe, for him instantaneously to sink down beneath the table with his tongue hanging out. Shout he could shout, squabble he could squabble, and oh *nudjh,* could he *nudjh!* But defend himself? against *me?* "Alex, keep this back talk up," my mother warns, as I depart from the roaring kitchen like Attila the Hun, run screaming from yet another half-eaten dinner, "continue with this disrespect and you will give that man a heart attack!" "Good!" I cry, slamming in her face the door to my room. "Fine!" I scream, extracting from my closet the zylon jacket I wear only with my collar up (a style she abhors as much as the filthy garment itself). "Wonderful!" I shout, and with streaming eyes run to the corner to vent my fury on the pinball machine.

Christ, in the face of my defiance—if my father had only been my mother! and my mother my father! But what a mix-up of the sexes in our house! Who should by rights be advancing on me, retreating—and who should be retreating, advancing! Who should be scolding, collapsing in helplessness, enfeebled totally by a tender heart! And who should be collapsing, instead scolding, correcting, reproving, criticizing, faultfinding without end! Filling the patriarchal vacuum! Oh, thank God! thank God! at least *he* had the cock and the balls! Preg-

nable (putting it mildly) as his masculinity was in this
world of *goyim* with golden hair and silver tongues, between his legs (God bless my father!) he was constructed
like a man of consequence, two big healthy balls such as a
king would be proud to put on display, and a *shlong* of
magisterial length and girth. And they were *his:* yes, of
this I am absolutely certain, they hung down off of, they
were connected on to, they could not be taken away from,
him!

Of course, around the house I saw less of his sexual
apparatus than I did of her erogenous zones. And once I
saw her menstrual blood . . . saw it shining darkly up at
me from the worn linoleum in front of the kitchen sink.
Just two red drops over a quarter of a century ago, but
they glow still in that icon of her that hangs, perpetually
illuminated, in my Modern Museum of Gripes and Grievances (along with the box of Kotex and the nylon stockings, which I want to come to in a moment). Also in this
icon is an endless dripping of blood down through a
drainboard into a dishpan. It is the blood she is draining
from the meat so as to make it kosher and fit for consump-
tion. Probably I am confusing things—I sound like a son
of the House of Atreus with all this talk of blood—but I
see her standing at the sink salting the meat so as to rid
it of its blood, when the attack of "woman's troubles" sends
her, with a most alarming moan, rushing off to her bedroom. I was no more than four or five, and yet those two
drops of blood that I beheld on the floor of her kitchen
are visible to me still . . . as is the box of Kotex . . . as

are the stockings sliding up her legs . . . as is—need I even say it?—the bread knife with which my own blood would be threatened when I refuse to eat my dinner. That knife! *That knife!* What gets me is that she herself did not even consider the use of it anything to be ashamed of, or particularly reticent about. From my bed I hear her babbling about her problems to the women around the mah-jongg game: *My Alex is suddenly such a bad eater I have to stand over him with a knife.* And none of them apparently finds this tactic of hers at all excessive. I have to stand over him with a knife! And not one of those women gets up from the mah-jongg table and walks out of her house! Because in their world, that is the way it is with bad eaters—you have to stand over them *with a knife!*

It was years later that she called from the bathroom, Run to the drugstore! Bring a box of Kotex! immediately! And the panic in her voice. Did I run! And then at home again, breathlessly handed the box to the white fingers that extended themselves at me through a narrow crack in the bathroom door . . . Though her menstrual troubles eventually had to be resolved by surgery, it is difficult nevertheless to forgive her for having sent me on that mission of mercy. Better she should have bled herself out on our cold bathroom floor, better *that,* than to have sent an eleven-year-old boy in hot pursuit of sanitary napkins! Where was my sister, for Christ's sake? Where was her own emergency supply? Why was this woman so grossly insensitive to the vulnerability of her own little boy— on the one hand so insensitive to my shame, and yet on the other, so attuned to my deepest desires!

. . . I am so small I hardly know what sex I am, or so you would imagine. It is early in the afternoon, spring of the year Four. Flowers are standing up in purple stalks in the patch of dirt outside our building. With the windows flung open the air in the apartment is fragrant, soft with the season—and yet electric too with my mother's vitality: she has finished the week's wash and hung it on the line; she has baked a marble cake for our dessert tonight, beautifully bleeding—there's that blood again! there's that knife again!—anyway expertly bleeding the chocolate in and out of the vanilla, an accomplishment that seems to me as much of a miracle as getting those peaches to hang there suspended in the shimmering mold of jello. She has done the laundry and baked the cake; she has scrubbed the kitchen and bathroom floors and laid them with newspapers; she has of course dusted; needless to say, she has vacuumed; she has cleared and washed our luncheon dishes and (with my cute little assistance) returned them to their place in the *milchiks* cabinet in the pantry—and whistling like a canary all the morning through, a tuneless melody of health and joy, of heedlessness and self-sufficiency. While I crayon a picture for her, she showers—and now in the sunshine of her bedroom, she is dressing to take me downtown. She sits on the edge of the bed in her padded bra and her girdle, rolling on her stockings and chattering away. Who is Mommy's good little boy? Who is the best little boy a mommy ever had? Who does Mommy love more than anything in the whole wide world? I am absolutely punchy with delight, and meanwhile follow in their tight, slow, agonizingly delicious

journey up her legs the transparent stockings that give
her flesh a hue of stirring dimensions. I sidle close enough
to smell the bath powder on her throat—also to appre-
ciate better the elastic intricacies of the dangling straps
to which the stockings will presently be hooked (undoubtedly with a flourish of trumpets). I smell the oil
with which she has polished the four gleaming posts of
the mahogany bedstead, where she sleeps with a man
who lives with us at night and on Sunday afternoons. My
father they say he is. On my fingertips, even though she
has washed each one of those little piggies with a warm
wet cloth, I smell my lunch, my tuna fish salad. Ah, it
might be cunt I'm sniffing. Maybe it is! Oh, I want to
growl with pleasure. Four years old, and yet I sense in
my blood—uh-huh, again with the blood—how rich with
passion is the moment, how dense with possibility. This
fat person with the long hair whom they call my sister is
away at school. This man, my father, is off somewhere
making money, as best he is able. These two are gone,
and who knows, maybe I'll be lucky, maybe they'll never
come back . . . In the meantime, it is afternoon, it is
spring, and for me and me alone a woman is rolling on
her stockings and singing a song of love. Who is going
to stay with Mommy forever and ever? *Me.* Who is it who
goes with Mommy wherever in the whole wide world
Mommy goes? *Why me, of course. What a silly question
—but don't get me wrong, I'll play the game!* Who had a
nice lunch with Mommy, who goes downtown like a good
boy on the bus with Mommy, who goes into the big store
with Mommy . . . and on and on and on . . . so that only

a week or so ago, upon my safe return from Europe, Mommy had this to say—

"Feel."

"*What?*"—even as she takes my hand in hers and draws it toward her body—"Mother—"

"I haven't gained five pounds," she says, "since you were born. Feel," she says, and holds my stiff fingers against the swell of her hips, which aren't bad . . .

And the stockings. More than twenty-five years have passed (the game is supposed to be over!), but Mommy still hitches up the stockings in front of her little boy. Now, however, he takes it upon himself to look the other way when the flag goes fluttering up the pole—and out of concern not just for his own mental health. That's the truth, I look away not for me but for the sake of that poor man, my father! Yet what preference does Father really have? If there in the living room their grown-up little boy were to tumble all at once onto the rug with his mommy, what would Daddy do? Pour a bucket of boiling water on the raging, maddened couple? Would he draw *his* knife— or would he go off to the other room and watch television until they were finished? "What are you looking away—?" asks my mother, amused in the midst of straightening her seams. "You'd think I was a twenty-one-year-old girl; you'd think I hadn't wiped your backside and kissed your little tushy for you all those years. Look at him"—this to my father, in case he hasn't been giving a hundred percent of his attention to the little floor show now being performed—"look, acting like his own mother is some sixty-year-old beauty queen."

Once a month my father took me with him down to the *shvitz* bath, there to endeavor to demolish—with the steam, and a rubdown, and a long deep sleep—the pyramid of aggravation he has built himself into during the previous weeks of work. Our street clothes we lock away in the dormitory on the top floor. On rows of iron cots running perpendicular to the lockers, the men who have already been through the wringer down below are flung out beneath white sheets like the fatalities of a violent catastrophe. If it were not for the abrupt thunderclap of a fart, or the snores sporadically shooting up around me like machine-gun fire, I would believe we were in a morgue, and for some strange reason undressing in front of the dead. I do not look at the bodies, but like a mouse hop frantically about on my toes, trying to clear my feet of my undershorts before anybody can peek inside, where, to my chagrin, to my bafflement, to my mortification, I always discover in the bottommost seam a pale and wispy brushstroke of my shit. Oh, Doctor, I wipe and I wipe and I wipe, I spend as much time wiping as I do crapping, maybe even more. I use toilet paper like it grew on trees—so says my envious father—I wipe until that little orifice of mine is red as a raspberry; but still, much as I would like to please my mother by dropping into her laundry hamper at the end of each day jockey shorts such as might have encased the asshole of an angel, I deliver forth instead (deliberately, Herr Doctor?—or just inevitably?) the fetid little drawers of a boy.

But here in a Turkish bath, why am I dancing around?

There are no women here. No women—and no *goyim*. Can it be? There is nothing to worry about!

Following the folds at the base of his white buttocks, I proceed out of the dormitory and down the metal stairs to that purgatory wherein the agonies that come of being an insurance agent, a family man, and a Jew will be steamed and beaten from my father's body. At the bottom landing we sidestep a pile of white sheets and a mound of sopping towels, my father pushes a shoulder against a heavy windowless door, and we enter a dark quiet region redolent of wintergreen. The sounds are of a tiny, unenthusiastic audience applauding the death scene in some tragedy: it is the two masseurs walloping and potching at the flesh of their victims, men half-clad in sheets and stretched out across marble slabs. They smack them and knead them and push them around, they slowly twist their limbs as though to remove them in a piece from their sockets—I am hypnotized, but continue to follow after my father as we pass alongside the pool, a small green cube of heart-stopping ice water, and come at last to the steam room.

The moment he pushes open the door the place speaks to me of prehistoric times, earlier even than the era of the cavemen and lake dwellers that I have studied in school, a time when above the oozing bog that was the earth, swirling white gasses choked out the sunlight, and aeons passed while the planet was drained for Man. I lose touch instantaneously with that ass-licking little boy who runs home after school with his A's in his hand, the little over-earnest innocent endlessly in search of the key to that unfathomable mystery, his mother's approbation, and am back in some sloppy watery time, before there were families such as we know them, before there were toilets and tragedies such as we know them, a time of amphibious creatures, plunging brainless hulking things, with wet meaty flanks and steaming torsos. It is as though all the Jewish men ducking beneath the cold dribble of shower off in the corner of the steam room, then lumbering back for more of the thick dense suffocating vapors, it is as though they have ridden the time-machine back to an age when they existed as some herd of Jewish animals, whose only utterance is *oy, oy* . . . for this is the sound they make as they drag themselves from the shower into the heavy gush of fumes. They appear, at long last, my father and his fellow sufferers, to have returned to the habitat in which they can be natural. A place without *goyim* and women.

I stand at attention between his legs as he coats me from head to toe with a thick lather of soap—and eye with admiration the baggy substantiality of what overhangs the marble bench upon which he is seated. His scrotum is like the long wrinkled face of some old man with an egg tucked into each of his sagging jowls—while mine might hang from the wrist of some little girl's dolly like a teeny pink purse. And as for his *shlong,* to me, with that fingertip of a prick that my mother likes to refer to in public (once, okay, but that once will last a lifetime) as my "little thing," his *shlong* brings to mind the fire hoses coiled along the corridors at school. *Shlong:* the word somehow catches exactly the brutishness, the *meatishness,* that I admire so, the sheer mindless, weighty, and unself-conscious dangle of that living piece of hose through which he passes streams of water as thick and strong as rope—while I deliver forth slender yellow threads that my euphemistic mother calls "a sis." A sis, I think, is undoubtedly what my sister makes, little yellow threads that you can sew with . . . "Do you want to make a nice sis?" she asks me—when I want to make a torrent, I want to make a flood: I want like he does to shift the tides of the toilet bowl! "Jack," my mother calls to him, "would you close that door, please? Some example you're setting for you know who." But if only that had been so, Mother! If only you-know-who could have found some inspiration in what's-his-name's coarseness! If only I could have nourished myself upon the depths of his vulgarity, instead of that too becoming a source of shame. Shame and shame and shame and shame—every place I turn something else to be ashamed of.

We are in my Uncle Nate's clothing store on Springfield Avenue in Newark. I want a bathing suit with a built-in athletic support. I am eleven years old and that is my secret: I want a jock. I know not to say anything, I just know to keep my mouth shut, but then how do you get it if you don't ask for it? Uncle Nate, a spiffy dresser with a mustache, removes from his showcase a pair of little boy's trunks, the exact style I have always worn. He indicates that this is the best suit for me, fast-drying and won't chafe. "What's your favorite color?" Uncle Nate asks—"maybe you want it in your school color, huh?" I

turn scarlet, though that is not my answer. "I don't want
that kind of suit any more," and oh, I can smell humiliation
in the wind, hear it rumbling in the distance—any minute
now it is going to crash upon my prepubescent head.
"Why not?" my father asks. "Didn't you hear your uncle,
this is the best—" "I want one with a jockstrap in it!" Yes,
sir, this just breaks my mother up. "For *your* little thing?"
she asks, with an amused smile.

Yes, Mother, imagine: for my little thing.

The potent man in the family—successful in business,
tyrannical at home—was my father's oldest brother,
Hymie, the only one of my aunts and uncles to have
been born on the other side and to talk with an accent.
Uncle Hymie was in the "soda-vater" business, bottler and
distributor of a sweet carbonated drink called Squeeze, the
vin ordinaire of our dinner table. With his neurasthenic
wife Clara, his son Harold, and his daughter Marcia, my
uncle lived in a densely Jewish section of Newark, on the
second floor of a two-family house that he owned, and
into whose bottom floor we moved in 1941, when my
father transferred to the Essex County office of Boston &
Northeastern.

We moved from Jersey City because of the anti-
Semitism. Just before the war, when the Bund was feeling its oats, the Nazis used to hold their picnics in a beer
garden only blocks from our house. When we drove by in
the car on Sundays, my father would curse them, loud
enough for me to hear, not quite loud enough for them to
hear. Then one night a swastika was painted on the front

of our building. Then a swastika was found carved into the desk of one of the Jewish children in Hannah's class. And Hannah herself was chased home from school one afternoon by a gang of boys, who it was assumed were anti-Semites on a rampage. My parents were beside themselves. But when Uncle Hymie heard the stories, he had to laugh: "This surprises you? Living surrounded on four sides by *goyim,* and this surprises you?" The only place for a Jew to live is among Jews, *especially,* he said with an emphasis whose significance did not entirely escape me, especially when children are growing up with people from the other sex. Uncle Hymie liked to lord it over my father, and took a certain pleasure in pointing out that in Jersey City only the building we lived in was exclusively Jewish, whereas in Newark, where *he* still lived, that was the case with the entire Weequahic neighborhood. In my cousin Marcia's graduating class from Weequahic High, out of the two hundred and fifty students, there were only eleven *goyim* and one colored. Go beat that, said Uncle Hymie . . . So my father, after much deliberation, put in for a transfer back to his native village, and although his immediate boss was reluctant to lose such a dedicated worker (and naturally shelved the request), my mother eventually made a long-distance phone call on her own, to the Home Office up in Boston, and following a mix-up that I don't even want to begin to go into, the request was granted: in 1941 we moved to Newark.

Harold, my cousin, was short and bullish in build—like all the men in our family, except me—and bore a strong resemblance to the actor John Garfield. My mother

adored him and was always making him blush (a talent
the lady possesses) by saying in his presence, "If a girl
had Heshele's dark lashes, believe me, she'd be in Hollywood with a million-dollar contract." In a corner of the
cellar, across from where Uncle Hymie had cases of
Squeeze piled to the ceiling, Heshie kept a set of York
weights with which he worked out every afternoon before the opening of the track season. He was one of the
stars of the team, and held a city record in the javelin
throw; his events were discus, shot, and javelin, though
once during a meet at School Stadium, he was put in
by the coach to run the low hurdles, as a substitute for a
sick teammate, and in a spill at the last jump, fell and
broke his wrist. My Aunt Clara at that time—or was it all
the time?—was going through one of her "nervous seiz-
ures"—in comparison to Aunt Clara, my own vivid
momma is a Gary Cooper—and when Heshie came home
at the end of the day with his arm in a cast, she dropped
in a faint to the kitchen floor. Heshie's cast was later referred to as "the straw that broke the camel's back,"
whatever that meant.

To me, Heshie was everything—that is, for the little
time I knew him. I used to dream that I too would someday be a member of the track team and wear scant white
shorts with a slit cut up either side to accommodate the
taut and bulging muscles of my thighs.

Just before he was drafted into the Army in 1943,
Heshie decided to become engaged to a girl named Alice
Dembosky, the head drum majorette of the high school
band. It was Alice's genius to be able to twirl not just one

but two silver batons simultaneously—to pass them over
her shoulders, glide them snakily between her legs, and
then toss them fifteen and twenty feet into the air, catch-
ing one, then the other, behind her back. Only rarely did
she drop a baton to the turf, and then she had a habit of
shaking her head petulantly and crying out in a little
voice, "Oh, Alice!" that only could have made Heshie love
her the more; it surely had that effect upon me. Oh-
Alice, with that long blond hair leaping up her back and
about her face! cavorting with such exuberance half the
length of the playing field! Oh-Alice, in her tiny white
skirt with the white satin bloomers, and the white boots
that come midway up the muscle of her lean, strong
calves! Oh Jesus, "Legs" Dembosky, in all her dumb,
blond *goyische* beauty! Another icon!

That Alice was so blatantly a *shikse* caused no end of
grief in Heshie's household, and even in my own; as for
the community at large, I believe there was actually a
kind of civic pride taken in the fact that a gentile could
have assumed a position of such high visibility in our high
school, whose faculty and student body were about
ninety-five percent Jewish. On the other hand, when Alice
performed what the loudspeaker described as her "piece
de resistance"—twirling a baton that had been wrapped
at either end in oil-soaked rags and then set afire—despite
all the solemn applause delivered by the Weequahic fans
in tribute to the girl's daring and concentration, despite
the grave *boom boom boom* of our bass drum and the
gasps and shrieks that went up when she seemed about

to set ablaze her two adorable breasts—despite this genuine display of admiration and concern, I think there was still a certain comic detachment experienced on our side of the field, grounded in the belief that this was precisely the kind of talent that only a *goy* would think to develop in the first place.

Which was more or less the prevailing attitude toward athletics in general, and football in particular, among the parents in the neighborhood: it was for the *goyim*. Let them knock their heads together for "glory," for victory in a ball game! As my Aunt Clara put it, in that taut, violin-string voice of hers, "Heshie! Please! I do not need *goyische naches!*" Didn't need, didn't want such ridiculous pleasures and satisfactions as made the gentiles happy . . . At football our Jewish high school was notoriously hopeless (though the band, may I say, was always winning prizes and commendations); our pathetic record was of course a disappointment to the young, no matter what the parents might feel, and yet even as a child one was able to understand that for us to lose at football was not exactly the ultimate catastrophe. Here, in fact, was a cheer that my cousin and his buddies used to send up from the stands at the end of a game in which Weequahic had once again met with seeming disaster. I used to chant it with them.

> Ikey, Mikey, Jake and Sam,
> We're the boys who eat no ham,
> We play football, we play soccer—
> And we keep matzohs in our locker!
> Aye, aye, aye, Weequahic High!

So what if we had lost? It turned out we had other things to be proud of. We ate no ham. We kept matzohs in our lockers. Not really, of course, but if we wanted to *we could, and we weren't ashamed to say that we actually did!* We were Jews—and we weren't ashamed to say it! We were Jews—and not only were we not inferior to the *goyim* who beat us at football, but the chances were that because we could not commit our hearts to victory in such a thuggish game, we were superior! We were Jews—*and we were superior!*

> White bread, rye bread,
> Pumpernickel, challah,
> All those for Weequahic,
> Stand up and hollah!

Another cheer I learned from Cousin Hesh, four more lines of poetry to deepen my understanding of the injustices we suffered . . . The outrage, the disgust inspired in my parents by the gentiles, was beginning to make some sense: the *goyim* pretended to be something special, while *we* were actually *their* moral superiors. And what made us superior was precisely the hatred and the disrespect they lavished so willingly upon us!

Only what about the hatred we lavished upon them?

And what about Heshie and Alice? What did *that* mean?

When all else failed, Rabbi Warshaw was asked to join with the family one Sunday afternoon, to urge our Heshie not to take his young life and turn it over to his own worst enemy. I watched from behind a shade in the

living room, as the rabbi strode impressively up the front
stoop in his big black coat. He had given Heshie his bar
mitzvah lessons, and I trembled to think that one day he
would give me mine. He remained in consultation with
the defiant boy and the blighted family for over an hour.
"Over an hour of his time," they all said later, as though
that alone should have changed Heshie's mind. But no
sooner did the rabbi depart than the flakes of plaster began falling once again from the ceiling overhead. A door
flew open—and I ran for the back of the house, to crouch
down behind the shade of my parents' bedroom. There
was Heshie into the yard, pulling at his own black hair.
Then came bald Uncle Hymie, one fist shaking violently
in the air—like Lenin he looked! And then the mob of
aunts and uncles and elder cousins, swarming between
the two so as to keep them from grinding one another
into a little heap of Jewish dust.

One Saturday early in May, after competing all day in
a statewide track meet in New Brunswick, Heshie got
back to the high school around dusk, and went immediately across to the local hangout to telephone Alice and
tell her that he had placed third in the state in the
javelin throw. She told him that she could never see him
again as long as he lived, and hung up.

At home Uncle Hymie was ready and waiting: what he
had done, he said, Heshie had forced him to do; what his
father had had to do that day, Harold had brought down
himself upon his own stubborn, stupid head. It was as
though a blockbuster had finally fallen upon Newark, so
terrifying was the sound that broke on the stairway: Hesh

came charging out of his parents' apartment, down the stairs, past our door, and into the cellar, and one long *boom* rolled after him. We saw later that he had ripped the cellar door from its topmost hinge with the force of a shoulder that surely seemed from that piece of evidence to be *at least* the third most powerful shoulder in the state. Beneath our floorboards the breaking of glass began almost immediately, as he hurled bottle after bottle of Squeeze from one dark end of the whitewashed cellar to the other.

When my uncle appeared at the top of the cellar steps, Heshie raised a bottle over his head and threatened to throw it in his father's face if he advanced so much as a step down the stairway. Uncle Hymie ignored the warning and started after him. Heshie now began to race in and out between the furnaces, to circle and circle the washing machines—still wielding the bottle of Squeeze. But my uncle stalked him into a corner, wrestled him to the floor, and held him there until Heshie had screamed his last obscenity—held him there (so Portnoy legend has it) *fifteen minutes*, until the tears of surrender at last appeared on his Heshie's long dark Hollywood lashes. We are not a family that takes defection lightly.

That morning Uncle Hymie had telephoned Alice Dembosky (in the basement flat of an apartment building on Goldsmith Avenue, where her father was the janitor) and told her that he wanted to meet her by the lake in Weequahic Park at noon; it was a very urgent matter involving Harold's health—he could not talk at length on the phone, as even Mrs. Portnoy didn't know all the facts. At the park, he drew the skinny blonde wearing the babushka into the front seat of the car, and with the windows rolled up, told her that his son had an incurable blood disease, a disease about which the poor boy himself did not even know. That was his story, bad blood, make of it what you will . . . It was the doctor's orders that he should not marry anyone, ever. How much longer Harold had to live no one really knew, but as far as Mr. Portnoy was concerned, he did not want to inflict the suffering that was to come, upon an innocent young person like herself. To soften the blow he wanted to offer the girl a gift, a little something that she could use however she wished, maybe even to help her find somebody new. He drew from his pocket an envelope containing five twenty-dollar bills. And dumb, frightened Alice Dembosky took it. Thus proving something that everybody but Heshie (and I) had surmised about the Polack from the beginning: that her plan was to take Heshie for all his father's money, and then ruin his life.

When Heshie was killed in the war, the only thing people could think to say to my Aunt Clara and my Uncle Hymie, to somehow mitigate the horror, to somehow console them in their grief, was, "At least he didn't leave you with a *shikse* wife. At least he didn't leave you with *goyische* children."

End of Heshie and his story.

Even if I consider myself too much of a big shot to set foot inside a synagogue for fifteen minutes—which is all he is asking—at least I should have respect enough to change into decent clothes for the day and not make a mockery of myself, my family, and my religion.

"I'm sorry," I mumble, my back (as is usual) all I will offer him to look at while I speak, "but just because it's your religion doesn't mean it's mine."

"What did you say? Turn around, mister, I want the courtesy of a reply from your mouth."

"I don't have a religion," I say, and obligingly turn in his direction, about a fraction of a degree.

"You don't eh?"

"I can't."

"And why not? You're something special? Look at me! You're somebody too special?"

"I don't believe in God."

"Get out of those dungarees, Alex, and put on some decent clothes."

"They're not dungarees, they're Levis."

"It's Rosh Hashanah, Alex, and to me you're wearing overalls! Get in there and put a tie on and a jacket on and a pair of trousers and a clean shirt, and come out looking like a human being. And shoes, Mister, hard shoes."

"My shirt *is* clean—"

"Oh, you're riding for a fall, Mr. Big. You're fourteen years old, and believe me, you don't know everything there is to know. Get out of those moccasins! What the hell are you supposed to be, some kind of Indian?"

"Look, I don't believe in God and I don't believe in the Jewish religion—or in any religion. They're all lies."

"Oh, they are, are they?"

"I'm not going to act like these holidays mean anything when they don't! And that's all I'm saying!"

"Maybe they don't mean anything because you don't know anything about them, Mr. Big Shot. What do you know about the history of Rosh Hashanah? One fact? Two facts maybe? What do you know about the history of the Jewish people, that you have the right to call their religion, that's been good enough for people a lot smarter than you and a lot older than you for two thousand years —that you can call all that suffering and heartache a lie!"

"There is no such thing as God, and there never was, and I'm sorry, but in my vocabulary that's a lie."

"Then who created the world, Alex?" he asks contemptuously. "It just happened, I suppose, according to you."

"Alex," says my sister, "all Daddy means is even if you don't want to go with him, if you would just change your clothes—"

"But for what?" I scream. "For something that never existed? Why don't you tell me to go outside and change my clothes for some alley cat or some tree—*because at least they exist!*"

"But you haven't answered me, Mr. Educated Wise Guy," my father says. "Don't try to change the issue. Who created the world and the people in it? Nobody?"

"Right! Nobody!"

"Oh, sure," says my father. "That's brilliant. I'm glad I didn't get to high school if that's how brilliant it makes you."

"Alex," my sister says, and softly—as is her way—softly, because she is already broken a little bit too—"maybe if you just put on a pair of shoes—"

"But you're as bad as he is, Hannah! If there's no God, what do shoes have to do with it!"

"One day a year you ask him to do something for you, and he's too big for it. And that's the whole story, Hannah, of your brother, of his respect and love . . ."

"Daddy, he's a good boy. He does respect you, he does love you—"

"And what about the Jewish people?" He is shouting now and waving his arms, hoping that this will prevent him from breaking into tears—because the word love has only to be whispered in our house for all eyes immediately to begin to overflow. "Does he respect them? Just as much as he respects me, just about as much . . ." Suddenly he is sizzling—he turns on me with another new and brilliant thought. "Tell me something, do you know Talmud, my educated son? Do you know history? One-two-three you were bar mitzvah, and that for you was the end of your religious education. Do you know men study their whole lives in the Jewish religion, and when they die they still haven't finished? Tell me, now that you are all finished at fourteen being a Jew, do you know a single thing about the wonderful history and heritage of the saga of your people?"

But there are already tears on his cheeks, and more are on the way from his eyes. "A's in school," he says, "but in life he's as ignorant as the day he was born."

Well, it looks as though the time has come at last—so I say it. It's something I've known for a little while now. "You're the ignorant one! You!"

"Alex!" cries my sister, grabbing for my hand, as though fearful I may actually raise it against him.

"But he is! With all that stupid saga shit!"

"Quiet! Still! Enough!" cries Hannah. "Go to your room—"

—While my father carries himself to the kitchen table, his head sunk forward and his body doubled over, as though he has just taken a hand grenade in his stomach. Which he has. Which I know. "You can wear rags for all I care, you can dress like a peddler, you can shame and embarrass me all you want, curse me, Alexander, defy me, hit me, hate me—"

The way it usually works, my mother cries in the kitchen, my father cries in the living room—hiding his eyes behind the *Newark News*—Hannah cries in the bathroom, and I cry on the run between our house and the pinball machine at the corner. But on this particular Rosh Hashanah everything is disarranged, and why my father is crying in the kitchen instead of my mother—why he sobs without protection of the newspaper, and with such pitiful fury—is because my mother is in a hospital bed recovering from surgery: this indeed accounts for his excruciating loneliness on this Rosh Hashanah, and his particular need of my affection and obedience. But at this moment in the history of our family, if he needs it, you can safely bet money that he is not going to get it from me. Because my need is not to give it to him! Oh, yes, we'll turn the tables on him, all right, won't we, Alex you little prick! Yes, Alex the little prick finds that his father's ordinary day-to-day vulnerability is somewhat aggravated by the fact that the man's wife (or so they tell me) has very nearly expired, and so Alex the little prick takes the opportunity to drive the dagger of his resentment just a few inches deeper into what is already a bleeding heart. Alexander the Great!

No! There's more here than just adolescent resentment and Oedipal rage—there's my integrity! I will not do what Heshie did! For I go through childhood *convinced* that had he only wanted to, my powerful cousin Heshie, the third best javelin thrower in all New Jersey (an honor, I would think, rich in symbolism for this growing boy, with visions of jockstraps dancing in his head), could easily have flipped my fifty-year-old uncle over onto his back, and pinned him to the cellar door. So then (I conclude) he must have lost on purpose. But why? For he knew—*I* surely knew it, even as a child—that his father had done something dishonorable. Was he then *afraid* to win? But why, when his own father had acted so vilely, and in Heshie's behalf! Was it cowardice? fear?—or perhaps was it Heshie's wisdom? Whenever the story is told of what my uncle was forced to do to make my dead cousin see the light, or whenever I have cause to reflect upon the event myself, I sense some enigma at its center, a profound moral truth, which if only I could grasp, might save me and my own father from some ultimate, but unimaginable, confrontation. *Why did Heshie capitulate? And should I?* But how can I, and still remain "true to myself"! Oh, but why don't I just try! Give it a little try, you little prick! So *don't* be so true to yourself for half an hour!

Yes, I must give in, I *must*, particularly as I know all my father has been through, what minute by minute mis-

ery there has been for him during these tens of thousands
of minutes it has taken the doctors to determine, first, that
there was something growing in my mother's uterus, and
second, whether the growth they finally located was malignant . . . whether what she had was . . . oh, that word
we cannot even speak in one another's presence! the word
we cannot even spell out in all its horrible entirety! the
word we allude to only by the euphemistic abbreviation
that she herself supplied us with before entering the hospital for her tests: C-A. And *genug!* The *n*, the *c*, the *e*,
the *r*, we don't need to hear to frighten us to Kingdom
Come! How brave she is, all our relatives agree, just to
utter those two letters! And aren't there enough whole
words as it is to whisper at each other behind closed doors?
There are! There are! Ugly and cold little words reeking
of the ether and alcohol of hospital corridors, words with
all the appeal of sterilized surgical instruments, words like
smear and *biopsy* . . . And then there are the words
that furtively, at home alone, I used to look up in the
dictionary just to *see* them there in print, the hard evidence of that most remote of all realities, words like *vulva*
and *vagina* and *cervix*, words whose definitions will never
again serve me as a source of illicit pleasure . . . And
then there is that word we wait and wait and wait to
hear, the word whose utterance will restore to our family
what now seems to have been the most wonderful and
satisfying of lives, that word that sounds to my ear like
Hebrew, like *b'nai* or *boruch*—benign! *Benign!* Boruch atoh
Adonai, *let it be benign!* Blessed art thou O Lord Our
God, *let it be benign!* Hear O Israel, and shine down thy

countenance, and the Lord is One, and honor thy father, and honor thy mother, and I will I will I promise I will—*only let it be benign!*

And it was. A copy of *Dragon Seed* by Pearl S. Buck is open on the table beside the bed, where there is also a half-empty glass of flat ginger ale. It's hot and I'm thirsty and my mother, my mind reader, says I should go ahead and drink what's left in her glass, I need it more than she does. But dry as I am, I don't want to drink from any glass to which she has put her lips—for the first time in my life the idea fills me with revulsion! "Take." "I'm not thirsty." "Look how you're perspiring." "I'm not thirsty." "Don't be polite all of a sudden." "But I don't *like* ginger ale." "You? Don't like ginger ale?" "*No.*" "Since when?" Oh, God! She's alive, and so we are at it again—she's alive, and right off the bat we're starting in!

She tells me how Rabbi Warshaw came and sat and talked with her for a whole half hour before—as she now so graphically puts it—she went under the knife. Wasn't that nice? Wasn't that thoughtful? (Only twenty-four hours out of the anesthetic, and she knows, you see, that I refused to change out of my Levis for the holiday!) The woman who is sharing the room with her, whose loving, devouring gaze I am trying to edge out of, and whose opinion, as I remember it, nobody had asked for, takes it upon herself to announce that Rabbi Warshaw is one of the most revered men in all of Newark. Re-ver-ed. Three syllables, as the rabbi himself would enunciate it, in his mighty Anglo-oracular style. I begin to lightly pound at the pocket of my baseball mitt, a signal that I am about

ready to go, if only someone will let me. "He loves baseball, he could play baseball twelve months a year," my
mother tells Mrs. Re-ver-ed. I mumble that I have "a
league game." "It's the finals. For the championship."
"Okay," says my mother, and lovingly, "you came, you
did your duty, now run—run to your league game." I
can hear in her voice how happy and relieved she is to
find herself alive on this beautiful September afternoon
. . . And isn't it a relief for me, too? Isn't this what I
prayed for, to a God I do not even believe is there? Wasn't
the unthinkable thing life without her to cook for us, to
clean for us, to . . . to *everything* for us! This is what I
prayed and wept for: that she should come out at the
other end of her operation, and be alive. And then come
home, to be once again our one and only mother. "Run,
my baby-boy," my mother croons to me, and sweetly—
oh, she can be so sweet and good to me, so motherly!
she will spend hour after hour playing canasta with me,
when I am sick and in bed as she is now: imagine, the
ginger ale the nurse has brought for her because she has
had a serious operation, she offers to *me*, because I'm overheated! Yes, she *will* give me the food out of her mouth,
that's a proven fact! And still I will not stay five full minutes at her bedside. "Run," says my mother, while Mrs.
Re-ver-ed, who in no time at all has managed to make
herself my enemy, and for the rest of my life, Mrs. Re-
ver-ed says, "Soon Mother will be home, soon everything
will be just like ordinary . . . Sure, run, run, they all run
these days," says the kind and understanding lady—oh,
they are all so kind and understanding, I want to strangle

them!—"walking they never heard of, God bless them."

So I run. Do I run! Having spent maybe two fretful minutes with her—two minutes of my precious time, even though just the day before, the doctors stuck right up her dress (so I imagined it, before my mother reminded me of "the knife," our knife) some kind of horrible shovel with which to scoop out what had gone rotten inside her body. They reached up and pulled down out of her just what she used to reach up and pull down out of the dead chicken. And threw it in the garbage can. Where I was conceived and carried, there now is *nothing*. A void! Poor Mother! How can I rush to leave her like this, after what she has just gone through? After all she has given me— my very life!—how can I be so cruel? "Will you leave me, my baby-boy, will you ever leave Mommy?" Never, I would answer, never, never, never . . . And yet now that she is hollowed out, I cannot even look her in the eye! And have avoided doing so ever since! Oh, there is her pale red hair, spread across the pillow in long strands of springy ringlets *that I might never have seen again.* There are the faint moons of freckles that she says used to cover her entire face when she was a small child, *and that I would never have seen again.* And there are those eyes of reddish brown, eyes the color of the crust of honey cake, *and still open, still loving me!* There was her ginger ale— and thirsty as I was, I could not have *forced* myself to drink it!

So I ran all right, out of the hospital and up to the playground and right out to center field, the position I play for a softball team that wears silky blue-and-gold jackets with the name of the club scrawled in big white felt letters from one shoulder to the other: S E A B E E S, A.C. Thank God for the Seabees A.C.! Thank God for center field! Doctor, you can't imagine how truly glorious it is out there, so alone in all that space . . . Do you know baseball at all? Because center field is like some observation post, a kind of control tower, where you are able to see everything and everyone, to understand what's happening the instant it happens, not only by the sound of the struck bat, but by the spark of movement that goes through the infielders in the first second that the ball comes flying at them; and once it gets beyond them, "It's mine," you call, "it's mine," and then after it you go. For in center field, if you can get to it, it *is* yours. Oh, how unlike my home it is to be in center field, where no one will appropriate unto himself anything that I say is *mine!*

Unfortunately, I was too anxious a hitter to make the high school team—I swung and missed at bad pitches so often during the tryouts for the freshman squad that eventually the ironical coach took me aside and said, "Sonny, are you sure you don't wear glasses?" and then sent me on my way. But did I have form! did I have style! And in my playground softball league, where the ball came in just a little slower and a little bigger, I am the star I dreamed I might become for the whole school. Of course, still in my ardent desire to excel I too frequently swing and miss, but when I connect, it goes great distances, Doctor, it flies over fences and is called a home run. Oh, and there is really nothing in life, nothing at all, that quite compares with that pleasure of rounding second base at a nice slow clip, because there's just no hurry any more, because that ball you've hit has just gone sailing out of sight . . . And I could field, too, and the farther I had to run, the better. "I got it! I got it! I got it!" and tear in toward second, to trap in the webbing of my glove—and barely an inch off the ground—a ball driven hard and low and right down the middle, a base hit, someone thought . . . Or back I go, "*I got it, I* got it—" back easily and gracefully toward that wire fence, moving practically in slow motion, and then that delicious Di Maggio sensation of grabbing it like something heaven-sent over one shoulder . . . Or running! turning! leaping! like little Al Gionfriddo—a baseball player, Doctor, who once did a very great thing . . . Or just standing nice and calm—nothing trembling, everything serene—standing there in the sunshine (as though in the middle of an empty field, or passing the time on the street corner), standing without a care in the world in the sunshine, like my king of kings, the Lord my God, The Duke Himself (Snider, Doctor, the name may come up again), standing there as loose and as easy, as happy as I will ever be, just waiting by myself under a high fly ball (*a towering fly ball,* I hear Red Barber say, as he watches from behind his microphone—hit out toward Portnoy; *Alex under it, under it*), just waiting there for the ball to fall into the glove I raise to it, and yup, there it is, *plock,* the third out of the inning (*and Alex gathers it in for out number three, and, folks, here's old C.D. for P. Lorillard and Company*), and then in one motion, while old Connie brings us a message from Old Golds, I start in toward the bench, holding the ball now with the five fingers of my bare left hand, and when I get to the in-field—having come down hard with one foot on the bag at second base—I shoot it gently, with just a flick of the wrist, at the opposing team's shortstop as he comes trot-ting out onto the field, and still without breaking stride, go loping in all the way, shoulders shifting, head hanging, a touch pigeon-toed, my knees coming slowly up and down in an altogether brilliant imitation of The Duke. Oh, the unruffled nonchalance of that game! There's not a movement that I don't know still down in the tissue of my muscles and the joints between my bones. How to bend over to pick up my glove and how to toss it away, how to test the weight of the bat, how to hold it and carry it and swing it around in the on-deck circle, how to raise that bat above my head and flex and loosen my shoulders and my neck before stepping in and planting my two feet exactly where my two feet belong in the batter's box—and how, when I take a called strike (which I have a tendency to do, it balances off nicely swinging at bad pitches), to step out and express, if only through a slight poking with the bat at the ground, just the right amount of exasperation with the powers that be . . . yes, every little detail so thoroughly studied and mastered, that it is simply beyond the realm of possibility for any situation to arise in which I do not know how to move, or where to move, or what to say or leave unsaid . . . And it's true, is it not?—incredible, but apparently true—there are people who feel in life the ease, the self-assurance, the simple and essential affiliation with what is going on, that

I used to feel as the center fielder for the Seabees? Because it wasn't, you see, that one was the best center fielder imaginable, only that one knew exactly, and down to the smallest particular, how a center fielder should conduct himself. And there are people like that walking the streets of the U.S. of A.? I ask you, why can't I be one! Why can't I exist now as I existed for the Seabees out there in center field! Oh, to be a center fielder, a center fielder—and nothing more!

But I am something more, or so they tell me. A Jew. No! No! An *atheist*, I cry. I am a nothing where religion is concerned, and I will not pretend to be anything that I am not! I don't care how lonely and needy my father is, the truth about me is the truth about me, and I'm sorry but he'll just have to swallow my apostasy whole! And I don't care how close we came to sitting *shiva* for my mother either—actually, I wonder now if maybe the whole hysterectomy has not been dramatized into C-A and out of it again solely for the sake of scaring the S-H out of me! Solely for the sake of humbling and frightening me into being once again an obedient and helpless little boy! And I find no argument for the existence of God, or for the benevolence and virtue of the Jews, in the fact that the most re-ver-ed man in all of Newark came to sit for "a whole half hour" beside my mother's bed. If he emptied her bedpan, if he fed her her meals, that might be the beginning of something, but to come for half an hour and sit beside a bed? What else has he got to do, Mother? To him, uttering beautiful banalities to people scared out of their wits—that is to him what playing baseball is to me! He loves it! And who wouldn't? Mother, Rabbi Warshaw is a fat, pompous, impatient fraud, with an absolute grotesque superiority complex, a character out of Dickens is what he is, someone who if you stood next to him on the bus and didn't know he was so revered, you would say, "That man stinks to high heaven of cigarettes," and that is *all* you would say. This is a man who somewhere along the line got the idea that the basic unit of meaning in the English language is the syllable. So no word he pronounces has less than three of them, not even the word *God*. You should hear the song and dance he makes out of *Israel*. For him it's as long as refrigerator! And do you remember him at my bar mitzvah, what a field day he had with Alexander Portnoy? Why, Mother, did he keep calling me by my whole name? Why, except to impress all you idiots in the audience with all those syllables! And it worked! It actually worked! Don't you understand, the synagogue is how he earns his living, *and that's all there is to it*. Coming to the hospital to be brilliant about life (syllable by syllable) to people who are shaking in their pajamas about death is his business, just as it is my father's business to sell life insurance! It is what they each do to earn a living, and if you want to feel pious about somebody, feel pious about my father, God damn it, and bow down to him the way you bow down to that big fat comical son of a bitch, because my father *really* works his balls off and doesn't happen to think that he is God's special assistant into the bargain. And doesn't speak in those fucking *syllables!* "I-a wan-tt to-a

wel-come-a you-ew tooo thee sy-no-gawg-a." Oh God, oh
Guh-ah-duh, if you're up there shining down your countenance, why not spare us from here on out the enunciation of the rabbis! Why not spare us the rabbis themselves!
Look, why not spare us religion, if only in the name of
our human dignity! Good Christ, Mother, the whole world
knows already, *so why don't you? Religion is the opiate
of the people!* And if believing that makes me a fourteen-
year-old Communist, then that's what I am, *and I'm proud
of it!* I would rather be a Communist in Russia than a
Jew in a synagogue any day—so I tell my father right to
his face, too. Another grenade to the gut is what it turns
out to be (I suspected as much), but I'm sorry, I happen
to believe in the rights of man, rights such as are extended
in the Soviet Union to *all* people, regardless of race, religion, or color. My communism, in fact, is why I now insist
on eating with the cleaning lady when I come home for
my lunch on Mondays and see that she is there—I will eat
with her, Mother, at the same table, *and the same food.*
Is that clear? If I get leftover pot roast warmed-up, then
she gets leftover pot roast warmed-up, and not creamy
Muenster or tuna either, served on a special glass plate
that doesn't absorb her germs! But no, no, Mother doesn't
get the idea, apparently. Too bizarre, apparently. Eat with
the *shvartze?* What could I be talking about? She whispers to me in the hallway, the instant I come in from
school, "Wait, the girl will be finished in a few minutes . . ." *But I will not treat any human being* (outside
my family) *as inferior!* Can't you grasp something of the
principle of equality, God damn it! And I tell you, if he

ever uses the word nigger in my presence again, I will drive a real dagger into his fucking bigoted heart! *Is that clear to everyone?* I don't care that his clothes stink so bad after he comes home from collecting the colored debit that they have to be hung in the cellar to air out. I don't care that they drive him nearly crazy letting their insurance lapse. That is only another reason to be compassionate, God damn it, to be sympathetic and understanding and to stop treating the cleaning lady as though she were some kind of mule, without the same passion for dignity that other people have! And that goes for the *goyim*, too! We all haven't been lucky enough to have been born Jews, you know. So a little *rachmones* on the less fortunate, okay? Because I am sick and tired of *goyische* this and *goyische* that! If it's bad it's the *goyim*, if it's good it's the Jews! Can't you see, my dear parents, from whose loins I somehow leaped, that such thinking is a trifle barbaric? That all you are expressing is your *fear?* The very first distinction I learned from you, I'm sure, was not night and day, or hot and cold, but *goyische* and Jewish! But now it turns out, my dear parents, relatives, and assembled friends who have gathered here to celebrate the occasion of my bar mitzvah, it turns out, you schmucks! you narrow-minded schmucks!—oh, how I hate you for your Jewish narrow-minded minds! including you, Rabbi Syllable, who have for the last time in your life sent me out to the corner for another pack of Pall Mall cigarettes, from which you *reek* in case nobody has ever told you—it turns out that there is just a little bit more to existence than what can be contained in those disgusting and useless categories! And instead of crying over he-who refuses at the age of fourteen ever to set foot inside a synagogue again, instead of wailing for he-who has turned his back on the saga of *his people*, weep for your own pathetic selves, why don't you, sucking and sucking on that sour grape of a religion! Jew Jew Jew Jew Jew Jew! It is coming out of my ears already, the saga of the suffering Jews! Do me a favor, my people, and stick your suffering heritage up your suffering ass—*I happen also to be a human being!*

But you *are* a Jew, my sister says. You are a Jewish boy, more than you know, and all you're doing is making yourself miserable, all you're doing is hollering into the wind . . . Through my tears I see her patiently explaining my predicament to me from the end of my bed. If I am fourteen, she is eighteen, and in her first year at Newark State Teacher's College, a big sallow-faced girl, oozing melancholy at every pore. Sometimes with another big, homely girl named Edna Tepper (who has, however, to recommend her, tits the size of my head), she goes to a folk dance at the Newark Y. This summer she is going to be crafts counselor in the Jewish Community Center day camp. I have seen her reading a paperback book with a greenish cover called *A Portrait of the Artist as a Young Man*. All I seem to know about her are these few facts, and of course the size and smell of her brassiere and panties. What years of confusion! And when will they be over? Can you give me a tentative date, please? When will I be cured of what I've got!

Do you know, she asks me, where you would be now if you had been born in Europe instead of America?

That isn't the issue, Hannah.

Dead, she says.

That isn't the issue!

Dead. Gassed, or shot, or incinerated, or butchered, or buried alive. Do you know that? And you could have screamed all you wanted that you were not a Jew, that you were a human being and had nothing whatever to do with their stupid suffering heritage, and still you would have been taken away to be disposed of. You would be dead, and I would be dead, and

But that isn't what I'm talking about!

And your mother and your father would be dead.

But why are you taking their side!

I'm not taking anybody's side, she says. I'm only telling you he's not such an ignorant person as you think.

And she isn't either, I suppose! I suppose the Nazis make everything she says and does smart and brilliant too! I suppose the Nazis are an excuse for everything that happens in this house!

Oh, I don't know, says my sister, maybe, maybe they are, and now she begins to cry too, and how monstrous I feel, for she sheds her tears for six million, or so I think, while I shed mine only for myself. Or so I think.

CUNT CRAZY

Did I mention that when I was fifteen I took it out of my pants and whacked off on the 107 bus from New York? I had been treated to a perfect day by my sister and Morty Feibish, her fiancé—a doubleheader at Ebbets Field, followed afterward by a seafood dinner at Sheepshead Bay. An exquisite day. Hannah and Morty were to stay overnight in Flatbush with Morty's family, and so I was put on a subway to Manhattan about ten o'clock—and there boarded the bus for New Jersey, upon which I took not just my cock in my hands but my whole life, when you think about it. The passengers were mostly drowsing off before we had even emerged from the Lincoln Tunnel —including the girl in the seat beside me, whose tartan skirt folds I had begun to press up against with the corduroy of my trouser legs—and I had it out and in my fist by the time we were climbing onto the Pulaski Skyway.

You might have thought that given the rich satisfactions of the day, I'd have had my fill of excitement and my dick would have been the last thing on my mind heading home that night. Bruce Edwards, a new catcher up from the minors—and just what we needed (we being Morty, myself, and Burt Shotton, the Dodger manager)—had gone something like six for eight in his first two games in the majors (or was it Furillo? at any rate, how insane whipping out my joint like that! imagine what would have been had I been caught red-handed! imagine if I had gone ahead and come all over that sleeping *shikse*'s golden arm!) and then for dinner Morty had ordered me a lobster, the first of my life.

Now, maybe the lobster is what did it. That taboo so easily and simply broken, confidence may have been given to the whole slimy, suicidal Dionysian side of my nature; the lesson may have been learned that to break the law, all you have to do is—just go ahead and break it! All you have to do is stop trembling and quaking and finding it unimaginable and beyond you: all you have to do, *is do it!* What else, I ask you, were all those prohibitive dietary rules and regulations all about to begin with, what else but to give us little Jewish children practice in being repressed? Practice, darling, practice, practice, practice. Inhibition doesn't grow on trees, you know—takes patience, takes concentration, takes a dedicated and self-sacrificing parent and a hard-working attentive little child to create in only a few years' time a really constrained and tight-ass human being. Why else the two sets of dishes? Why else the kosher soap and salt? Why else, I ask you, but to remind us three times a day that life is boundaries and restrictions if it's anything, hundreds of thousands of little rules laid down by none other than None Other, rules which either you obey without question, regardless of how idiotic they may appear (and thus remain, by obeying, in His good graces), or you transgress, most likely in the name of outraged common sense—which you transgress because even a child doesn't like to go around feeling like an absolute moron and schmuck—yes, you transgress, only with the strong likelihood (my father assures me) that comes next Yom Kippur and the names are written in the big book where He writes the names of those who are going to get to live until the following September (a scene which manages somehow to engrave itself upon my imagination), and lo, your own precious name ain't among them. Now who's the schmuck, huh? And it doesn't make any difference either (this I understand from the outset, about the way this God, Who runs things, reasons) how big or how small the rule is that you break: it's the breaking alone that gets His goat—it's the simple fact of waywardness, and that alone, that He absolutely cannot stand, and which He does not forget either, when He sits angrily down (fuming probably, and surely with a smashing miserable headache, like my father at the height of his constipation) and begins to leave the names out of that book.

When duty, discipline, and obedience give way—ah, here, *here* is the message I take in each Passover with my mother's *matzoh brei*—what follows, there is no predicting. Renunciation is all, cries the koshered and bloodless piece of steak my family and I sit down to eat at dinner time. Self-control, sobriety, sanctions—this is the key to a human life, saith all those endless dietary laws. Let the *goyim* sink *their* teeth into whatever lowly creature crawls and grunts across the face of the dirty earth, we will not contaminate our humanity thus. Let *them* (if you know who I mean) gorge themselves upon anything and

everything that moves, no matter how odious and abject
the animal, no matter how grotesque or *shmutzig* or dumb
the creature in question happens to be. Let them eat eels
and frogs and pigs and crabs and lobsters; let them eat
vulture, let them eat ape-meat and skunk if they like—a
diet of abominable creatures well befits a breed of mankind so hopelessly shallow and empty-headed as to drink,
to divorce, and to fight with their fists. All they know,
these imbecilic eaters of the execrable, is to swagger, to
insult, to sneer, and sooner or later to hit. Oh, also they
know how to go out into the woods with a gun, these
geniuses, and kill innocent wild deer, deer who themselves *nosh* quietly on berries and grasses and then go on
their way, bothering no one. You stupid *goyim!* Reeking
of beer and empty of ammunition, home you head, a
dead animal (formerly *alive*) strapped to each fender, so
that all the motorists along the way can see how strong
and manly you are; and then, in your houses, you take
these deer—who have done you, who have done nothing
in all of nature, not the least bit of harm—you take these
deer, cut them up into pieces, and cook them in a pot.
There isn't enough to eat in this world, they have to eat
up the *deer* as well! They will eat *anything*, anything they
can get their big *goy* hands on! And the terrifying corollary, *they will do anything as well*. Deer eat what deer
eat, and Jews eat what Jews eat, but not these *goyim*.
Crawling animals, wallowing animals, leaping and an-
gelic animals—it makes no difference to them—what they
want they take, and to hell with the other thing's feelings
(let alone kindness and compassion). Yes, it's all written

down in history, what they have done, our illustrious neighbors who own the world and know absolutely nothing of human boundaries and limits.

. . . Thus saith the kosher laws, at least to the child I was, growing up under the tutelage of Sophie and Jack P., and in a school district of Newark where in my entire class there are only two little Christian children, and they live in houses I do not enter, on the far fringes of our neighborhood . . . thus saith the kosher laws, and who am I to argue that they're wrong? For look at Alex himself, the subject of *our* every syllable—age fifteen, he sucks one night on a lobster's claw and within the hour his cock is out and aimed at a *shikse* on a Public Service bus. And his superior Jewish brain might as well be *made* of *matzoh brei!*

Such a creature, needless to say, has never been boiled alive in our house—the lobster, I refer to. A *shikse* has never been in our house period, and so it's a matter of conjecture in what condition she might emerge from my mother's kitchen. The cleaning lady is obviously a *shikse*, but she doesn't count because she's black.

Ha ha. A *shikse* has never been in our house because *I* have brought her there, is what I mean to say. I do recall one that my own father brought home with him for dinner one night when I was still a boy: a thin, tense, shy, deferential, soft-spoken, aging cashier from his office named Anne McCaffery.

Doctor, could he have been slipping it to her? I can't believe it! Only it suddenly occurs to me. Could my father have been slipping it to this lady on the side? I can still remember how she sat down beside me on the sofa, and in her nervousness made a lengthy to-do of spelling her first name, and of pointing out to me how it ended with an E, which wasn't always the case with someone called Anne—and so on and so forth . . . and meanwhile, though her arms were long and white and skinny and freckled (Irish arms, I thought) inside her smooth white blouse, I could see she had breasts that were nice and substantial— and I kept taking peeks at her legs, too. I was only eight or nine, but she really did have such a terrific pair of legs that I couldn't keep my eyes away from them, the kind of legs that every once in a while it surprises you to find some pale spinster with a pinched face walking around on top of . . . With those legs—why, *of course* he was *shtupping* her . . . *Wasn't* he?

Why he brought her home, *he* said, was "for a real Jewish meal." For weeks he had been jabbering about the new *goyische* cashier ("a very plain drab person," he said, "who dresses in *shmattas*") who had been pester- ing him—so went the story he couldn't stop telling us— for a real Jewish meal from the day she had come to work in the Boston & Northeastern office. Finally my mother couldn't take any more. "All right, bring her already—she needs it so bad, so I'll give her one." Was he caught a little by surprise? Who will ever know.

At any rate, a Jewish meal is what she got all right. I don't think I have ever heard the word "Jewish" spoken so many times in one evening in my life, and let me tell you, I am a person who has heard the word "Jewish" spoken.

"This is your real Jewish chopped liver, Anne. Have you ever had real Jewish chopped liver before? Well, my wife makes the real thing, you can bet your life on that. Here, you eat it with a piece of bread. This is real Jewish rye bread, with seeds. That's it, Anne, you're doing very good, ain't she doing good, Sophie, for her first time? That's it, take a nice piece of real Jewish rye, now take a big fork full of the real Jewish chopped liver"—and on and on, right down to the jello—"that's right, Anne, the jello is kosher too, sure, of course, has to be—oh no, oh no, no cream in your coffee, not after meat, ha ha, hear what Anne wanted, Alex—?"

But babble-babble all you want, Dad dear, a question has just occurred to me, twenty-five years later (not that I have a single shred of evidence, not that until this moment I have ever imagined my father capable of even the slightest infraction of domestic law . . . but since infraction seems to hold for me a certain fascination), a question has arisen in the audience: why *did* you bring a *shikse*, of all things, into our home? Because you couldn't bear that a gentile woman should go through life without the experience of eating a dish of Jewish jello? Or because you could no longer live your own life without making Jewish confession? Without confronting your wife with your crime, so she might accuse, castigate, humiliate, punish, and thus bleed you forever of your forbidden lusts! Yes, a regular Jewish desperado, my father. I recognize the syndrome perfectly. Come, someone, anyone, find me out and condemn me—I did the most terrible thing you can think of: I took what I am not supposed to have!

Chose pleasure for myself over duty to my loved ones!
Please, catch me, incarcerate me, before God forbid I
get away with it completely—and go out and do again
something I actually like!

And did my mother oblige? Did Sophie put together
the two tits and the two legs and come up with four? Me
it seems to have taken two and a half decades to do such
steep calculation. Oh, I must be making this up, really.
My father . . . and a *shikse?* Can't be. Was beyond his
ken. My own father—fucked *shikses?* I'll admit under
duress that he fucked my mother . . . but *shikses?* I can
no more imagine him knocking over a gas station.

But then why is she shouting at him so, what is this
scene of accusation and denial, of castigation and threat
and unending tears . . . what is this all about except
that he has done something that is very bad and maybe
even unforgivable? The scene itself is like some piece of
heavy furniture that sits in my mind and will not budge
—which leads me to believe that, yes, it actually did
happen. My sister, I see, is hiding behind my mother:
Hannah is clutching her around the middle and whimpering, while my mother's own tears are tremendous and
fall from her face all the way to the linoleum floor. Simultaneously with the tears she is screaming so loud at him
that her veins stand out—and screaming at me, too, because, looking further into this thing, I find that while
Hannah hides behind my mother, *I take refuge behind
the culprit himself.* Oh, this is pure fantasy, this is right
out of the casebook, is it not? No, no, that is nobody else's
father but my own who now brings his fist down on the

kitchen table and shouts back at her, "I did no such thing!
That is a lie and wrong!" Only wait a minute—it's *me*
who is screaming "I didn't do it!" *The culprit is me!*
And why my mother weeps so is because my father refuses to *potch* my behind, which she promised would be
potched, "and good," when he found out the terrible
thing *I* had done.

When I am bad and rotten in small ways she can manage me herself: she has, you recall—I know *I* recall!—only
to put me in my coat and galoshes—oh, nice touch, Mom,
those galoshes!—lock me out of the house (*lock me out
of the house!*) and announce through the door that she
is never going to let me in again, so I might as well be
off and into my new life; she has only to take that simple
and swift course of action to get instantaneously a confession, a self-scorification, and, if she should want it, a
signed warranty that I will be one hundred percent pure
and good for the rest of my life—all this if only I am
allowed back inside that door, where they happen to have
my bed and my clothes and *the refrigerator*. But when
I am really wicked, so evil that she can only raise her
arms to God Almighty to ask Him what she has done to
deserve such a child, at such times my father is called in
to mete out justice; my mother is herself too sensitive,
too fine a creature, it turns out, to administer corporal
punishment: "It hurts me," I hear her explain to my
Aunt Clara, "more than it hurts him. That's the kind of
person I am. I can't do it, and that's that." Oh, poor Mother.

But look, what is going on here after all? Surely, Doctor, we can figure this thing out, two smart Jewish boys

like ourselves . . . A terrible act has been committed, and it has been committed by either my father or me. The wrongdoer, in other words, is one of the two members of the family who owns a penis. Okay. So far so good. Now: did he fuck between those luscious legs the gentile cashier from the office, or have I eaten my sister's chocolate pudding? You see, she *didn't* want it at dinner, but apparently *did* want it saved so she could have it before she went to bed. Well, good Christ, how was I supposed to know all that, Hannah? Who looks into the fine points when he's hungry? I'm eight years old and chocolate pudding happens to get me hot. All I have to do is see that deep chocolatey surface gleaming out at me from the refrigerator, and my life isn't my own. Furthermore, I *thought* it was *left over!* And that's the truth! Jesus Christ, is that what this screaming and *shrying* is all about, that I ate that sad sack's chocolate pudding? Even if I did, I didn't mean it! I thought it was something else! I swear, I swear, I didn't mean to do it! . . . But *is* that me—or my father hollering out his defense before the jury? Sure, that's him—he did it, okay, okay, Sophie, leave me alone already, I did it, *but I didn't mean it!* Shit, the next thing he'll tell her is why he should be forgiven is because he didn't *like* it either. What do you mean, you didn't *mean* it, schmuck—you stuck it in there, didn't you? Then stick up for yourself now, like a man! Tell her, tell her: "That's right, Sophie, I slipped it to the *shikse*, and what you think and don't think on the subject don't mean shit to me. Because the way it works, in case you ain't heard, is that I am the man around here, *and I call the shots!*" And slug

her if you have to! Deck her, Jake! Surely that's what a
goy would do, would he not? Do you think one of those
big-shot deer hunters with a gun collapses in a chair when
he gets caught committing the seventh and starts weeping and begging his wife to be *forgiven?*—forgiven for
what? What after all does it consist of? You put your
dick some place and moved it back and forth and stuff
came out the front. So, Jake, what's the big deal? How long
did the whole thing last that you should suffer such damna-
tion from her mouth—such guilt, such recrimination and
self-loathing! Poppa, why do we have to have such guilty
deference to women, you and me—when we don't! We
mustn't! Who should run the show, Poppa, is *us!* "Daddy
has done a terrible terrible thing," cries my mother—or
is that my imagination? Isn't what she is saying more like,
"Oh, little Alex has done a terrible thing again, Daddy—"
Whatever, she lifts Hannah (of all people, Hannah!),
who until that moment I had never really taken seriously
as a genuine object of anybody's love, takes her up into
her arms and starts kissing her all over her sad and unloved face, saying that her little girl is the only one in
the whole wide world she can really trust . . . But if I
am eight, Hannah is twelve, and nobody is picking her
up, I assure you, because the poor kid's problem is that
she is overweight, "and how," my mother says. She's not
even supposed to *eat* chocolate pudding. Yeah, *that's*
why I took it! Tough shit, Hannah, it's what the *doctor*
ordered, not me. I can't help it if you're fat and "sluggish"
and I'm skinny and brilliant. I can't help it that I'm so
beautiful they stop Mother when she is wheeling me in

my carriage so as to get a good look at my gorgeous
punim—you hear her tell that story, it's something I myself had nothing to do with, it's a simple fact of nature,
that I was born beautiful and you were born, if not
ugly, certainly not something people wanted to take
special looks at. And is that my fault, too? How you were
born, four whole years before I even entered the world?
Apparently this is the way God wants it to be, Hannah!
In the big book!

But the fact of the matter is, she doesn't seem to hold
me responsible for anything: she just goes on being good
to her darling little baby brother, and never once strikes
me or calls me a dirty name. I take her chocolate pudding,
and she takes my shit, and never says a word in protest.
Just kisses me before I go to bed, and carefully crosses me
going to school, and then stands back and obligingly al-
lows herself to be swallowed up by the wall (I guess
that's where she is) when I am imitating for my beaming
parents all the voices on "Allen's Alley," or being heralded
to relatives from one end of North Jersey to the other for
my perfect report card. Because when I am not being
punished, Doctor, I am being carried around that house
like the Pope through the streets of Rome . . .

You know, I can really come up with no more than a
dozen memories involving my sister from those early years
of my childhood. Mostly, until she emerges in my adolescence as the only sane person in that lunatic asylum
whom I can talk to, it is as though she is someone we see
maybe once or twice a year—for a night or two she visits

with us, eating at our table, sleeping in one of our beds, and then, poor fat thing, she just blessedly disappears.

Even in the Chinese restaurant, where the Lord has lifted the ban on pork dishes for the obedient children of Israel, the eating of lobster Cantonese is considered by God (Whose mouthpiece on earth, in matters pertaining to food, is my Mom) to be totally out of the question. Why we can eat pig on Pell Street and not at home is because . . . frankly I still haven't got the whole thing figured out, but at the time I believe it has largely to do with the fact that the elderly man who owns the place, and whom amongst ourselves we call *"Shmendrick,"* isn't somebody whose opinion of us we have cause to worry about. Yes, the only people in the world whom it seems to me the Jews are not afraid of are the Chinese. Because, one, the way they speak English makes my father sound like Lord Chesterfield; two, the insides of their heads are just so much fried rice anyway; and three, to them we are not Jews but *white*—and maybe even Anglo-Saxon. Imagine! No wonder the waiters can't intimidate us. To them we're just some big-nosed variety of WASP! Boy, do we eat! Suddenly even the pig is no threat—though, to be sure, it comes to us so chopped and shredded, and is then set afloat on our plates in such oceans of soy sauce, as to bear no resemblance at all to a pork chop, or a hambone, or, most disgusting of all, a *sausage* (ucchh!) . . . But why then can't we eat a lobster, too, disguised as something else? Allow my mother a logical explanation. The syllogism, Doctor, as used by Sophie Portnoy. Ready? Why we can't eat lobster. "Because it can kill you! Because I ate it once, and I nearly died!"

Yes, she too has committed her transgressions, and has been duly punished. In her wild youth (which all took place before I got to know her) she had allowed herself to be bamboozled (which is to say, flattered and shamed simultaneously) into eating lobster Newburg by a mischievous, attractive insurance agent who worked with my father for Boston & Northeastern, a lush named (could it be better?) Doyle.

It was at a convention held by the company in Atlantic City, at a noisy farewell banquet, that Doyle led my mother to believe that even though that wasn't what it smelled like, the plate the waiter had shoved in front of her corsage contained nothing but chicken à la king. To be sure, she sensed that something was up even then, suspected even as the handsome drunken Doyle tried to feed her with her own fork that tragedy, as she calls it, was lurking in the wings. But high herself on the fruit of two whiskey sours, she rashly turned up her long Jewish nose to a very genuine premonition of foul play, and—oh, hotheaded bitch! wanton hussy! improvident adventuress! —surrendered herself wholly to the spirit of reckless abandon that apparently had taken possession of this hall full of insurance agents and their wives. Not until the sherbet arrived did Doyle—who my mother also describes as "in looks a second Errol Flynn, and not just in looks"—did Doyle reveal to her what it was she had actually ingested.

Subsequently she was over the toilet all night throwing up. "My *kishkas* came out from that thing! Some practical joker! That's why to this day I tell you, Alex, never to commit a practical joke—because the consequences can be tragic! I was so sick, Alex," she used to love to remind herself and me, and my father too, five, ten, fifteen years after the cataclysm itself, "that your father, Mr. Brave One here, had to call the hotel doctor out of a sound sleep to come to the room. See how I'm holding my fingers? I was throwing up so hard, they got stiff just like this, like I was *paralyzed,* and *ask* your father—Jack, tell him, tell him what you thought when you saw what happened to my fingers from the lobster Newburg." "What lobster Newburg?" "That your friend Doyle forced down my throat." "Doyle? What Doyle?" "Doyle, The *Shicker Goy* Who They Had To Transfer To The Wilds of South Jersey He Was Such A Run-Around. Doyle! Who Looked Like Errol Flynn! Tell Alex what happened to my fingers, that you *thought* happened—" "Look, I don't even know what you're talking about," which is probably the case: not everybody quite senses my mother's life to be the high drama she herself experiences—also, there is always a possibility that this story has more to do with imagination than reality (more to do, needless to say, with the dangerous Doyle than the forbidden lobster). And then, of course, my father is a man who has a certain amount of worrying to do each day, and sometimes he just has to forgo listening to the conversations going on around him in order to fulfill his anxiety requirement. It can well be that he hasn't really heard a word she's been saying.

But on it goes, my mother's monologue. As other children hear the story of Scrooge every year, or are read to

nightly from some favorite book, I am continually
shtupped full of the suspense-filled chapters of her peril-
ous life. This in fact is the literature of my childhood,
these stories of my mother's—the only bound books in the
house, aside from schoolbooks, are those that have been
given as presents to my parents when one or the other
was recuperating in the hospital. One third of our library
consists of *Dragon Seed* (her hysterectomy) (moral:
nothing is never ironic, there's always a laugh lurking
somewhere) and the other two thirds are *Argentine Diary*
by William L. Shirer and (same moral) *The Memoirs
of Casanova* (his appendectomy). Otherwise our books
are written by Sophie Portnoy, each an addition to that
famous series of hers entitled, *You Know Me, I'll Try Anything Once.* For the idea that seems to generate and
inform her works is that she is some sort of daredevil who
goes exuberantly out into life in search of the new and
the thrilling, only to be slapped down for her pioneering
spirit. She actually seems to think of herself as a woman at
the very frontiers of experience, some doomed dazzling
combination of Marie Curie, Anna Karenina, and Ame-
lia Earhart. At any rate, that is the sort of romantic image
of her which this little boy goes to bed with, after she has
buttoned him into his pajamas and tucked him between
the sheets with the story of how she learned to drive a car
when she was pregnant with my sister, and the very first
day that she had her license—"the very first *hour*, Alex"
—"some maniac" slammed into her rear bumper, and consequently she has never driven a car from that moment
on. Or the story of how she was searching for the gold-

fish in a pond at Saratoga Springs, New York, where she had been taken at the age of ten to visit an old sick aunt, and accidentally fell in, right to the bottom of the filthy pond, and has not gone into the water since, not even down the shore, when it's low tide and a lifeguard is on duty. And then there is the lobster, which even in her drunkenness she knew wasn't chicken à la king, but only "to shut up the mouth on that Doyle" had forced down her throat, and subsequently the near-tragedy happened, and she has not of course eaten anything even faintly resembling lobster since. And does not want me to either. Ever. Not, she says, if I know what is good for me. "There are plenty of good things to eat in the world, Alex, without eating a thing like a lobster and running the risk of having paralyzed hands for the rest of your life."

Whew! Have I got grievances! Do I harbor hatreds I didn't even know were there! Is it the process, Doctor, or is it what we call "the material"? All I do is complain, the repugnance seems bottomless, and I'm beginning to wonder if maybe enough isn't enough. I hear myself indulging in the kind of ritualized bellyaching that is just what gives psychoanalytic patients such a bad name with the general public. Could I really have detested this childhood and resented these poor parents of mine to the same degree then as I seem to now, looking backward upon what I was from the vantage point of what I am—and am not? Is this truth I'm delivering up, or is it just plain *kvetching*? Or is *kvetching* for people like me a *form* of truth? Regardless, my conscience wishes to make it known, before the beefing begins anew, that *at the time* my boyhood was not this thing I feel so estranged from and resentful of now. Vast as my confusion was, deep as my inner turmoil seems to appear in retrospect, I don't remember that I was one of those kids who went around wishing he lived in another house with other people, whatever my unconscious yearnings may have been in that direction. After all, where else would I find an audience like those two for my imitations? I used to leave them in the aisles at mealtime—my mother once actually wet her pants, Doctor, and had to go running in hysterical laughter to the bathroom from my impression of Mister Kitzel on "The Jack Benny Show." What else? Walks, walks with my father in Weequahic Park on Sundays that I still haven't forgotten. You know, I can't go off to the country and find an acorn on the ground without thinking of him and those walks. And that's not nothing, nearly thirty years later.

And have I mentioned, vis-à-vis my mother, the running conversation we two had in those years before I was even old enough to go off by myself to a school? During those five years when we had each other alone all day long, I do believe we covered just about every subject known to man. "Talking to Alex," she used to tell my father when he walked in exhausted at night, "I can do a whole afternoon of ironing, and never even notice the time go by." And mind you, I am only *four*.

And as for the hollering, the cowering, the crying, even that had vividness and excitement to recommend it; moreover, that nothing was ever simply nothing but always

SOMETHING, that the most ordinary kind of occurrence could explode without warning into A TERRIBLE CRISIS, this was to me *the way life is.* The novelist, what's his name, Markfield, has written in a story somewhere that until he was fourteen he believed "aggravation" to be a Jewish word. Well, this was what I thought about "tumult" and "bedlam," two favorite nouns of my mother's. Also "spatula." I was already the darling of the first grade, and in every schoolroom competition, expected to win hands down, when I was asked by the teacher one day to identify a picture of what I knew perfectly well my mother referred to as a "spatula." But for the life of me I could not think of the word in English. Stammering and flushing, I sank defeated into my seat, not nearly so stunned as my teacher but badly shaken up just the same . . . and that's how far back my fate goes, how early in the game it was "normal" for me to be in a state resembling torment—in this particular instance over something as monumental as a kitchen utensil.

Oh, all that conflict over a spatula, Momma,
Imagine how I feel about you!

I am reminded at this joyous little juncture of when we lived in Jersey City, back when I was still very much my mother's papoose, still very much a sniffer of her body perfumes and a total slave to her *kugel* and *grieben* and *ruggelech*—there was a suicide in our building. A fifteen-year-old boy named Ronald Nimkin, who had been crowned by the women in the building "José Iturbi the Second," hanged himself from the shower head in his bathroom. "With those golden hands!" the women wailed, referring of course to his piano playing—"With that talent!" Followed by, "You couldn't look for a boy more in love with his mother than Ronald!"

I swear to you, this is not bullshit or a screen memory, these are the very words these women use. The great dark operatic themes of human suffering and passion come rolling out of those mouths like the prices of Oxydol and Del Monte canned corn! My own mother, let me remind you, when I returned this past summer from my adventure in Europe, greets me over the phone with the following salutation: "Well, how's my lover?" Her *lover* she calls me, while her husband is listening on the other extension! And it never occurs to her, if I'm her lover, who is he, the *schmegeggy* she lives with? No, you don't have to go digging where these people are concerned—they wear the old unconscious on their *sleeves!*

Mrs. Nimkin, weeping in our kitchen: "Why? Why? Why did he do this to us?" Hear? Not what might *we* have done to *him*, oh no, never that—why did he do this *to us?* To us! Who would have given our arms and legs to make him happy and a famous concert pianist into the bargain! Really, can they be this blind? Can people be so abysmally stupid and live? Do you *believe* it? Can they actually be equipped with all the machinery, a brain, a spinal cord, and the four apertures for the ears and eyes—equipment, Mrs. Nimkin, nearly as impressive as color TV—and still go through life without a single clue about the feelings and yearnings of anyone other than themselves? Mrs. Nimkin, you shit, I remember you, I was only six, but I remember you, and what killed your Ronald, the concert-pianist-to-be is obvious: YOUR FUCKING SELFISHNESS AND STUPIDITY! "All the lessons we gave him," weeps Mrs. Nimkin . . . Oh look, look, why do I carry on like this? Maybe she means well, surely she must—at a time of grief, what can I expect of these simple people? It's only because in her misery she doesn't know what else to say that she says that God-awful thing about all the lessons they gave to somebody who is now a corpse. What are they, after all, these Jewish women who raised us up as children? In Calabria you see their suffering counterparts sitting like stones in the churches, swallowing all that hideous Catholic bullshit; in Calcutta they beg in the streets, or if they are lucky, are off somewhere in a dusty field hitched up to a plow . . . Only in America, Rabbi Golden, do these peasants, our mothers, get their hair dyed platinum at the age of sixty, and walk up and down Collins Avenue in Florida in pedalpushers and mink stoles—and with opinions on every subject under the sun. It isn't their fault they were given a gift like speech— look, if cows could talk, they would say things just as idiotic. Yes, yes, maybe that's the solution then: think of them as cows, who have been given the twin miracles of speech and mah-jongg. Why not be charitable in one's thinking, right, Doctor?

My favorite detail from the Ronald Nimkin suicide: even as he is swinging from the shower head, there is a note pinned to the dead young pianist's short-sleeved shirt —which is what I remember most about Ronald: this tall emaciated teen-age catatonic, swimming around all by

himself in those oversized short-sleeved sport shirts, and
with their lapels starched and ironed back so fiercely
they looked to have been bulletproofed . . . And Ronald
himself, every limb strung so tight to his backbone that
if you touched him, he would probably have begun to
hum . . . and the fingers, of course, those long white
grotesqueries, seven knuckles at least before you got down
to the nicely gnawed nail, those Bela Lugosi hands that
my mother would tell me—and tell me—*and tell me*—because nothing is ever said once—nothing!—were "the hands
of a born pianist."

Pianist! Oh, that's one of the words they just love, almost as much as *doctor*, Doctor. And *residency*. And best
of all, *his own office. He opened his own office in Living-
ston.* "Do you remember Seymour Schmuck, Alex?" she
asks me, or Aaron Putz or Howard Shlong, or some yo-yo
I am supposed to have known in grade school twenty-five
years ago, and of whom I have no recollection whatsoever.
"Well, I met his mother on the street today, and she told
me that Seymour is now the biggest brain surgeon in the
entire Western Hemisphere. He owns six different split-
level ranch-type houses made all of fieldstone in Living-
ston, and belongs to the boards of eleven synagogues, all
brand-new and designed by Marc Kugel, and last year
with his wife and his two little daughters, who are so
beautiful that they are already under contract to Metro,
and so brilliant that they should be in college—he took
them all to Europe for an eighty-million-dollar tour of
seven thousand countries, some of them you never even
heard of, that they made them just to honor Seymour, and

on top of that, he's so important, Seymour, that in every single city in Europe that they visited he was asked by the mayor himself to stop and do an impossible operation on a brain in hospitals that they also built for him right on the spot, and—listen to this—where they pumped into the operating room during the operation the theme song from *Exodus* so everybody should know what religion he is—and that's how big your friend Seymour is today! *And how happy he makes his parents!"*

And you, the implication is, when are *you* going to get married already? In Newark and the surrounding suburbs this apparently is the question on everybody's lips: WHEN IS ALEXANDER PORTNOY GOING TO STOP BEING SELFISH AND GIVE HIS PARENTS, WHO ARE SUCH WONDERFUL PEOPLE, GRANDCHIL-DREN? "Well," says my father, the tears brimming up in his eyes, "well," he asks, *every single time I see him,* "is there a serious girl in the picture, Big Shot? Excuse me for asking, I'm only your father, but since I'm not going to be alive forever, and you in case you forgot carry the family name, I wonder if maybe you could let me in on the secret."

Yes, shame, shame, on Alex P., the only member of his graduating class who hasn't made grandparents of his Mommy and his Daddy. While everybody else has been marrying nice Jewish girls, and having children, and buy-ing houses, and (my father's phrase) *putting down roots,* while all the other sons have been carrying forward the family name, what he has been doing is—chasing cunt. And *shikse* cunt, to boot! Chasing it, sniffing it, lapping it, *shtupping* it, but above all, *thinking about it.* Day and

night, at work and on the street—thirty-three years old
and still he is roaming the streets with his eyes popping. A
wonder he hasn't been ground to mush by a taxicab, given
how he makes his way across the major arteries of Manhattan during the lunch hour. Thirty-three, and still
ogling and daydreaming about every girl who crosses
her legs opposite him in the subway! Still cursing himself
for speaking not a word to the succulent pair of tits that
rode twenty-five floors alone with him in an elevator!
Then cursing himself for the opposite as well! For he has
been known to walk up to thoroughly respectable-looking
girls in the street, and despite the fact that since his appearance on Sunday morning TV his face is not entirely
unknown to an enlightened segment of the public—despite the fact that he may be on his way to his current
mistress' apartment for his dinner—he has been known on
one or two occasions to mutter, "Look, would you like
to come home with me?" *Of course* she is going to say
"No." Of course she is going to scream, "Get out of here,
you!" or answer curtly, "I have a nice home of my own,
thank you, with a husband in it." What is he doing to himself, this fool! this idiot! this furtive *boy!* This sex maniac!
He simply cannot—*will* not—control the fires in his putz,
the fevers in his brain, the desire continually burning
within for the new, the wild, the unthought-of and, if you
can imagine such a thing, *the undreamt-of.* Where cunt
is concerned he lives in a condition that has neither dimin-
ished nor in any significant way been refined from what
it was when he was fifteen years old and could not get
up from his seat in the classroom without hiding a hard-on

beneath his three-ring notebook. Every girl he sees turns out (hold your hats) to be carrying around between her legs—a real cunt. Amazing! Astonishing! Still can't get over the fantastic idea that when you are looking at a girl, you are looking at somebody who is guaranteed to have on her—a cunt! *They all have cunts!* Right under their dresses! Cunts—for fucking! And, Doctor, Your Honor, whatever your name is—it seems to make no difference how much the poor bastard actually gets, for he is dreaming about tomorrow's pussy even while pumping away at today's!

Do I exaggerate? Am I doing myself in only as a clever way of showing off? Or boasting perhaps? Do I really experience this restlessness, this horniness, as an affliction —or as an accomplishment? Both? Could be. Or is it only a means of evasion? Look, at least I don't find myself still in my early thirties locked into a marriage with some nice person whose body has ceased to be of any genuine interest to me—at least I don't have to get into bed every night with somebody who by and large I fuck out of obligation instead of lust. I mean, the nightmarish depression some people suffer at bedtime . . . On the other hand, even I must admit that there is maybe, from a certain perspective, something a little depressing about my situation, too. Of course you can't have everything, or so I understand—but the question I am willing to face is: have I anything? How much longer do I go on conducting these experiments with women? How much longer do I go on sticking this thing into the holes that come available to it—first this hole, then when I tire of this hole, that hole over there . . . and so on. When will it end? Only *why* should it end! To please a father and mother? To conform to the norm? Why on earth should I be so defensive about being what was honorably called some years ago, a bachelor? After all, that's all this is, you know—bachelorhood. So what's the crime? Sexual freedom? In this day and age? Why should *I* bend to the bourgeoisie? Do I ask them to bend to me? Maybe I've been touched by the tarbrush of Bohemia a little—is that so awful? Whom am I harming with my lusts? I don't blackjack the ladies, I don't twist arms to get them into bed with me. I am, if I may say so, an honest and compassionate man; let me tell you, as men go I am . . . But why must I explain myself! *Excuse* myself! Why must I justify with my Honesty and Compassion my desires! So I have desires—only they're endless. Endless! And that, that may not be such a blessing, taking for the moment a psychoanalytic point of view . . . But then all the unconscious can do anyway, so Freud tells us, is *want*. *And* want! *And* WANT! Oh, Freud, do I know! This one has a nice ass, but she talks too much. On the other hand, this one here doesn't talk at all, at least not so that she makes any sense—but, boy, can she suck! What cock know-how! While here is a honey of a girl, with the softest, pinkest, most touching nipples I have ever drawn between my lips, only she won't go down on me. Isn't that odd? And yet—go understand people—it is her pleasure while being boffed to have one or the other of my forefingers lodged snugly up her anus. What a mysterious business it is! The endless fascination of these apertures and openings! You see, I just can't stop! Or tie myself to any *one*. I have affairs that last as long as a year, a year and a half, months and months of love, both tender and voluptuous, but in the end—it is as inevitable as death—time marches on and lust peters out. In the end, I just cannot take that step into marriage. But why should I? *Why?* Is there a law saying Alex Portnoy has to be somebody's husband and father? Doctor, they can stand on the window ledge and threaten to splatter themselves on the pavement below, they can pile the Seconal to the ceiling—I may have to live for weeks and weeks on end in terror of these marriage-bent girls throwing themselves beneath the subway train, but I simply cannot, I simply *will* not, enter into a contract to sleep with just one woman for the rest of my days. Imagine it: suppose I were to go ahead and marry A, with her sweet tits and so on, what will happen when B appears, whose are even sweeter—or, at any rate, newer? Or C, who knows how to move her ass in some special way I have never experienced; or D, or E, of F. I'm trying to be honest with you, Doctor—because with sex the human imagination runs to Z, and then beyond! Tits and cunts and legs and lips and mouths and tongues and assholes! How can I give up what I have never even had, for a girl, who delicious and provocative as once she may have been, will inevitably grow as familiar to me as a loaf of bread? For love? What love? Is that what binds all these couples we know together—the ones who even bother to let themselves be bound? Isn't it something more like weakness? Isn't it rather convenience and apathy and guilt? Isn't it rather fear and exhaustion and inertia, gutlessness plain and simple, far far more than that "love" that the marriage counselors and the songwriters and the psychotherapists are forever dreaming about? Please, let us not bullshit one another about "love" and its duration. Which is why I ask: how can I marry someone I "love" knowing full well that five, six, seven years hence I am going to be out on the streets hunting down the fresh new pussy—all the while my devoted wife, who has made me such a lovely home, et cetera, bravely suffers her loneliness and rejection? How could I face her terrible tears? I couldn't. How could I face my adoring children? And then the divorce, right? The *child* support. The *alimony*. The *visitation* rights. Wonderful prospect, just wonderful. And as for anybody who kills herself because I prefer not to be blind to the future, well, she is her worry—she has to be! There is surely no need or justification for anybody to threaten suicide just because I am wise enough to see what frustrations and recriminations lie ahead . . . Baby, please, don't howl like that please—somebody is going to think you're being strangled to death. Oh baby (I hear myself pleading, last year, this year, every year of my life!), you're going to be all right, really, truly you are; you're going to be just fine and dandy and much better off, so please, you bitch, come back inside this room *and let me go!* "You! You and your filthy cock!" cries the most recently disappointed (and self-appointed) bride-to-be, my strange, lanky, and very batty friend, who used to earn as much in an hour posing for underwear ads as her illiterate father would earn in a week in the coal mines of West Virginia: "I thought you were supposed to be a superior person, you muff-diving, mother-fucking son of a bitch!" This beautiful girl, who has got me all wrong, is called The Monkey, a nickname that derives from a little perversion she once engaged in shortly before meeting me and going on to grander things. Doctor, I had never had anybody like her in my life, she was the fulfillment of my most lascivious adolescent dreams—but marry her, can she be serious? You see, for all her preening and perfumes, she has a very low opinion of herself, and simultaneously—and here is the source of much of our trouble—a ridiculously high opinion of me. And simultaneously, a very *low* opinion of me! She is one confused Monkey, and, I'm afraid, not too very bright. "An intellectual!" she screams. "An educated, spiritual person! You mean, miserable hard-on you, you care more about the niggers in Harlem that you don't even know, than you do about me, who's been sucking you off for a solid year!" Confused, heartbroken, and also out of her mind. For all this comes to me from the balcony of our hotel room in Athens, as I stand in the doorway, suitcases in hand, begging her to *please* come back inside so that I can catch a plane out of that place. Then the angry little manager, all olive oil, mustache, and outraged respectability, is running up the stairway waving his arms in the air—and so, taking a deep breath, I say, "Look, you want to jump, jump!" and out I go—and the last words I hear have to do with the fact that it was only out of love for me ("*Love!*" she screams) that she allowed herself to do the degrading things I forced quote unquote upon her.

Which is not the case, Doctor! Not the case at all!
Which is an attempt on this sly bitch's part to break me
on the rack of guilt—and thus get herself a husband. Because at twenty-nine that's what she wants, you see—but
that does not mean, you see, that I have to oblige. "In
September, you son of a bitch, I am going to be thirty
years old!" Correct, Monkey, correct! Which is precisely
why it is you and not me who is responsible for your
expectations and your dreams! Is that clear? *You!* "I'll
tell the world about you, you cold-hearted prick! I'll tell
them what a filthy pervert you are, and the dirty things
you made me do!"

The cunt! I'm lucky really that I came out of that affair *alive.* If I have!

But back to my parents, and how it seems that by re-
maining in my single state I bring these people, too,
nothing but grief. That I happen, Mommy and Daddy, just
happen to have recently been appointed by the Mayor to
be Assistant Commissioner for The City of New York Commission on Human Opportunity apparently doesn't mean
shit to you in terms of accomplishment and stature—
though this is not exactly the case, I know, for, to be
truthful, whenever my name now appears in a news story
in the *Times,* they bombard every living relative with a
copy of the clipping. Half my father's retirement pay goes
down the drain in postage, and my mother is on the
phone for days at a stretch and has to be fed intravenously,
her mouth is going at such a rate about her Alex. In fact,
it is exactly as it always has been: they can't get over what

a success and a genius I am, my name in the paper, an
associate now of the glamorous new Mayor, on the side
of Truth and Justice, enemy of slumlords and bigots and
rats ("to encourage equality of treatment, to prevent discrimination, to foster mutual understanding and respect—"
my commission's humane purpose, as decreed by act of
the City Council) . . . but still, if you know what I mean,
still somehow not entirely perfect.

Now, can you beat that for a serpent's tooth? All they
have sacrificed for me and done for me and how they
boast about me and are the best public relations firm
(they tell me) any child could have, and it turns out
that I still won't be perfect. Did you ever hear of such
a thing in your life? I just refuse to be perfect. What a
pricky kid.

They come to visit: "Where did you get a rug like this?"
my father asks, making a face. "Did you get this thing in
a junk shop or did somebody give it to you?"

"I like this rug."

"What are you talking," my father says, "it's a worn-out
rug."

Light-hearted. "It's worn, but not out. Okay? Enough?"

"Alex, please," my mother says, "it is a very worn rug."

"You'll trip on that thing," my father says, "and throw
your knee out of whack, and then you'll really be in
trouble."

"And with your knee," says my mother meaningfully,
"that wouldn't be a picnic."

At this rate they are going to roll the thing up any

minute now, the two of them, and push it out the window.
And then take me home!

"The rug is fine. My *knee* is fine."

"It wasn't so fine," my mother is quick to remind me,
"when you had the cast on, darling, up to your hip. How
he *shlepped* that thing around! How miserable he was!"

"I was fourteen years old then, Mother."

"Yeah, and you came out of that thing," my father says,
"you couldn't bend your leg, I thought you were going to
be a cripple for the rest of your life. I told him, 'Bend it!
Bend it!' I practically begged him morning, noon, and
night, 'Do you want to be a cripple forever? Bend that
leg!'"

"You scared the *daylights* out of us with that knee."

"But that was in nineteen hundred and forty-seven.
And this is nineteen sixty-six. The cast has been off nearly
twenty years!"

My mother's cogent reply? "You'll see, someday
you'll be a parent, and you'll know what it's like. And
then maybe you won't sneer at your family any more."

The legend engraved on the face of the Jewish nickel—
on the body of every Jewish child!—not IN GOD WE
TRUST, but SOMEDAY YOU'LL BE A PARENT AND
YOU'LL KNOW WHAT IT'S LIKE.

"You think," my father the ironist asks, "it'll be in our
lifetime, Alex? You think it'll happen before I go down
into the grave? No—he'd rather take chances with a worn-
out rug!" The ironist—and logician! "—And crack his head
open! And let me ask you something else, my independent son—who would even know you were here if you were

lying bleeding to death on the floor? Half the time you don't answer the phone, I see you lying here with God only knows what's wrong—and who is there to take care of you? Who is there even to bring you a bowl of soup, if God forbid something terrible should happen?"

"I can take care of myself! I don't go around like some people"—boy, still pretty tough with the old man, eh, Al?—"some people I know in continual anticipation of total catastrophe!"

"You'll see," he says, nodding miserably, "you'll get sick"—and suddenly a squeal of anger, a whine out of nowhere of absolute hatred *of me!*—*"you'll get old, and you won't be such an independent big shot then!"*

"Alex, Alex," begins my mother, as my father walks to my window to recover himself, and in passing, to comment contemptuously about "the neighborhood he lives in." I work *for* New York, and he still wants me to live in beautiful Newark!

"Mother, I'm thirty-three! I am the Assistant Commissioner of Human Opportunity for the City of New York! I graduated first in my law school class! Remember? I have graduated first from every class I've ever *been* in! At twenty-five I was already special counsel to a House Subcommittee—of the United States Congress, Mother! Of America! If I wanted Wall Street, Mother, I could be on Wall Street! I am a highly respected man in my profession, that should be obvious! Right this minute, Mother, I am conducting an investigation of unlawful discriminatory practices in the building trades in New York—*racial discrimination!* Trying to get the Ironworkers' Union,

Mother, to tell me their little secrets! That's what I did
just today! Look, *I* helped solve the television quiz scandal, do you *remember—?*" Oh, why go on? Why go on
in my strangled high-pitched adolescent voice? Good
Christ, a Jewish man with parents alive is a fifteen-year-
old boy, and will remain a fifteen-year-old boy till *they
die!*

Anyway, Sophie has by this time taken my hand, and
with hooded eyes, waits until I sputter out the last accomplishment I can think of, the last virtuous deed I have
done, then speaks: "But to us, to us you're still a baby,
darling." And next comes the whisper, Sophie's famous
whisper that everybody in the room can hear without
even straining, she's so considerate: "Tell him you're
sorry. Give him a kiss. A kiss from you would change the
world."

A kiss from me *would change the world!* Doctor! Doctor! Did I say fifteen? Excuse me, I meant ten! I meant
five! I meant zero! A Jewish man with his parents alive is
half the time a helpless *infant!* Listen, come to my aid,
will you—and quick! Spring me from this role I play of the
smothered son in the Jewish joke! Because it's beginning
to pall a little, at thirty-three! And also it *hoits*, you
know, there is *pain* involved, a little human suffering is
being felt, if I may take it upon myself to say so—only
that's the part Sam Levenson leaves *out!* Sure, they sit in
the casino at the Concord, the women in their minks and
the men in their phosphorescent suits, and boy, do they
laugh, laugh and laugh and laugh—"Help, help, my son the
doctor is drowning!"—ha ha *ha,* ha ha *ha,* only what

about the *pain*, Myron Cohen! What about the guy who
is actually drowning! Actually sinking beneath an ocean
of parental relentlessness! What about him—who happens, Myron Cohen, to be *me!* Doctor, *please*, I can't live
any more in a world given its meaning and dimension by
some vulgar nightclub clown. By some—some *black humor-
ist!* Because that's who the black humorists are—of course!
—the Henny Youngmans and the Milton Berles breaking
them up down there in the Fountainebleau, and with
what? Stories of murder and mutilation! "Help," cries the
woman running along the sand at Miami Beach, "help,
my son the doctor is drowning!" Ha ha ha—only it is *my
son the patient*, lady! And is he drowning! Doctor, get
these people off my ass, will you please? The macabre is
very funny on the stage—but not to live it, thank you! So
just tell me how, and I'll do it! Just tell me what, and I'll
say it right to their faces! Scat, Sophie! Fuck off, Jack!
Go *away* from me already!

I mean here's a joke for you, for instance. Three Jews
are walking down the street, my mother, my father, and
me. It's this past summer, just before I am to leave on
my vacation. We have had our dinner ("You got a piece
of fish?" my father asks the waiter in the fancy French
restaurant I take them to, *to show I am grown-up*—"*Oui,
monsieur*, we have—" "All right, give me a piece of fish,"
says my father, "*and make sure it's hot*"), we have had
our dinner, and afterward, chewing on my Titralac (for
relief of gastric hyperacidity), I walk a ways with them
before putting them in a taxi for the Port Authority Bus
Terminal. Immediately my father starts in about how I

haven't come to visit in five weeks (ground I thought we two had already covered in the restaurant, while my mother was whispering to the waiter to make sure her "big boy's" piece of fish—that's me, folks!—was well-done), and now I am going away for a whole month, and all in all when do they ever see their own son? They see their daughter, and their daughter's children, and not infrequently, but that is not successful either. "With that son-in-law," my father says, "if you don't say the right psychological thing to his kids, if I don't talk straight psychology to my own granddaughters, he wants to put me in jail! I don't care what he calls himself, he still thinks like a Communist to me. My own grandchildren, and everything I say has to pass by him, Mr. Censor!" No, their daughter is now Mrs. Feibish, and her little daughters are Feibishes too. Where are the Portnoys he dreamed of? In my nuts. "Look," I cry in my strangulated way, "you're seeing me *now!* You're with me *right this minute!*" But he is off and running, and now that he hasn't fishbones to worry about choking on, there is no reining him in—Mr. and Mrs. Schmuck have Seymour and his beautiful wife and their seven thousand brilliant and beautiful children who come to them *every single Friday night*—"Look, I am a very busy person! I have a briefcase full of important things to do—!" "Come on," he replies, "you gotta eat, you can come for a meal once a week, because you gotta eat anyway comes six o'clock—well, don't you?" Whereupon who pipes up but Sophie, informing him that when she was a little girl her family was always telling her to do this and do that, and how unhappy and resentful it sometimes would cause her to feel, and how my father shouldn't insist with me because, she concludes, "Alexander is a big boy, Jack, he has a right to make his own decisions, that's something I always told him." You always *what? What* did she say?

Oh, why go on? Why be so obsessed like this? Why be so petty? Why not be a sport like Sam Levenson and laugh it all off—right?

Only let me finish. So they get into the taxi. "Kiss him," mother whispers, "you're going all the way to Europe."

Of course my father overhears—that's why she lowers her voice, so we'll all listen—and panic sweeps over him. Every year, from September on, he is perpetually asking me what my plans are for the following August—now he realizes that he has been outfoxed: bad enough I am leaving on a midnight plane for another continent, but worse, he hasn't the slightest idea of my itinerary. I did it! I made it!

"—But where in Europe? Europe is half the whole globe—" he cries, as I begin to close the taxi door from the outside.

"I told you, I don't know."

"What do you mean? You *gotta* know! How will you get there yourself, if you 'don't know'—"

"Sorry, sorry—"

Desperately now his body comes lurching across my mother's—just as I slam shut the door—*oy*, not on his fingers, please! Jesus, this father! Whom I have had forever! Whom I used to find in the morning fast asleep on the toilet bowl, his pajamas around his knees and his chin hanging onto his chest. Up at quarter to six in the morn-

ing, so as to give himself a full uninterrupted hour on the
can, in the fervent hope that if he is so kind and thoughtful as this to his bowels, they will relent, they will give in,
they will say finally, "Okay, Jack, you win," and make a
present to the poor bastard of five or six measly lumps of
shit. "Jesus Christ!" he groans, when I awaken him so as
to wash up for school, and he realizes that it is nearly seven-
thirty and down in the bowl over which he has been
sleeping for an hour, there is, if he's lucky, one brown
angry little pellet such as you expect from the rectum of a
rabbit maybe—but not from the rear-end of a man who
now has to go out all clogged up to put in a twelve-hour
day. "Seven-*thirty?* Why didn't you say something!"
Zoom, he's dressed, and in his hat and coat, and with his
big black collection book in one hand he bolts his stewed
prunes and his bran flakes standing up, and fills a pocket
with a handful of dried fruits that would bring on in an
ordinary human being something resembling dysentery.
"I ought to stick a hand grenade up my ass, if you want the
truth," he whispers privately to me, while my mother oc-
cupies the bathroom and my sister dresses for school in her
"room," the sun parlor—"I got enough All-Bran in me
to launch a battleship. It's backed up to my throat, for
Christ's sake." Here, because he has got me snickering, and
is amusing himself too in his own mordant way, he opens
his mouth and points downward inside himself with a
thumb. "Take a look. See where it starts to get dark? That
ain't just dark—that's all those prunes rising up where my
tonsils used to be. Thank God I had those things out,
otherwise there wouldn't be room."

"Very nice talk," my mother calls from the bathroom. "Very nice talk to a child."

"Talk?" he cries. "It's the *truth*," and in the very next instant is thomping angrily around the house hollering, "My hat, I'm late, where's my hat? who saw my hat?" and my mother comes into the kitchen and gives me her patient, eternal, all-knowing sphinx-look . . . and waits . . . and soon he is back in the hallway, apoplectic and moaning, practically in grief, "Where is my hat? *Where is that hat!*" until softly, from the depths of her omniscient soul, she answers him, "Dummy, it's on your head." Momentarily his eyes seem to empty of all signs of human experience and understanding; he stands there, a blank, a thing, a body full of shit and no more. Then consciousness returns—yes, he will have to go out into the world after all, for his hat has been found, on his head of all places. "Oh yeah," he says, reaching up in wonderment —and then out of the house and into the Kaiser, and Superman is gone until dark.

The Kaiser, time for my story about the Kaiser: how he proudly took me with him when he went after the war to trade in the '39 Dodge for a new automobile, new make, new model, new everything—what a perfect way for an American dad to impress his American son!—and how the fast-talking salesman acted as though he just couldn't believe his ears, was simply incredulous, each time my father said "No" to one after another of the thousand little accessories the cock-sucker wanted to sell us to hang on the car. "Well, I'll tell you my opinion for whatever it's worth," says that worthless son of a bitch, "she'd look two

hun-erd percent better with the whitewalls—don't you
think so, young fella? Wouldn't you like your dad to get
the whitewalls, at least?" At least. Ah, you slimy prick,
you! Turning to me like that, to stick it into my old man—
you miserable lowlife thieving son of a bitch! Just who the
fuck are you, I wonder, to lord it over us—a God damn
Kaiser-Fraser salesman! Where are you *now,* you intimi-
dating bastard? "No, no whitewalls," mumbles my hum-
bled father, and I simply shrug my shoulders in embarrass-
ment over his inability to provide me and my family with
the beautiful things in life.

Anyway, anyway—off to work in the radio-less white-
wall-less Kaiser, there to be let into the office by the
cleaning lady. Now, I ask you, why must he be the one
to raise the shades in that office in the morning? Why
must he work the longest day of any insurance agent in
history? For whom? *Me?* Oh, if so, if so, if that is his reason, then it is all really too fucking tragic to bear. The
misunderstanding is too great! For *me?* Do me a favor *and
don't do it for me!* Don't please look around for a reason
for your life being what it is and come up with Alex!
Because I am not the be-all and end-all of everybody's
existence! I refuse to *shlep those* bags around for the rest
of *my* life! Do you hear me? I refuse! Stop finding it incomprehensible that I should be flying to Europe, thousands and thousands of miles away, just when you have
turned sixty-six and are all ready to keel over at any minute, like you read about first thing every morning in the
Times. Men his age and younger, *they die*—one minute
they're alive, and the next dead, and apparently what he

thinks is that if I am only across the Hudson instead of the Atlantic . . . Listen, what *does* he think? That with me around it simply won't happen? That I'll race to his side, take hold of his hand, and thereby restore him to life? Does he actually believe that I somehow have the power to destroy death? That I am the resurrection and the life? My dad, a real believing Christer! And doesn't even know it!

His death. His death and his bowels: the truth is I am hardly less preoccupied with either than he is himself. I never get a telegram, never get a phone call after midnight, that I do not feel my own stomach empty out like a washbasin, and say aloud—aloud!—"He's dead." Because apparently I believe it too, believe that I can somehow save him from annihilation—can, and must! But where did we all get this ridiculous and absurd idea that I am so—powerful, so precious, so necessary to everybody's survival! What was it with these Jewish parents—because I am not in this boat alone, oh no, I am on the biggest troop ship afloat . . . only look in through the portholes and see us there, stacked to the bulkheads in our bunks, moaning and groaning with such pity for ourselves, the sad and watery-eyed sons of Jewish parents, sick to the gills from rolling through these heavy seas of guilt—so I sometimes envision us, me and my fellow wailers, melancholics, and wise guys, still in steerage, like our forebears —and oh sick, sick as dogs, we cry out intermittently, one of us or another, "Poppa, how could you?" "Momma, why did you?" and the stories we tell, as the big ship pitches and rolls, the vying we do—who had the most castrating mother, who the most benighted father, I can match you, you bastard, humiliation for humiliation, shame for shame . . . the retching in the toilets after meals, the hysterical deathbed laughter from the bunks, and the tears— here a puddle wept in contrition, here a puddle from indignation—in the blinking of an eye, the body of a man (with the brain of a boy) rises in impotent rage to flail at the mattress above, only to fall instantly back, lashing itself with reproaches. Oh, my Jewish men friends! My dirty-mouthed guilt-ridden brethren! My sweethearts! My mates! Will this fucking ship ever stop pitching? When? *When,* so that we can leave off complaining how sick we are—and go out into the air, and live!

Doctor Spielvogel, it alleviates nothing fixing the blame —blaming is still ailing, of course, of course—but nonetheless, what *was* it with these Jewish parents, *what,* that they were able to make us little Jewish boys believe ourselves to be princes on the one hand, unique as unicorns on the one hand, geniuses and brilliant like nobody has ever been brilliant and beautiful before in the history of childhood—saviors and sheer perfection on the one hand, and such bumbling, incompetent, thoughtless, helpless, selfish, evil little shits, little *ingrates,* on the other!

"But in Europe *where*—?" he calls after me, as the taxi pulls away from the curb.

"I don't *know* where," I call after him, gleefully waving farewell. I am thirty-three, and free at last of my mother and father! For a month.

"But how will we know your address?"

Joy! Sheer joy! "You won't!"

"But what if in the meantime—?"

"What if what?" I laugh. "What if what are you worried about now?"

"What if—?" And my God, does he really actually shout it out of the taxi window? Is his fear, his greed, his need and belief in me so great that he actually shouts these words out into the streets of New York? "What if I die?"

Because that is what I hear, Doctor. The last words I hear before flying off to Europe—and with The Monkey, somebody whom I have kept a total secret from them. "What if I die?" and then off I go for my orgiastic holiday abroad.

. . . Now, whether the words I hear are the words spoken is something else again. And whether what I hear I hear out of compassion for him, out of my agony over the inevitability of this horrific occurrence, his death, or out of my eager anticipation of that event, is also something else again. But this of course you understand, this of course is your bread and your butter.

I was saying that the detail of Ronald Nimkin's suicide that most appeals to me is the note to his mother found pinned to that roomy straitjacket, his nice stiffly laundered sports shirt. Know what it said? Guess. The last message from Ronald to his momma? Guess.

Mrs. Blumenthal called. Please bring your mah-jongg rules to the game tonight.

Ronald

Now, how's *that* for good to the last drop? How's that
for a good boy, a thoughtful boy, a kind and courteous
and well-behaved boy, a nice Jewish boy such as no one
will ever have cause to be ashamed of? Say thank you,
darling. Say you're welcome, darling. Say you're sorry,
Alex. Say you're sorry! *Apologize!* Yeah, for what? What
have I done now? Hey, I'm hiding under my bed, my back
to the wall, refusing to say I'm sorry, refusing, too, to
come out and take the consequences. *Refusing!* And she is
after me with a broom, trying to sweep my rotten carcass
into the open. Why, shades of Gregor Samsa! Hello Alex,
goodbye Franz! "You better tell me you're sorry, you, or
else! And I don't mean maybe either!" I am five, maybe
six, and she is or-elsing me and not-meaning-maybe as
though the firing squad is already outside, lining the
street with newspaper preparatory to my execution.

And now comes the father: after a pleasant day of trying to sell life insurance to black people who aren't even
exactly sure they're alive, home to a hysterical wife and
a metamorphosed child—because what did I do, me, the
soul of goodness? Incredible, beyond belief, but either
I kicked her in the shins, or I bit her. I don't want to sound
like I'm boasting, but I do believe it was *both.*

"Why?" she demands to know, kneeling on the floor
to shine a flashlight in my eyes, "why do you do such a
thing?" Oh, simple, why did Ronald Nimkin give up his
ghost and the piano? BECAUSE WE CAN'T TAKE ANY
MORE! BECAUSE YOU FUCKING JEWISH MOTH-
ERS ARE JUST TOO FUCKING MUCH TO BEAR! I
have read Freud on Leonardo, Doctor, and pardon the

hubris, but my fantasies exactly: this big smothering bird beating frantic wings about my face and mouth *so that I cannot even get my breath.* What do we want, me and Ronald and Leonardo? *To be left alone!* If only for half an hour at a time! Stop already *hocking* us to be *good! hocking* us to be *nice!* Just leave us alone, God damn it, to pull our little dongs in peace and think our little selfish thoughts—stop already with the respectabilizing of our hands and our tushies and our mouths! Fuck the vitamins and the cod liver oil! Just give us each day our daily flesh! And forgive us our trespasses—which aren't even trespasses to begin with!

"—a little boy you want to be who kicks his own mother in the shins—?" My father speaking . . . and look at his arms, will you? I have never really noticed before the size of the forearms the man has got on him. He may not have whitewall tires or a high school education, but he has arms on him that are no joke. And, Jesus, is he angry. But why? In part, you schmuck, I kicked her for *you!*

"—a human bite is worse than a dog bite, do you know that, you? Get out from under that bed! Do you hear me, what you did to your mother is worse than a dog could do!" And so loud is his roar, and so convincing, that my normally placid sister runs to the kitchen, great gruntfuls of fear erupting from her mouth, and in what we now call the fetal position crouches down between the refrigerator and the wall. Or so I seem to remember it—though it would make sense, I think, to ask how I know what is going on in the kitchen if I am still hiding beneath my bed.

"The bite I can live with, the shins I can live with"— her broom still relentlessly trying to poke me out from my cave—"but what am I going to do with a child who won't even say he's sorry? Who won't tell his own mother that he's sorry and will never never do such a thing again, *ever!* What are we going to do, Daddy, with such a little boy in our house!"

Is she *kidding?* Is she *serious?* Why doesn't she call the cops and get me shipped off to children's prison, if this is how incorrigible I really am? "Alexander Portnoy, aged five, you are hereby sentenced to hang by your neck until you are dead for refusing to say you are sorry to your mother." You'd think the child lapping up their milk and taking baths with his duck and his boats in their tub was the most wanted criminal in America. When actually what we are playing in that house is some farce version of *King Lear,* with me in the role of Cordelia! On the phone she is perpetually telling whosoever isn't listening on the other end about her biggest fault being that she's too good. Because *surely* they're not listening—*surely* they're not sitting there nodding and taking down on their telephone pads this kind of transparent, self-serving, insane horseshit that even a pre-school-age child can see through. "You know what my biggest fault is, Rose? I hate to say it about myself, but I'm too good." These are actual words, Doctor, tape-recorded these many years in my brain. And killing me still! These are the actual messages that these Roses and Sophies and Goldies and Pearls transmit to one another *daily!* "I give my everything to other people," she admits, sighing, "and I get kicked in the teeth in return —and my fault is that as many times as I get slapped in the face, I can't stop being good."

Shit, Sophie, just *try,* why don't you? Why don't we *all* try! Because to be *bad,* Mother, that is the real struggle: to be bad—and to enjoy it! That is what makes men of us boys, Mother. But what my conscience, so-called, has done to my sexuality, my spontaneity, my courage! Never mind some of the things I try so hard to get away with— because the fact remains, *I don't.* I am marked like a road map from head to toe with my repressions. You can travel the length and breadth of my body over superhighways of shame and inhibition and fear. See, I am too good too, Mother, I too am moral to the bursting point—just like you! Did you ever see me try to smoke a cigarette? I look like Bette Davis. Today boys and girls not even old enough to be bar-mitzvahed are sucking on marijuana like it's peppermint candy, and I'm still all thumbs with a Lucky Strike. Yes, that's how good *I* am, Momma. Can't smoke, hardly drink, no drugs, don't borrow money or play cards, can't tell a lie without beginning to sweat as though I'm passing over the equator. Sure, I say *fuck* a lot, but I assure you, that's about the sum of my success with transgressing. Look what I have done with The Monkey—given her up, run from her in fear, the girl whose cunt I have been dreaming about lapping all my life. Why is a little turbulence so beyond my means? Why must the least deviation from respectable conventions cause me such inner hell? When I *hate* those fucking conventions! When I know *better* than the taboos! Doctor, my doctor, what do you say, LET'S PUT THE ID BACK IN YID! Liberate this nice Jewish boy's libido, will you please? Raise the prices if you have to—I'll pay anything! Only enough cowering in the face of the deep, dark pleasures! Ma, Ma, what was it you wanted to turn me into anyway, a walking zombie like Ronald Nimkin? Where did you get the idea that the most wonderful thing I could be in life was *obedient?* A little *gentleman?* Of all the aspirations for a creature of lusts and desires! "Alex," you say, as we leave the Weequahic Diner—and don't get me wrong, I eat it up: praise is praise, and I take it however it comes—"Alex," you say to me all dressed up in my clip-on tie and my two-tone "loafer" jacket, "the way you cut your meat! the way you ate that baked potato without spilling! I could kiss you, I never *saw* such a little gentleman with his little napkin in his lap like that!" *Fruitcake*, Mother. Little *fruitcake* is what you saw—and exactly what the training program was designed to produce. Of course! Of course! The mystery really is not that I'm not dead like Ronald Nimkin, but that I'm not like all the nice young men I see strolling hand in hand in Bloomingdale's on Saturday mornings. Mother, the beach at Fire Island is strewn with the bodies of nice Jewish boys, in bikinis and Bain de Soleil, also little gentlemen in restaurants, I'm sure, also who helped mommies set up mah-jongg tiles when the ladies came on Monday night to play. Christ Almighty! After all those years of setting up those tiles— one bam! two crack! mah-jongg!—how I made it into the world of pussy at all, *that's* the mystery. I close my eyes, and it's not so awfully hard—I see myself sharing a house at Ocean Beach with somebody in eye make-up named Sheldon. "Oh, fuck you, Shelly, they're *your* friends, *you* make the garlic bread." Mother, your little gentlemen are all grown up now, and there on lavender beach towels they lie, in all their furious narcissism. And *oy Gut,* one is calling out—to me! "Alex? Alexander the King? Baby, did you see where I put my tarragon?" There he is, Ma, your little gentleman, kissing someone named Sheldon on the lips! Because of his herb dressing! "Do you know what I read in *Cosmopolitan?*" says my mother to my father. "That there are women who are homosexual persons." "Come on," grumbles Poppa Bear, "what kind of garbage is that, what kind of crap is that—?" "Jack, please, I'm not making it up. I *read* it in *Cosmo!* I'll *show* you the article!" "Come on, they print that stuff for the circulation—" Momma! Poppa! There is worse even than that—there are people who fuck chickens! There are men who screw stiffs! You simply cannot imagine how some people will respond to having served fifteen- and twenty-year sentences as some crazy bastard's idea of "good"! So if I kicked you in the shins, Ma-má, if I sunk my teeth into your wrist clear through to the *bone,* count your blessings! For had I kept it *all* inside me, believe me, you too might have arrived home to find a pimply adolescent corpse swinging over the bathtub by his father's belt. Worse yet, this last summer, instead of sitting *shiva* over a son running off to faraway Europe, you might have found yourself dining out on my "deck" on Fire Island—the two of you, me, and Sheldon. And if you remember what that *goyische* lobster did to your *kishkas,* imagine what it would have been like trying to keep down Shelly's *sauce béarnaise.*

So *there.*

What a pantomime I had to perform to get my zylon windbreaker off my back and into my lap so as to cover my joint that night I bared it to the elements. All for the benefit of the driver, within whose Polack power it lay merely to flip on the overhead lights and thus destroy in a single moment fifteen years of neat notebooks and good grades and teeth-cleaning twice a day and never eating a piece of fruit without thoroughly washing it beforehand . . . Is it hot in here! Whew, is it hot! Boy oh boy, I guess I just better get this jacket off and put it right down here in a neat litle pile in my lap . . . Only what am I *doing?* A Polack's day, my father has suggested to me, isn't complete until he had dragged his big dumb feet across the bones of a Jew. Why am I taking this chance in front of my worst enemy? What will become of me if I'm caught!

Half the length of the tunnel it takes me to unzip my zipper silently—and there it is again, up it pops again, as always swollen, bursting with demands, like some idiot macrocephalic making his parents' life a misery with his simpleton's insatiable needs.

"Jerk me off," I am told by the silky monster. *"Here? Now?"* "Of course here and now. When would you expect an opportunity like this to present itself a second time? Don't you know what that girl is who is asleep beside you? Just look at that nose." "What nose?" "That's the point—it's hardly even there. Look at that hair, like off a spinning wheel. Remember 'flax' that you studied in school? That's human flax! Schmuck, this is the real Mc-Coy. A *shikse!* And asleep! Or maybe she's just faking it is a strong possibility too. Faking it, but saying under her breath, 'C'mon, Big Boy, do all the different dirty things to me you ever wanted to do.'" "Could that be *so?*" "Darling," croons my cock, "let me just begin to list the many different dirty things she would like you to start off with: she wants you to take her hard little *shikse* titties in your hands, for one." "She does?" "She wants you to finger-fuck her *shikse* cunt till she faints." "Oh God. Till she faints!" "This is an opportunity such as may never occur again. So long as you live." "Ah, but that's the point, how long is that likely to be? The driver's name is all X's and Y's—if my father is right, these Polish people are direct descendants from the ox!"

But who wins an argument with a hard-on? *Ven der putz shteht, ligt der sechel in drerd.* Know that famous proverb? When the prick stands up, the brains get buried in the ground! When the pricks stands up, the brains are as good as dead! And 'tis so! Up it jumps, a dog through a hoop, right into the bracelet of middle finger, index finger, and thumb that I have provided for the occasion. A three-finger hand-job with staccato half-inch strokes up from the base—this will be best for a bus, this will (hopefully) cause my zylon jacket to do a minimal amount of hopping and jumping around. To be sure, such a technique means forgoing the sensitive tip, but that much of life is sacrifice and self-control is a fact that even a sex fiend cannot afford to be blind to.

The three-finger hand-job is what I have devised for
jerking off in public places—already I have employed it at
the Empire Burlesque house in downtown Newark. One
Sunday morning—following the example of Smolka, my
Tom Sawyer—I leave the house for the schoolyard, whistling and carrying a baseball glove, and when no one is
looking (obviously a state of affairs I hardly believe in) I
jump aboard an empty 14 bus, and crouch in my seat the
length of the journey. You can just imagine the crowd
outside the burlesque house on a Sunday morning. Downtown Newark is as empty of life and movement as the
Sahara, except for those outside the Empire, who look like
the crew off a ship stricken with scurvy. Am I crazy to be
going in there? God only knows what kind of disease I am
going to pick up off those seats! "Go in anyway, fuck the
disease," says the maniac who speaks into the microphone
of my jockey shorts, "don't you understand what you're
going to see inside there? A woman's snatch." "A *snatch?*"
"The whole thing, right, all hot and dripping and ready to
go." "But I'll come down with the syph from just touching
the ticket. I'll pick it up on the bottom of my sneaks and
track it into my own house. Some nut will go berserk and
stab me to death for the Trojan in my wallet. What if the
cops come? Waving pistols—and somebody runs—and
they shoot *me* by mistake! Because I'm underage. What if
I get killed—or even worse, arrested! What about my parents!" "Look, do you want to see a cunt or don't you want
to see a cunt?" "I want to! I want to!" "They have a whore
in there, kid, who fucks the curtain with her bare twat."
Okay—I'll risk the syph! I'll risk having my brain curdle

and spending the rest of my days in an insane asylum playing handball with my own shit—only what about my picture in the *Newark Evening News!* When the cops throw on the lights and cry, "Okay, freaks, this is a raid!" —what if the flashbulbs go off! And get me—*me*, already president of the International Relations Club in my second year of high school! Me, who skipped two grades of grammar school! Why, in 1946, because they wouldn't let Marian Anderson sing in Convention Hall, I led my entire eighth-grade class in refusing to participate in the annual patriotic-essay contest sponsored by the D.A.R. I was and still am the twelve-year-old boy who, in honor of his courageous stand against bigotry and hatred, was invited to the Essex House in Newark to attend the convention of the C.I.O. Political Action Committee—to mount the platform and to shake the hand of Dr. Frank Kingdon, the renowned columnist whom I read every day in *PM*. How can I be contemplating going into a burlesque house with all these degenerates to see some sixty-year-old lady pretend to make love to a hunk of asbestos, when on the stage of the Essex House ballroom, Dr. Frank Kingdon himself took my hand, and while the whole P.A.C. rose to applaud my opposition to the D.A.R., Dr. Kingdon said to me, "Young man, you are going to see democracy in action here this morning." And with my brother-in-law-to-be, Morty Feibish, I have already attended meetings of the American Veterans Committee, I have helped Morty, who is Membership chairman, set up the bridge chairs for a chapter meeting. I have read *Citizen Tom Paine* by Howard Fast, I have read Bellamy's *Looking Backward*, and *Finnley Wren* by Philip Wylie. With my sister and Morty, I have listened to the record of marching songs by the gallant Red Army Chorus. Rankin and Bilbo and Martin Dies, Gerald L. K. Smith and Father Coughlin, all those Fascist sons of bitches are my mortal enemies. So what in God's name am I doing in a side seat at the burlesque house jerking off into the pocket of my fielder's glove? What if there's violence! What if there's germs!

Yes, only what if later, after the show, that one over there with the enormous boobies, *what if* . . . In sixty seconds I have imagined a full and wonderful life of utter degradation that we lead together on a chenille spread in a shabby hotel room, me (the enemy of America First) and Thereal McCoy, which is the name I attach to the sluttiest-looking slut in the chorus line. And what a life it is, too, under our bare bulb (HOTEL flashing just outside our window). She pushes Drake's Daredevil Cupcakes (chocolate with a white creamy center) down over my cock and then eats them off of me, flake by flake. She pours maple syrup out of the Log Cabin can and then licks it from my tender balls until they're clean again as a little baby boy's. Her favorite line of English prose is a masterpiece: "Fuck my pussy, Fuckface, till I faint." When I fart in the bathtub, she kneels naked on the tile floor, leans all the way over, and kisses the bubbles. She sits on my cock while I take a shit, plunging into my mouth a nipple the size of a tollhouse cookie, and all the while whispering every filthy word she knows viciously in my ear. She puts ice cubes in her mouth until her tongue and lips are freezing, then sucks me off—then switches to hot tea! Everything, everything I have ever thought of, she has thought of too, *and will do*. The biggest whore (rhymes in Newark with *poor*) there ever was. And she's mine! "Oh, Thereal, I'm coming, I'm coming, you fucking whore," and so become the only person ever to ejaculate into the pocket of a baseball mitt at the Empire Burlesque house in Newark. Maybe.

The big thing at the Empire is hats. Down the aisle from me a fellow-addict fifty years my senior is dropping his load in his hat. His *hat*, Doctor! *Oy*, I'm sick. I want to cry. Not into your hat, you *shvantz*, you got to put that thing on your head! You've got to put it on now and go back outside and walk around downtown Newark dripping gissum down your forehead. How will you eat your lunch in that hat!

What misery descends upon me as the last drop dribbles into my mitt. The depression is overwhelming; even my cock is ashamed and doesn't give me a single word of back talk as I start from the burlesque house, chastising myself ruthlessly, moaning aloud, "oh, no, *no*," not unlike a man who has just felt his sole skid through a pile of dog turds—sole of his shoe, but take the pun, who cares, who cares . . . Ach! Disgusting! Into his hat, for Christ's sake. *Ven der putz shteht! Ven der putz shteht!* Into the hat that he wears on his *head!*

I suddenly remember how my mother taught me to piss standing up! Listen, this may well be the piece of information we've been waiting for, the key to what determined my character, what causes me to be living in this predicament, torn by desires that are repugnant to my conscience, and a conscience repugnant to my desires. Here is how I learned to pee into the bowl like a big man. Just listen to this!

I stand over the circle of water, my baby's weeny jutting cutely forth, while my momma sits beside the toilet on the rim of the bathtub, one hand controlling the tap of the tub (from which a trickle runs that I am supposed to imitate) and her own hand tickling the underside of my prick. I repeat: *tickling my prickling!* I guess she thinks that's how to get stuff to come out of the front of that thing, and let me tell you, the lady is right. "Make a nice sis, *bubala,* make a nice little sissy for Mommy," sings Mommy to me, while in actuality what I am standing there making with her hand on my prong is in all probability my future! Imagine! The *ludicrousness!* A man's character is being forged, a destiny is being shaped . . . oh, maybe not . . . At any rate, for what the information is worth, in the presence of another man I simply cannot draw my water. To this very day. My bladder may be distended to watermelon proportions, but interrupted by another presence before the stream has begun (you want to hear everything, okay, I'm telling everything) which is that in Rome, Doctor, The Monkey and I picked up a common whore in the street and took her back to bed with us. Well, now that's out. It seems to have taken me some time.

The bus, the bus, what intervened on the bus to prevent me from coming all over the sleeping *shikse's* arm—I don't know. Common sense, you think? Common decency? My right mind, as they say, coming to the fore? Well, where is this right mind on that afternoon I came home from school to find my mother out of the house, and our refrigerator stocked with a big purplish piece of raw liver? I believe that I have already confessed to the piece of liver that I bought in a butcher shop and banged behind a billboard on the way to a bar mitzvah lesson. Well, I wish to make a clean breast of it, Your Holiness. That—she—it—wasn't my first piece. My first piece I had in the privacy of my own home, rolled round my cock in the bathroom at three-thirty—and then had again on the end of a fork, at five-thirty, along with the other members of that poor innocent family of mine.

So. Now you know the worst thing I have ever done. I fucked my own family's dinner.

Unless you share with The Monkey her contention that the most heinous crime of my career was abandoning her in Greece. Second most heinous: leading her into that triumvirate in Rome. In *her* estimation—some estimation, that!—I am solely responsible for making that *ménage*, because mine is the stronger and more moral nature. "The Great Humanitarian!" she cries. "The one whose *job* it is to protect the poor poor people against their landlords! You, who gave me that *U.S.A.* to read! *You're* why I got that application blank to Hunter! *You're* why I'm killing myself to be something more than just somebody's dumb and stupid piece of ass! And now you want to treat me like I'm nothing but just some hump, to *use*—use for every kinky weirdo thing you want to do—and like *you're* supposed to be the superior intellectual! Who goes on educational fucking *television!*"

You see, in this Monkey's estimation it was my mission to pull her up from those very abysses of frivolity and waste, of perversity and wildness and lust, into which I myself have been so vainly trying all my life successfully to sink—I am supposed to rescue her from those very temptations I have been struggling all these years to *yield* to! And it is of no consequence to her whatsoever that in bed she herself has been fantasying about this arrangement no less feverishly than I have. Doctor, I ask you, who was it that made the suggestion in the first place? Since the night we met, just who has been tempting whom with the prospect of yet another woman in our bed? Believe me, I'm not trying to slither out of my slime—I am trying to slither *into* it!—but it must be made absolutely clear, to you and me if not to her, that this hopelessly neurotic woman, this pathetic screwy hillbilly cunt, is hardly what could be called *my* victim. I simply will not bend to that *victim* shit! Now she's thirty, wants to be married and a mother, wants to be respectable and live in a house with a husband (particularly as the high-paying years of her glamorous career appear to be just about over), but it does not follow that just because she imagines herself victimized and deprived and exploited (and may even be, taking a long view of her life), that I am the one upon whom they are going to pin the rap. *I* didn't make her thirty years old and single. *I* didn't take her from the coal fields of West Virginia and make her my personal charge—and I didn't put her in bed with that streetwalker either! The fact is that it was The Monkey herself, speaking her high-fashion Italian, who leaned out of our rented car and explained to the whore what it was we wanted and how much we were willing to pay. I simply sat there behind the wheel, one foot on the gas pedal, like the getaway driver that I am . . . And, believe me, when that whore climbed into the back seat, I thought no; and at the hotel, where we managed to send her up alone to our room, by way of the bar, I thought no again. No! No! No!

She wasn't bad-looking, this whore, sort of round and dumpy, but in her early twenties and with a big pleasant open face—and just stupendous tits. Those were what we'd picked her out for, after driving slowly up and down the Via Veneto examining the merchandise on parade. The whore, whose name was Lina, took her dress off standing in the middle of the room; underneath she wore a "merry widow" corset, from which the breasts bubbled up at one end, and the more than ample thighs rippled out at the other. I was astonished by the garment and its theatricality—but then I was astonished by everything, above all, that we had gone ahead after all these months of talking, and finally done it.

The Monkey came out of the bathroom in her short chemise (ordinarily a sight that made me very hot, that cream-colored silk chemise with a beautiful Monkey in it), and I meanwhile took off all my clothes and sat naked at the foot of the bed. That Lina spoke not a word of English only intensified the feeling that began to ebb and flow between The Monkey and myself, a kind of restrained sadism: we could speak to one another, exchange secrets and plans without the whore's understanding—as she and The Monkey could whisper in Italian without my knowledge of what they might be saying, or plotting . . . Lina spoke first and The Monkey turned to translate. "She says you have a big one." "I'll bet she says that to all the boys." Then they stood there in their underwear looking my way—*waiting*. But so was I waiting too. And was my heart pounding. It had to come to pass, two women and me . . . so now what happens? Still, you see, I'm saying to myself *No!*

"She wants to know," said The Monkey, after Lina had spoken a second time, "where the *signore* would like her to begin." "The *signore*," said I, "wishes her to begin at the beginning . . ." Oh, very witty that reply, very non-chalant indeed, only we continue to sit there motionless, me and my hard-on, all undressed and no place to go. Finally it is The Monkey who sets our lust in motion. She moves across to Lina, above whom she towers (oh God, isn't she enough? isn't she really sufficient for my needs? how many cocks have I got?), and puts her hand between the whore's legs. We had imagined it beforehand in all its possibilities, dreamed it all out loud for many many months now, and yet I am dumbstruck at the sight of The Monkey's middle finger disappearing up into Lina's cunt.

I can best describe the state I subsequently entered as one of unrelieved *busy-ness*. Boy, was I busy! I mean there was just so much to do. You go here and I'll go there—okay, now you go here and *I'll* go there—all right, now she goes down that way, while I head up this way, and you sort of half turn around on this . . . and so it

went, Doctor, until I came my third and final time. The
Monkey was by then the one with her back on the bed,
and I the one with my ass to the chandelier (and the
cameras, I fleetingly thought)—and in the middle, feeding her tits into my Monkey's mouth, was our whore. Into
whose hole, into what *sort* of hole, I deposited my final
load is entirely a matter for conjecture. It could be that
in the end I wound up fucking some dank, odoriferous
combination of sopping Italian pubic hair, greasy American buttock, and absolutely rank bedsheet. Then I got up,
went into the bathroom, and, you'll all be happy to know,
regurgitated my dinner. My *kishkas*, Mother—threw them
right up into the toilet bowl. Isn't that a good boy?

When I came out of the bathroom, The Monkey and
Lina were lying asleep in one another's arms.

The Monkey's pathetic weeping, the recriminations
and the accusations, began immediately after Lina had
dressed and departed. I had delivered her into evil. "*Me?
You're* the one who stuck your finger up her snatch and
got the ball rolling! *You* kissed her on the fucking lips—!"
"Because," she screamed, "if I'm going to do something,
then like I *do* it! But that doesn't mean I *want* to!" And
then, Doctor, she began to berate me about Lina's tits,
how I hadn't *played* with them enough. "All you ever talk
about and think about is tits! *Other people's tits!* Mine are
so small and everybody else's in the world you see are so
huge—so you finally get a pair that are *tremendous*, and
what do you do? *Nothing!*" "Nothing is an exaggeration,
Monkey—the fact of the matter is that I couldn't always
fight my way *past* you—" "I am not a lesbian! Don't you
dare call me a lesbian! Because if I am, *you made me*

one!" "*Oh Jesus, no—!"* "I did it for you, *yes*—and now you
hate me for it!" "Then we won't do it again, for *me*, all
right? Not if this is the fucking ridiculous result!"

Except the next night we got each other very steamed
up at dinner—as in the early days of our courtship, The
Monkey retired at one point to the ladies' room at
Ranieri's and returned to the table with a finger redolent
of pussy, which I held beneath my nose to sniff and kiss at
till the main dish arrived—and after a couple of brandies
at Doney's, accosted Lina once again at her station and
took her with us to the hotel for round two. Only this time
I relieved Lina of her undergarments myself and mounted
her even before The Monkey had come back into the bedroom from the john. If I'm going to do it, I thought, I'm
going to do it! All the way! Everything! And no vomiting,
either! You're not in Weequahic High School any more!
You're nowhere *near* New Jersey!

When The Monkey stepped out of the bathroom and
saw that the ball game was already under way, she wasn't
entirely pleased. She sat down on the edge of the bed, her
little features smaller than I had ever seen them, and
declining an invitation to participate, silently watched
until I had had my orgasm and Lina had finished faking
hers. Obligingly then—sweetly, really—Lina made for between my mistress' long legs, but The Monkey pushed her
away and went off to sit and sulk in a chair by the window. So Lina—not a person overly sensitive to interper-
sonal struggle—lay back on the pillow beside me and
began to tell us all about herself. The bane of existence
was the abortions. She was the mother of one child, a boy,

with whom she lived on Monte Mario ("in a beautiful
new building," The Monkey translated). Unfortunately
she could not manage, in her situation, any more than
one—"though she loves children"—and so was always in
and out of the abortionist's office. Her only precautionary
device seemed to be a spermicidal douche of no great
reliability.

I couldn't believe that she had never heard of either the
diaphragm or the birth-control pill. I told The Monkey to
explain to her about modern means of contraception that
she could surely avail herself of, probably with only a
little ingenuity. I got from my mistress a very wry look.
The whore listened but was skeptical. It distressed me
considerably that she should be so ignorant about a matter pertaining to her own well-being (there on the bed
with her fingers wandering around in my damp pubic
hair): That fucking Catholic church, I thought . . .

So, when she left us that night, she had not only fifteen
thousand of my lire in her handbag, but a month's supply
of The Monkey's Enovid—that I had given to her.

"Oh, you are some savior!" The Monkey shouted, after
Lina had left.

"What do you want her to do—get knocked up every
other week? What sense does that make?"

"What do I care what happens to *her!*" said The
Monkey, her voice turning rural and mean. "*She's* the
whore! And all *you* really wanted to do was to fuck *her!*
You couldn't even wait until I was out of the john to
do it! And then you gave her *my* pills!"

"And what's that mean, huh? What exactly are you try-

ing to say? You know, one of the things you don't always
display, Monkey, is a talent for reason. A talent for frank-
ness, yes—for reason, no!"

"Then leave me! You've got what you wanted! Leave!"

"Maybe I will!"

"To you I'm just another *her*, anyway! You, with all
your big words and big shit holy ideals and all I am in
your eyes is just a cunt—and a lesbian!—and a whore!"

Skip the fight. It's boring. Sunday: we emerge from the
elevator, and who should be coming through the front
door of the hotel but our Lina—and with her a child of
about seven or eight, a fat little boy made out of alabaster,
dressed all in ruffles and velvet and patent leather. Lina's
hair is down and her dark eyes, fresh from church, have a
familiarly Italian mournful expression. A nice-looking person really. A sweet person (I can't get over this!). And
she has to come to show off her *bambino!* Or so it looks.

Pointing to the little boy, she whispers to The Monkey,
"Molto elegante, no?" But then she follows us out to our
car, and while the child is preoccupied with the door-
man's uniform, suggests that maybe we would like to
come to her apartment on Monte Mario this afternoon
and all of us do it with another man. She has a friend, she
says—mind you, I get all this through my translator—she
has a friend who she is sure, she says, would like to fuck
the *signorina*. I can see the tears sliding out from beneath
The Monkey's dark glasses, even as she says to me, "Well,
what do I tell her, yes or no?" "No, of course. Positively
not." The Monkey exchanges some words with Lina and

then turns to me once again: "She says it wouldn't be for money, it would just be for—"

"No! No!"

All the way to the Villa Adriana she weeps: "I want a child too! And a home! And a husband! I am not a lesbian! I am not a whore!" She reminds me of the evening the previous spring when I took her up to the Bronx with me, to what we at the H. O. commission call "Equal Opportunity Night." "All those poor Puerto Rican people being overcharged in the supermarket! In Spanish you spoke, and oh I was so impressed! Tell me about your bad sanitation, tell me about your rats and vermin, tell me about your police protection! Because discrimination is against the law! A year in prison or a five-hundred-dollar fine! And that poor Puerto Rican man stood up and shouted, 'Both!' Oh, you fake, Alex! You hypocrite and phony! Big shit to a bunch of stupid spics, but I know the truth, Alex! *You make women sleep with whores!*"

"I don't make anybody do anything they don't want to do."

"Human opportunities! *Human!* How you love that word! But do you know what it means, you son of a bitch pimp! I'll *teach* you what it means! Pull this car over, Alex!"

"Sorry, no."

"Yes! Yes! Because I'm getting out! I'm finding a phone! I'm going to call long-distance to John Lindsay and tell him what you made me do."

"The fuck you will."

"I'll expose you, Alex—I'll call Jimmy Breslin!"

Then in Athens she threatens to jump from the balcony unless I marry her. So I leave.

Shikses! In winter, when the polio germs are hibernating and I can bank upon surviving outside of an iron lung until the end of the school year, I ice-skate on the lake in Irvington Park. In the last light of the weekday afternoons, then all day long on crisply shining Saturdays and Sundays, I skate round and round in circles behind the *shikses* who live in Irvington, the town across the city line from the streets and houses of my safe and friendly Jewish quarter. I know where the *shikses* live from the kinds of curtains their mothers hang in the windows. Also, the *goyim* hang a little white cloth with a star in the front window, in honor of themselves and their boys away in the service—a blue star if the son is living, a gold star if he is dead. "A Gold Star Mom," says Ralph Edwards, solemnly introducing a contestant on "Truth or Consequences," who in just two minutes is going to get a bottle of seltzer squirted at her snatch, followed by a brand-new refrigerator for her kitchen . . . A Gold Star Mom is what my Aunt Clara upstairs is too, except here is the difference—she has no gold star in her window, for a dead son doesn't leave her feeling proud or noble, or feeling anything, for that matter. It seems instead to have turned her, in my father's words, into "a nervous case" for life. Not a day has passed since Heshie was killed in the Normandy invasion that Aunt Clara has not spent most of it in bed, and sobbing so badly that Doctor Izzie has sometimes to come and give her a shot to calm her hysteria down . . .

But the curtains—the curtains are embroidered with lace, or "fancy" in some other way that my mother describes derisively as *"goyische* taste." At Christmastime, when I have no school and can go off to ice-skate at night under the lights, I see the trees blinking on and off behind the gentile curtains. Not on our block—God forbid!—or on Leslie Street, or Schley Street, or even Fabian Place, but as I approach the Irvington line, here is a *goy,* and there is a *goy,* and there still another—and then I am into Irvington and it is simply awful: not only is there a tree conspicuously ablaze in every parlor, but the houses themselves are outlined with colored bulbs advertising Christianity, and phonographs are pumping "Silent Night" out into the street as though—as though?—it were the national anthem, and on the snowy lawns are set up little cut-out models of the scene in the manger—really, it's enough to make you sick. How can they possibly *believe* this shit? Not just children but grownups, too, stand around on the snowy lawns smiling down at pieces of wood six inches high that are called Mary and Joseph and little Jesus—and the little cut-out cows and horses are smiling too! God! The idiocy of the Jews all year long, and then the idiocy of the *goyim* on these holidays! What a country! Is it any wonder we're all of us half nuts?

But the *shikses,* ah, the *shikses* are something else again. Between the smell of damp sawdust and wet wool in the overheated boathouse, and the sight of their fresh cold blond hair spilling out of their kerchiefs and caps, I am ecstatic. Amidst these flushed and giggling girls, I lace up my skates with weak, trembling fingers, and then out

into the cold and after them I move, down the wooden
gangplank on my toes and off onto the ice behind a fluttering covey of them—a nosegay of *shikses*, a garland of
gentile girls. I am so awed that I am in a state of desire
beyond a hard-on. My circumcised little dong is simply
shriveled up with veneration. Maybe it's dread. How do
they get so gorgeous, so healthy, so *blond?* My contempt
for what they believe in is more than neutralized by my
adoration of the way they look, the way they move and
laugh and speak—the lives they must lead behind those
goyische curtains! Maybe a pride of *shikses* is more like
it—or is it a pride of *shkotzim?* For these are the girls
whose older brothers are the engaging, good-natured,
confident, clean, swift, and powerful halfbacks for the
college football teams called *Northwestern* and *Texas
Christian* and *UCLA*. Their fathers are men with white
hair and deep voices who never use double negatives,
and their mothers the ladies with the kindly smiles and
the wonderful manners who say things like, "I do believe,
Mary, that we sold thirty-five cakes at the Bake Sale."
"Don't be too late, dear," they sing out sweetly to their
little tulips as they go bouncing off in their bouffant taffeta
dresses to the Junior Prom with boys whose names are
right out of the grade-school reader, not Aaron and Arnold and Marvin, but Johnny and Billy and Jimmy and
Tod. Not Portnoy or Pincus, but Smith and Jones and
Brown! These people are the *Americans*, Doctor—like
Henry Aldrich and Homer, like the Great Gildersleeve
and his nephew LeRoy, like Corliss and Veronica, like
"Oogie Pringle" who gets to sing beneath Jane Powell's

window in *A Date with Judy*—these are the people for whom Nat "King" Cole sings every Christmastime, "Chestnuts roasting on an open fire, Jack Frost nipping at your nose . . ." An open fire, in *my* house? No, no, theirs are the noses whereof he speaks. Not his flat black one or my long bumpy one, but those tiny bridgeless wonders whose nostrils point northward automatically at birth. And stay that way for life! These are the children from the coloring books come to life, the children they mean on the signs we pass in Union, New Jersey, that say CHILDREN AT PLAY and DRIVE CAREFULLY, WE LOVE OUR CHILDREN—these are the girls and boys who live "next door," the kids who are always asking for "the jalopy" and getting into "jams" and then out of them again in time for the final commercial—the kids whose neighbors aren't the Silversteins and the Landaus, but Fibber McGee and Molly, and Ozzie and Harriet, and Ethel and Albert, and Lorenzo Jones and his wife Belle, and Jack Armstrong! Jack Armstrong, the All-American *Goy!*—and Jack as in John, not Jack as in Jake, like my father . . . Look, we ate our meals with that radio blaring away right through to the dessert, the glow of the yellow station band is the last light I see each night before sleep—so don't tell me we're just as good as anybody else, don't tell me we're Americans just like they are. No, no, these blond-haired Christians are the legitimate residents and owners of this place, and they can pump any song they want into the streets and no one is going to stop them either. O America! America! it may have been gold in the streets to my grandparents, it may have been a chicken in every pot to my

father and mother, but to me, a child whose earliest movie
memories are of Ann Rutherford and Alice Faye, America
is a *shikse* nestling under your arm whispering love love
love love love!

So: dusk on the frozen lake of a city park, skating behind the puffy red earmuffs and the fluttering yellow ringlets of a strange *shikse* teaches me the meaning of the
word *longing*. It is almost more than an angry thirteen-
year-old little Jewish Momma's Boy can bear. Forgive
the luxuriating, but these are probably the most poignant
hours of my life I'm talking about—I learn the meaning of
the word longing, I learn the meaning of the word *pang*.
There go the darling things dashing up the embankment,
clattering along the shoveled walk between the ever-
greens—and so here I go too (if I dare!). The sun is almost all the way down, and everything is purple (including my prose) as I follow at a safe distance until they
cross the street on their skates, and go giggling into the
little park-side candy store. By the time I get up the nerve
to come through the door—every eye will surely be upon
me!—they have already loosened their mufflers and un-
zipped their jackets, and are raising cups of hot chocolate
between their smooth and burning cheeks—and those
noses, mystery of mysteries! each disappears entirely into
a cup full of chocolate and marshmallows and comes out
at the other end unblemished by liquid! Jesus, look how
guiltlessly they eat between meals! What girls! Crazily,
impetuously, I order a cup of chocolate myself—and proceed to ruin my appetite for dinner, served promptly by
my jumping-jack mother at five-thirty, when my father

walks into the house "starved." Then I follow them back to the lake. Then I follow them around the lake. Then at last my ecstasy is over—they go home to the grammatical fathers and the composed mothers and the self-assured brothers who all live with them in harmony and bliss behind their *goyische* curtains, and I start back to Newark, to my palpitating life with my family, lived now behind the aluminum "Venetians" for which my mother has been saving out of her table-money for years.

What a rise in social class we have made with those blinds! Headlong, my mother seems to feel, we have been catapulted into high society. A good part of her life is now given over to the dusting and polishing of the slats of the blinds; she is behind them wiping away during the day, and at dusk, looks out from between her clean slats at the snow, where it has begun to fall through the light of the street lamp—and begins pumping up the worry-machine. It is usually only a matter of minutes before she is appropriately frantic. "Where *is* he already?" she moans, each time a pair of headlights comes sweeping up the street and are not his. Where, oh where, our Odysseus! Upstairs Uncle Hymie is home, across the street Landau is home, next door Silverstein is home—everybody is home by five forty-five except my father, and the radio says that a blizzard is already bearing down on Newark from the North Pole. Well, there is just no doubt about it, we might as well call Tuckerman & Farber about the funeral arrangements, and start inviting the guests. Yes, it needs only for the roads to begin to glisten with ice for the assumption to be made that my father, fifteen minutes late for dinner, is crunched up against a telegraph pole somewhere, lying dead in a pool of his own blood. My mother comes into the kitchen, her face by now a face out of El Greco. "My two starving Armenians," she says in a breaking voice, "eat, go ahead, darlings—start, there's no sense waiting—" And who wouldn't be grief-struck? Just think of the years to come—her two babies without a father, herself without a husband and provider, all because out of nowhere, just as that poor man was starting home, it had to begin to snow.

Meanwhile I wonder if with my father dead I will have to get a job after school and Saturdays, and consequently give up skating at Irvington Park—give up skating with my *shikses* before I have even spoken a single word to a one of them. I am afraid to open my mouth for fear that if I do no words will come out—or the *wrong* words. "Portnoy, yes, it's an old French name, a corruption of *porte noir,* meaning black door or gate. Apparently in the Middle Ages in France the door to our family manor house was painted . . ." et cetera and so forth. No, no, they will hear the *oy* at the end, and the jig will be up. Al Port then, Al Parsons! "How do you do, Miss McCoy, mind if I skate alongside, my name is Al Parsons—" but isn't Alan as Jewish and foreign as Alexander? I know there's Alan Ladd, but there's also my friend Alan Rubin, the shortstop for our softball team. And wait'll she hears I'm from Weequahic. Oh, what's the difference anyway, I can lie about my name, I can lie about my school, but how am I going to lie about this fucking nose? "You seem like a very nice person, Mr. Porte-Noir, but why do you go around covering the middle of your face like that?" Because suddenly it has taken off, the middle of my face! Because gone is the button of my childhood years, that pretty little thing that people used to look at in my carriage, and lo and behold, the middle of my face has begun to reach out toward God! Porte-Noir and Parsons my ass, kid, you have got J-E-W written right across the middle of that face—look at the schnoz on him, for God's sakes! That ain't a nose, it's a hose! Screw off, Jewboy! Get off the ice and leave these girls alone!

And it's true. I lower my head to the kitchen table and on a piece of my father's office stationery outline my profile with a pencil. And it's *terrible*. How has this happened to me who was so gorgeous in that carriage, Mother! At the top it has begun to aim toward the heavens, while simultaneously, where the cartilage ends halfway down the slope, it is beginning to bend back toward my mouth. A couple of years and I won't even be able to eat, this thing will be directly in the path of the *food!* No! No! It can't be! I go into the bathroom and stand before the mirror, I press the nostrils upward with two fingers. From the side it's not too bad either, but in front, where my upper lip used to be, there is now just teeth and gum. Some *goy*. I look like Bugs Bunny! I cut pieces from the cardboard that comes back in the shirts from the laundry and Scotch-tape them to either side of my nose, thus restoring in profile the nice upward curve that I sported all through my childhood . . . but which is now gone! It actually seems that this sprouting of my beak dates exactly from the time that I discovered the *shikses* skating

in Irvington Park—as though my own nose bone has taken
it upon itself to act as my parents' agent! Skating with
shikses? Just you try it, wise guy. Remember Pinocchio?
Well, that is nothing compared with what is going to
happen to you. They'll laugh and laugh, howl and hoot
—and worse, calling you Goldberg in the bargain, send
you on your way roasting with fury and resentment. Who
do you think they're always giggling about as it is? You!
The skinny Yid and his shnoz following them around the
ice every single afternoon—and can't talk! "Please, will
you stop playing with your nose," my mother says. "I'm
not interested, Alex, in what's growing up inside there,
not at dinner." "But it's too *big*." "What? What's too big?"
says my father. "My *nose!*" I scream. "Please, it gives you
character," my mother says, "so leave it alone!"

But who wants character? I want Thereal McCoy! In
her blue parka and her red earmuffs and her big white
mittens—Miss America, on blades! With her mistletoe and
her plum pudding (whatever that may be), and her one-
family house with a banister and a staircase, and parents
who are tranquil and patient and *dignified*, and also a
brother Billy who knows how to take motors apart and
says "Much obliged," and isn't afraid of anything physical,
and oh the way she'll cuddle next to me on the sofa in her
Angora sweater with her legs pulled back up beneath her
tartan skirt, and the way she'll turn at the doorway and
say to me, "And thank you ever so much for a wonderful
wonderful evening," and then this amazing creature—to
whom no one has ever said "*Shah!*" or "I only hope your
children will do the same to you someday!"—this perfect,

perfect-stranger, who is as smooth and shiny and cool as custard, will kiss me—raising up one shapely calf behind her—and my nose and my name will have become as nothing.

Look, I'm not asking for the world—I just don't see why I should get any less out of life than some schmuck like Oogie Pringle or Henry Aldrich. I want Jane Powell too, God damn it! And Corliss and Veronica. I too want to be the boyfriend of Debbie Reynolds—it's the Eddie Fisher in me coming out, that's all, the longing in all us swarthy Jewboys for those bland blond exotics called *shikses* . . . Only what I don't know yet in these feverish years is that for every Eddie yearning for a Debbie, there is a Debbie yearning for an Eddie—a Marilyn Monroe yearning for her Arthur Miller—even an Alice Faye yearning for Phil Harris. Even Jayne Mansfield was about to marry one, remember, when she was suddenly killed in a car crash? Who knew, you see, who knew back when we were watching *National Velvet,* that this stupendous purple-eyed girl who had the supreme *goyische* gift of all, the courage and know-how to get up and ride around on a horse (as opposed to having one pull your wagon, like the rag-seller for whom I am named)—who would have believed that this girl on the horse with the riding breeches and the perfect enunciation was lusting for our kind no less than we for hers? Because you know what Mike Todd was—a cheap facsimile of my Uncle Hymie upstairs! And who in his right mind would ever have believed that Elizabeth Taylor had the hots for Uncle Hymie? Who knew that the secret to a *shikse*'s heart (and box) was not to

pretend to be some hook-nosed variety of *goy*, as boring
and vacuous as her own brother, but to be what one's
uncle was, to be what one's father was, to be whatever
one was oneself, instead of doing some pathetic little Jewish imitation of one of those half-dead, ice-cold *shaygets*
pricks, Jimmy or Johnny or Tod, who look, who think,
who feel, who talk like fighter-bomber pilots!

Look at The Monkey, my old pal and partner in crime.
Doctor, just saying her name, just bringing her to mind,
gives me a hard-on on the spot! But I know I shouldn't
call her or see her ever again. Because the bitch is crazy!
The sex-crazed bitch is out of her mind! Pure trouble!
But—what, what was I supposed to be but *her* Jewish
savior? The Knight on the Big White Steed, the fellow
in the Shining Armor the little girls used to dream would
come to rescue them from the castles in which they were
always imagining themselves to be imprisoned, well, as
far as a certain school of *shikse* is concerned (of whom
The Monkey is a gorgeous example), this knight turns
out to be none other than a brainy, balding, beaky Jew,
with a strong social conscience and black hair on his balls,
who neither drinks nor gambles nor keeps show girls on
the side; a man guaranteed to give them kiddies to rear
and Kafka to read—a regular domestic Messiah! Sure, he
may as a kind of tribute to his rebellious adolescence say
shit and *fuck* a lot around the house—in front of the children even—but the indisputable and heartwarming fact is
that *he is always around the house*. No bars, no brothels,
no race tracks, no backgammon all night long at the

Racquet Club (about which she knows from her stylish past) or beer till all hours down at the American Legion (which she can remember from her mean and squalid youth). No, no indeed—what we have before us, ladies and gentlemen, direct from a long record-breaking engagement with his own family, is a Jewish boy just dying in his every cell to be Good, Responsible, & Dutiful to a family of his own. The same people who brought you Harry Golden's *For 2¢ Plain* bring you now—The Alexander Portnoy Show! If you liked Arthur Miller as a savior of *shikses,* you'll just love Alex! You see, my background was in every way that was crucial to The Monkey the very opposite of what she had had to endure eighteen miles south of Wheeling, in a coal town called Moundsville—while I was up in New Jersey drowning in schmaltz (lolling in Jewish "warmth," as The Monkey would have it), she was down in West Virginia virtually freezing to death, nothing but chattel really to a father who was, as she describes him, himself little more than first cousin to a mule, and some kind of incomprehensible bundle of needs to a mother who was as well-meaning as it was possible to be if you were a hillbilly one generation removed from the Alleghenies, a woman who could neither read nor write nor count all that high, and to top things off, hadn't a single molar in her head.

A story of The Monkey's which made a strong impression on me (not that all her stories didn't compel this particular neurotic's attention, with their themes of cruelty, ignorance, and exploitation): Once when she was eleven, and against her father's will had sneaked off on a

Saturday to a ballet class given by the local "artiste" (called Mr. Maurice), the old man came after her with a belt, beat her with it around the ankles all the way home, and then locked her in the closet for the rest of the day— and with her feet *tied* together for good measure. "Ketch you down by that queer again, you, and won't just tie 'em up, I'll do more'n that, don't you worry!"

When she first arrived in New York, she was eighteen and hadn't any back teeth to speak of, either. They had all been extracted (for a reason she still can't fathom) by the local Moundsville practitioner, as gifted a dentist as she remembers Mr. Maurice to have been a dancer. When we two met, nearly a year ago now, The Monkey had already been through her marriage and her divorce. Her husband had been a fifty-year-old French industrialist, who had courted and married her one week in Florence, where she was modeling in a show at the Pitti Palace. Subsequent to the marriage, his sex life consisted of getting into bed with his young and beautiful bride and jerking off into a copy of a magazine called *Garter Belt,* which he had flown over to him from Forty-second Street. The Monkey has at her disposal a kind of dumb, mean, rural twang which she sometimes likes to use, and would invariably drop down into it when describing the excesses to which she was expected to be a witness as the tycoon's wife. She could be very funny about the fourteen months she had spent with him, despite the fact that it was probably a grim if not terrifying experience. But he had flown her to London after the marriage for five thousand dollars' worth of dental work, and then back in Paris, hung around her neck several hundred thousand dollars more in jewelry, and for the longest while, says The Monkey, this caused her to feel loyal to him. As she put it (before I forbade her ever again to say *like*, and *man*, and *swinger*, and *crazy*, and *a groove*): "It was, like ethics."

What caused her finally to run for her life were the little orgies he began to arrange after jerking off into *Garter Belt* (or was it *Spiked Heels?*) became a bore to both of them. A woman, preferably black, would be engaged for a very high sum to squat naked upon a glass coffee table and take a crap while the tycoon lay flat on his back, directly beneath the table, and jerked his dong off. And as the shit splattered on the glass six inches above her beloved's nose, The Monkey, our poor Monkey, was expected to sit on the red damask sofa, fully clothed, sipping cognac and watching.

It was a couple of years after her return to New York—I suppose she's about twenty-four or twenty-five by this time—that The Monkey tried to kill herself a little by making a pass at her wrists with a razor, all on account of the way she had been treated at Le Club, or El Morocco, or maybe L'Interdit, by her current boyfriend, one or another of the hundred best-dressed men in the world. Thus she found her way to the illustrious Dr. Morris Frankel, henceforth to be known in these confessions as Harpo. Off and on during these past five years The Monkey has thrashed around on Harpo's couch, waiting for him to tell her what she must do to become somebody's wife and somebody's mother. Why, cries The Monkey to Harpo, why must she always be involved with such hideous and cold-hearted shits, instead of with *men?* Why? Harpo, speak! Say something to me! *Anything!* "Oh, I know he's alive," The Monkey used to say, her little features scrunched up in anguish, "I just know it. I mean, who ever heard of a dead man with an answering service?" So, in and out of therapy (if that's what it is) The Monkey goes —in whenever some new shit has broken her heart, out whenever the next likely knight has made his appearance.

I was "a breakthrough." Harpo of course didn't say yes, but then he didn't say no, either, when she suggested that this was who I might be. He did cough, however, and this The Monkey takes as her confirmation. Sometimes he coughs, sometimes he grunts, sometimes he belches, once in a while he farts, whether voluntarily or not who knows, though I hold that a fart has to be interpreted as a nega- tive transference reaction on his part. "Breakie, you're so *brilliant!*" "Breakie" when she is being my sex kitten and cat—and when she is fighting for her life: "You big son of a bitch Jew! I want to be married and human!"

So, I was to be her breakthrough . . . but wasn't she to be mine? Who like The Monkey had ever happened to me before—or will again? Not that I had not prayed, of course. No, you pray and you pray and you pray, you lift your impassioned prayers to God on the altar of the toilet seat, throughout your adolescence you deliver up to Him the living sacrifice of your spermatazoa by the *gallon*— and then one night, around midnight, on the corner of Lexington and Fifty-second, when you have come really to the point of losing faith in the existence of such a crea- ture as you have been imagining for yourself even unto your thirty-second year, there she is, wearing a tan pants suit, and trying to hail a cab—lanky, with dark and abundant hair, and smallish features that give her face a kind of petulant expression, and an absolutely fantastic ass.

Why not? What's lost? What's gained, however? Go ahead, you shackled and fettered son of a bitch, *speak to her*. She has an ass on her with the swell and the cleft of the world's most perfect nectarine! *Speak!*

"Hi"—softly, and with a little surprise, as though I might have met her somewhere before . . .

"What do *you* want?"

"To buy you a drink," I said.

"A real swinger," she said, sneering.

Sneering! Two seconds—and two insults! To the Assistant Commissioner of Human Opportunity for this whole city! "To eat your pussy, baby, how's that?" My God! She's going to call a cop! Who'll turn me in to the Mayor!

"That's better," she replied.

And so a cab pulled up, and we went to her apartment, where she took off her clothes and said, "Go ahead."

My incredulity! That such a thing was happening to me! Did I eat! It was suddenly as though my life were taking place in the middle of a wet dream. There I was, going down at last on the star of all those pornographic films that I had been producing in my head since I first laid a hand upon my own joint . . . "Now me you," she said, "—one good turn deserves another," and, Doctor, this stranger then proceeded to suck me off with a mouth that might have gone to a special college to learn all the wonderful things it knew. What a find, I thought, she takes it right down to the root! What a mouth I have fallen into! Talk about opportunities! And simultaneously: *Get out! Go! Who and what can this person be!*

Later we had a long, serious, very stirring conversation about perversions. She began by asking if I had ever done it with a man. I said no. I asked (as I gathered she wanted me to) if she had ever done it with another woman.

". . . Nope."

". . . Would you like to?"

". . . Would you like me to?"

". . . Why not, sure."

". . . Would you like to watch?"

". . . I suppose so."

". . . Then maybe it could be arranged."

". . . Yes?"

". . . Yes."

". . . Well, I might like that."

"Oh," she said, with a nice sarcastic edge, "I think you might."

She told me then that only a month before, when she had been ill with a virus, a couple she knew had come by to make dinner for her. After the meal they said they wanted her to watch them screw. So she did. She sat up on the bed with a temperature of 102, and they took off their clothes and went at it on the bedroom rug—"And you know what they wanted me to do, while they were making it?"

"No."

"I had some bananas on the counter in the kitchen, and they wanted me to eat one. While I watched."

"For the arcane symbolism, no doubt."

"The *what?*"

"Why did they want you to eat the banana?"

"Man, I don't know. I guess they wanted to know I was really *there*. They wanted to like *hear* me. Chewing. Look, do you just suck, or do you fuck, too?"

The real McCoy! My slut from the Empire Burlesque —without the tits, but so beautiful!

"I fuck too."

"Well, so do I."

"Isn't that a coincidence," I said, "us running into each other."

She laughed for the first time, and instead of that finally putting me at my ease, suddenly I *knew*—some big spade was going to leap out of the bedroom closet and spring for my heart with his knife—or she herself was going to go berserk, the laughter would erupt into wild hysterics—and God only knew what catastrophe would follow. Eddie Waitkus!

Was she a call girl? A maniac? Was she in cahoots with some Puerto Rican pusher who was about to make his entrance into my life? Enter it—and end it, for the forty dollars in my wallet and a watch from Korvette's?

"Look," I said, in my clever way, "do you do this, more or less, all the time . . . ?"

"What kind of question is that! What kind of shit-eating remark is that supposed to be! Are you another heartless bastard too? Don't you think I have feelings *too!*"

"I'm sorry. Excuse me."

But suddenly, where there had been fury and outrage, there were only tears. Did I need any more evidence that this girl was, to say the least, a little erratic psychologically? Any man in his right mind would surely then have gotten up, gotten dressed, and gotten the hell out in one piece. And counting his blessings. But don't you see—my right mind is just another name for my fears! My right mind is simply that inheritance of terror that I bring with me out of my ridiculous past! That tyrant, my superego, he should be strung up, that son of a bitch, hung by his fucking storm-trooper's boots till he's dead! In the street, who had been trembling, me or the girl? Me! Who had the boldness, the daring, the guts, me or the girl? The girl! The fucking *girl!*

"Look," she said, wiping away the tears with the pillowcase, "look, I lied to you before, in case you're interested, in case you're writing this down or something."

"Yeah? About what?" And here he comes, I thought, my *shvartze*, out of the closet,—eyes, teeth, and razor blade flashing! Here comes the headline: ASST HUMAN OPP'Y COMMISH FOUND HEADLESS IN GO-GO GIRL'S APT!

"I mean like what the fuck did I lie for, to *you?*"

"I don't know what you're talking about, so I can't tell you."

"I mean *they* didn't want me to eat the banana. My friends didn't want me to eat any banana. *I* wanted to."

Thus: The Monkey.

As for why she did lie, to *me?* I think it was her way of informing herself right off—semiconsciously, I suppose—

that she had somehow fallen upon a higher-type person:
that pickup on the street notwithstanding, and the whole-
hearted suck in her bed notwithstanding—followed by
that heart-stirring swallow—and the discussion of perversions that followed that . . . still, she really hadn't wanted
me to think of her as given over *wholly* to sexual excess
and adventurism . . . Because a glimpse of me was apparently all it took for her to leap imaginatively ahead into
the life that might now be hers . . . No more narcissistic
playboys in their Cardin suits; no more married, desper-
ate advertising executives in overnight from Connecticut;
no more faggots in British warmers for lunch at Seren-
dipity, or aging lechers from the cosmetics industry drool-
ing into their hundred-dollar dinners at Le Pavillon at
night . . . No, at long last the figure who had dwelled
these many years at the heart of *her* dreams (so it turned
out), a man who would be good to a wife and to children
. . . a Jew. And what a Jew! First he eats her, and then,
immediately after, comes slithering on up and begins talking and explaining things, making judgments left and
right, advising her what books to read and how to vote,
telling her how life should and should not be lived. "How
do you know that?" she used to ask warily. "I mean that's
just your *opinion.*" "What do you mean *opinion*—it's not
my opinion, girlie, it's the truth." "I mean, is that like
something everybody knows . . . or just you?" A Jewish
man, who cared about the welfare of the poor of the
City of New York, was eating her pussy! Someone who
had appeared on educational TV was shooting off into
her mouth! In a flash, Doctor, she must have seen it all

—can that be? Are women *that* calculating? Am I actually
a naïf about cunt? Saw and planned it all, did she, right
out there on Lexington Avenue? . . . The gentle fire
burning in the book-lined living room of our country
home, the Irish nanny bathing the children before
Mother puts them to bed, and the willowy ex-model, jet-
setter, and sex deviant, daughter of the mines and mills
of West Virginia, self-styled victim of a dozen real bastards, seen here in her Saint Laurent pajamas and her
crushed-kid boots, dipping thoughtfully into a novel by
Samuel Beckett . . . seen here on a fur rug with her husband, whom People Are Talking About, The Saintliest
Commissioner of the City of New York . . . seen here
with his pipe and his thinning kinky black Hebe hair, in
all his Jewish messianic fervor and charm . . .

What happened finally at Irvington Park: late on a Saturday afternoon I found myself virtually alone on the
frozen lake with a darling fourteen-year-old *shikseleh*
whom I had been watching practicing her figure eights
since after lunch, a girl who seemed to me to possess the
middle-class charms of Margaret O'Brien—that quickness
and cuteness around the sparkling eyes and the freckled
nose—*and* the simplicity and plainness, the lower-class
availability, the lank blond hair of Peggy Ann Garner.
You see, what looked like movie stars to everyone else
were just different kinds of *shikses* to me. Often I came
out of the movies trying to figure out what high school in
Newark Jeanne Crain (and her cleavage) or Kathryn
Grayson (and her cleavage) would be going to if they

were my age. And where would I find a *shikse* like Gene
Tierney, who I used to think might even be a Jew, if she
wasn't actually part Chinese. Meanwhile Peggy Ann
O'Brien has made her last figure eight and is coasting
lazily off for the boathouse, and I have done nothing
about her, or about any of them, nothing all winter long,
and now March is almost upon us—the red skating flag
will come down over the park and once again we will be
into polio season. I may not even live into the following
winter, *so what am I waiting for?* "Now! Or never!" So
after her—when she is safely out of sight—I madly begin
to skate. "Excuse me," I will say, "but would you mind
if I walk you home?" If I *walked*, or if I *walk*—which is
more correct? Because I have to speak absolutely perfect
English. Not a word of Jew in it. "Would you care perhaps
to have a hot chocolate? May I have your phone number
and come to call some evening? My name? I am Alton
Peterson"—a name I had picked for myself out of the
Montclair section of the Essex County phone book—
totally *goy* I was sure, and sounds like Hans Christian
Andersen into the bargain. What a coup! Secretly I have
been practicing writing "Alton Peterson" all winter
long, practicing on sheets of paper that I subsequently
tear from my notebook after school and burn so that they
won't have to be explained to anybody in my house. I
am Alton Peterson, I am Alton Peterson—Alton Christian
Peterson? Or is that going a little too far? Alton *C.*
Peterson? And so preoccupied am I with not forgetting
whom I would now like to be, so anxious to make it to
the boathouse while she is still changing out of her skates

—and wondering, too, what I'll say when she asks about the middle of my face and what happened to it (old hockey injury? Fell off my horse while playing polo after church one Sunday morning—too many sausages for breakfast, ha ha ha!)—I reach the edge of the lake with the tip of one skate a little sooner than I had planned—and so go hurtling forward onto the frostbitten ground, chipping one front tooth and smashing the bony protrusion at the top of my tibia.

My right leg is in a cast, from ankle to hip, for six weeks. I have something that the doctor calls Osgood Shlatterer's Disease. After the cast comes off, I drag the leg along behind me like a war injury—while my father cries, "Bend it! Do you want to go through life like that? Bend it! Walk natural, will you! Stop favoring that Oscar Shattered leg, Alex, or you are going to wind up a cripple for the rest of your days!"

For skating after *shikses*, under an alias, I would be a cripple for the rest of my days.

With a life like mine, Doctor, who needs dreams?

Bubbles Girardi, an eighteen-year-old girl who had been thrown out of Hillside High School and was subsequently found floating in the swimming pool at Olympic Park by my lascivious classmate, Smolka, the tailor's son . . .

For myself, I wouldn't go near that pool if you paid me—it is a breeding ground for polio and spinal meningitis, not to mention diseases of the skin, the scalp, and the asshole—it is even rumored that some kid from Weequahic once stepped into the footbath between the locker room and the pool and actually came out at the other end without his toenails. And yet that is where you find the girls who fuck. Wouldn't you know it? That is the place to find the kinds of *shikses* Who Will Do Anything! If only a person is willing to risk polio from the poor, gangrene from the footbath, ptomaine from the hot dogs, and elephantiasis from the soap and the towels, he might possibly get laid.

We sit in the kitchen, where Bubbles was working over the ironing board when we arrived—in her slip! Mandel and I leaf through back numbers of *Ring* magazine, while in the living room Smolka tries to talk Bubbles into taking on his two friends as a special favor to him. Bubbles' brother, who in a former life was a paratrooper, is nobody we have to worry about, Smolka assures us, because he is off in Hoboken boxing in a feature event under the name Johnny "Geronimo" Girardi. Her father drives a taxi during the day, and a car for The Mob at night—he is out somewhere chauffeuring gangsters around and doesn't get home until the early hours, and the mother we don't have to worry about because she's dead. Perfect, Smolka, perfect, I couldn't feel more secure. Now I have absolutely nothing to worry about except the Trojan I have been carrying around so long in my wallet that inside its tinfoil wrapper it has probably been half eaten away by mold. One spurt and the whole thing will go flying in pieces all over the inside of Bubbles Girardi's box—and *then* what do I do?

To be sure that these Trojans really hold up under pressure, I have been down in my cellar all week filling them with quart after quart of water—expensive as it is, I have been using them to jerk off into, to see if they will stand up under simulated fucking conditions. So far so good. Only what about the sacred one that has by now left an indelible imprint of its shape upon my wallet, the very special one I have been saving to get laid with, with the lubricated tip? How can I possibly expect no damage to have been done after sitting on it in school—crushing it in that wallet—for nearly six months? And who says Geronimo is going to be all night in Hoboken? And what if the person the gangsters are supposed to murder has already dropped dead from fright by the time they arrive, and Mr. Girardi is sent home early for a good night's rest? What if the girl has the syph! But then Smolka must have it too!—Smolka, who is always dragging drinks out of everybody else's bottle of cream soda, and grabbing with his hand at your putz! That's all I need, with my mother! I'd never hear the end of it! "Alex, what is that you're hiding under your foot?" "Nothing." "Alex, please, I heard a definite clink. What is that that fell out of your trousers that you're stepping on it with your foot? Out of your good trousers!" "Nothing! My shoe! Leave me alone!" "Young man, what are you—oh my God! Jack! Come quick! Look—look on the floor by his shoe!" With his pants around his knees, and the *Newark News* turned back to the obituary page and clutched in his hand, he rushes into the kitchen from the bathroom—"*Now* what?" She screams (that's her answer) and points beneath my chair. "What is that, Mister—some smart high-school joke?" demands my father, in a fury—"what is that black plastic thing doing on the kitchen floor?" "It's not a plastic one," I say, and break into sobs. "It's my own. I caught the syph from an eighteen-year-old Italian girl in Hillside, and now, now, I have no more p-p-p-penis!" "His little thing," screams my mother, "that I used to tickle it to make him go wee-wee—" "DON'T TOUCH IT NOBODY MOVE," cries my father, for my mother seems about to leap forward onto the floor, like a woman into her husband's grave—"call—the Humane Society—" "Like for a rabies *dog?*" she weeps. "Sophie, what else are you going to do? Save it in a drawer somewhere? To show his children? He ain't going to *have* no children!" She begins to howl pathetically, a grieving animal, while my father . . . but the scene fades quickly, for in a matter of seconds I am blind, and within the hour my brain is the consistency of hot Farina.

Tacked above the Girardi sink is a picture of Jesus Christ floating up to Heaven in a pink nightgown. How disgusting can human beings be! The Jews I despise for their narrow-mindedness, their self-righteousness, the incredibly bizarre sense that these cave men who are my parents and relatives have somehow gotten of their superiority—but when it comes to tawdriness and cheapness, to beliefs that would shame even a gorilla, you simply cannot top the *goyim*. What kind of base and brainless schmucks are these people to worship somebody who, number one, never existed, and number two, if he did, looking as he does in that picture, was without a doubt The Pansy of Palestine. In a pageboy haircut, with a

Palmolive complexion—and wearing a gown that I realize today must have come from Fredericks of Hollywood! Enough of God and the rest of that garbage! Down with religion and human groveling! Up with socialism and the dignity of man! Actually, why I should be visiting the Girardi home is not so as to lay their daughter—please God!—but to evangelize for Henry Wallace and Glen Taylor. Of course! For who are the Girardis if not *the people*, on whose behalf, for whose rights and liberties and dignities, I and my brother-in-law-to-be wind up arguing every Sunday afternoon with our hopelessly ignorant elders (who vote Democratic and think Neanderthal), my father and my uncle. If we don't like it here, they tell us, why don't we go back to Russia where everything is hunky-dory? "You're going to turn that kid into a Communist," my father warns Morty, whereupon I cry out, "You don't understand! All men are brothers!" Christ, I could strangle him on the spot for being so blind to human brotherhood!

Now that he is marrying my sister, Morty drives the truck and works in the warehouse for my uncle, and in a manner of speaking, so do I: three Saturdays in a row now I have risen before dawn to go out with him delivering cases of Squeeze to general stores off in the rural wilds where New Jersey joins with the Poconos. I have written a radio play, inspired by my master, Norman Corwin, and his celebration of V-E Day, *On a Note of Triumph* (a copy of which Morty has bought me for my birthday). *So the enemy is dead in an alley back of the Wilhelmstrasse; take a bow, G.I., take a bow, little guy* . . . Just the rhythm alone can cause my flesh to ripple, like the beat of the marching song of the victorious Red Army, and the song we learned in grade school during the war, which our teachers called "The Chinese National Anthem." "Arise, ye who refuse to be bond-slaves, with our very flesh and blood"—oh, that defiant cadence! I remember every single heroic word!—"we will build a new great wall!" And then my favorite line, commencing as it does with my favorite word in the English language: "*In*-dig-*na*-tion fills the hearts of all of our coun-try-*men! A-rise! A-rise!* A-RISE!"

I open to the first page of my play and begin to read aloud to Morty as we start off in the truck, through Irvington, the Oranges, on toward the West—Illinois! Indiana! Iowa! O my America of the plains and the mountains and the valleys and the rivers and the canyons . . . It is with just such patriotic incantations as these that I have begun to put myself to sleep at night, after jerking off into my sock. My radio play is called *Let Freedom Ring!* It is a morality play (now I know) whose two major characters are named Prejudice and Tolerance, and it is written in what I call "prose-poetry." We pull into a diner in Dover, New Jersey, just as Tolerance begins to defend Negroes for the way they smell. The sound of my own humane, compassionate, Latinate, alliterative rhetoric, inflated almost beyond recognition by Roget's *Thesaurus* (a birthday gift from my sister)—plus the fact of the dawn and my being out in it—plus the tattooed counterman in the diner whom Morty calls "Chief"—plus eating for the first time in my life home-fried potatoes for breakfast—plus swinging back up into the cab of the truck in my Levis

and lumberjacket and moccasins (which out on the highway no longer seem the costume that they do in the halls
of the high school)—plus the sun just beginning to shine
over the hilly farmlands of New Jersey, my state!—I am
reborn! Free, I find, of shameful secrets! So clean-feeling,
so strong and virtuous-feeling—so American! Morty pulls
back onto the highway, and right then and there I take
my vow, I swear that I will dedicate my life to the righting of wrongs, to the elevation of the downtrodden and
the underprivileged, to the liberation of the unjustly imprisoned. With Morty as my witness—my manly left-wing
new-found older brother, the living proof that it is possible to love mankind and baseball both (and who loves
my older sister, whom I am ready to love now, too, for
the escape hatch with which she has provided the two
of us), who is my link through the A.V.C. to Bill Mauldin,
as much my hero as Corwin or Howard Fast—to Morty,
with tears of love (for him, for me) in my eyes, I vow
to use "the power of the pen" to liberate from injustice
and exploitation, from humiliation and poverty and ignorance, the people I now think of (giving myself goose-
flesh) as *The People.*

I am icy with fear. Of the girl and her syph! of the
father and his friends! of the brother and his fists! (even
though Smolka has tried to get me to believe what strikes
me as wholly incredible, even for *goyim:* that both brother
and father know, and neither cares, that Bubbles is a
"hoor"). And fear, too, that beneath the kitchen window,
which I plan to leap out of if I should hear so much as a
footstep on the stairway, is an iron picket fence upon

which I will be impaled. Of course, the fence I am thinking of surrounds the Catholic orphanage on Lyons Avenue, but I am by now halfway between hallucination and
coma, and somewhat woozy, as though I've gone too long
without food. I see the photograph in the *Newark News,*
of the fence and the dark puddle of my blood on the
sidewalk, and the caption from which my family will
never recover: INSURANCE MAN'S SON LEAPS TO
DEATH.

While I sit freezing in my igloo, Mandel is basting in
his own perspiration—and smells it. The body odor of
Negroes fills me with compassion, with "prose-poetry"—
Mandel I am less indulgent of: "he nauseates me" (as
my mother says of him), which isn't to suggest that he is
any less hypnotic a creature to me than Smolka is. Sixteen
and Jewish just like me, but there all resemblance ends:
he wears his hair in a duck's ass, has sideburns down to
his jawbone, and sports one-button roll suits and pointy
black shoes, and Billy Eckstine collars bigger than Billy
Eckstine's! But Jewish. Incredible! A moralistic teacher
has leaked to us that Arnold Mandel has the I.Q. of a
genius yet prefers instead to take rides in stolen cars,
smoke cigarettes, and get sick on bottles of beer. Can you
believe it? A Jewish boy? He is also a participant in the
circle-jerks held with the shades pulled down in Smolka's
living room after school, while both elder Smolkas are
slaving away in the tailor shop. I have heard the stories,
but still (despite my own onanism, exhibitionism, and
voyeurism—not to mention fetishism) I can't and won't
believe it: four or five guys sit around in a circle on the

floor, and at Smolka's signal, each begins to pull off—and the first one to come gets the pot, a buck a head.

What pigs.

The only explanation I have for Mandel's behavior is that his father died when Mandel was only ten. And this of course is what mesmerizes me most of all: *a boy without a father.*

How do I account for Smolka and *his* daring? He has *a mother who works.* Mine, remember, patrols the six rooms of our apartment the way a guerilla army moves across its own countryside—there's not a single closet or drawer of mine whose contents she hasn't a photographic sense of. Smolka's mother, on the other hand, sits all day by a little light in a little chair in the corner of his father's store, taking seams in and out, and by the time she gets home at night, hasn't the strength to get out her Geiger counter and start in hunting for her child's hair-raising collection of French ticklers. The Smolkas, you must understand, are not so rich as we—and therein lies the final difference. A mother who works and no Venetian blinds . . . yes, this sufficiently explains everything to me—how come he swims at Olympic Park as well as why he is always grabbing at everybody else's putz. He lives on Hostess cupcakes and his own wits. I get a hot lunch and all the inhibitions thereof. But don't get me wrong (as though that were possible): during a winter snowstorm what is more thrilling, while stamping off the slush on the back landing at lunchtime, than to hear "Aunt Jenny" coming over the kitchen radio, and to smell cream of tomato soup heating up on the stove? What beats freshly laundered and ironed pajamas any season of the year, and a bedroom fragrant with furniture polish? How would I like my underwear all gray and jumbled up in my drawer, as Smolka's always is? I wouldn't. How would I like socks without toes and nobody to bring me hot lemonade and honey when my throat is sore?

Conversely, how would I like Bubbles Girardi to come to my own house in the afternoon and blow me, as she did Smolka, on his own bed?

Of some ironic interest. Last spring, whom do I run in to down on Worth Street, but the old circle-jerker himself, Mr. Mandel, carrying a sample case full of trusses, braces, and supports. And do you know? That he was still living and breathing absolutely astonished me. I couldn't get over it—I haven't yet. And married too, domesticated, with a wife and two little children—and a "ranch" house in Maplewood, New Jersey. Mandel lives, owns a length of garden hose, he tells me, and a barbecue and briquets! Mandel, who, out of awe of Pupi Campo and Tito Valdez, went off to City Hall the day after quitting high school and had his first name officially changed from Arnold to Ba-ba-lu. Mandel, who drank "six-packs" of beer! Miraculous. Can't be! How on earth did it happen that retribution passed him by? There he was, year in and year out, standing in idleness and ignorance on the corner of Chancellor and Leslie, perched like some greaser over his bongo drums, his duck's ass bare to the heavens—and nothing and nobody struck him down! And now he is thirty-three, like me, and a salesman for his wife's father, who has a surgical supply house on Market Street in Newark. And what about me, he asks, what do I do for a living? Really, doesn't he know? Isn't he on my parents' mailing list? Doesn't everyone know I am now the most moral man in all of New York, all pure motives and humane and compassionate ideals? Doesn't he know that what I do for a living is I'm *good?* "Civil Service," I answered, pointing across to Thirty Worth. Mister Modesty.

"You still see any of the guys?" Ba-ba-lu asked. "You married?"

"No, no."

Inside the new jowls, the old furtive Latin-American greaser comes to life. "So, uh, what do you do for pussy?"

"I have affairs, Arn, and I beat my meat."

Mistake, I think instantly. Mistake! What if he blabs to the *Daily News?* ASST HUMAN OPP'Y COMMISH FLOGS DUMMY, *Also Lives in Sin, Reports Old School Chum.*

The headlines. Always the headlines revealing my filthy secrets to a shocked and disapproving world.

"Hey," said Ba-ba-lu, "remember Rita Girardi? Bubbles? Who used to suck us all off?"

". . . What about her?" Lower your voice, Ba-ba-lu! "What about her?"

"Didn't you read in the *News?*"

"—What *News?*"

"The *Newark News.*"

"I don't see the Newark papers any more. What happened to her?"

"She got murdered. In a bar on Hawthorne Avenue,

right down from The Annex. She was with some boogey and then some other boogey came in and shot them both in the head. How do you like that? Fucking for boogies."

"Wow," I said, and meant it. Then suddenly—"Listen, Ba-ba-lu, whatever happened to Smolka?"

"Don't know," says Ba-ba-lu. "Ain't he a professor? I think I heard he was a professor."

"A professor? *Smolka?*"

"I think he is some kind of college teacher."

"Oh, can't be," I say with my superior sneer.

"Yeah. That's what somebody said. Down at Princeton."

"Princeton?"

But can't be! Without hot tomato soup for lunch on freezing afternoons? Who slept in those putrid pajamas? The owner of all those red rubber thimbles with the angry little spiky projections that he told us drove the girls up the walls of Paris? Smolka, who swam in the pool at Olympic Park, he's alive *too?* And a professor at Princeton *noch?* In what department, classical languages or astrophysics? Ba-ba-lu, you sound like my mother. You must mean plumber, or electrician. Because I will not believe it! I mean down in my *kishkas,* in my deep emotions and my old beliefs, down beneath the me who knows very well that of course Smolka and Mandel continue to enjoy the ranch houses and the professional opportunities available to men on this planet, I simply cannot believe in the survival, let alone the middle-class success, of these two bad boys. Why, they're supposed to be in jail—or the gutter. They didn't do their homework, damn it! Smolka used to cheat off me in Spanish, and Mandel didn't even give enough of a shit to bother to do that, and as for washing their hands before eating . . . Don't you understand, these two boys are supposed to be dead! Like Bubbles. Now there at least is a career that makes some sense. There's a case of cause and effect that confirms my ideas about human consequence! Bad enough, rotten enough, and you get your cock-sucking head blown off by boogies. Now that's the way the world's *supposed* to be run!

Smolka comes back into the kitchen and tells us she doesn't want to do it.

"But you said we were going to get laid!" cries Mandel. "You said we were going to get blowed! Reamed, steamed, and dry-cleaned, that's what you *said!*"

"Fuck it," I say, "if she doesn't want to do it, who needs her, let's go—"

"But I've been pounding off over this for a week! I ain't going anywhere! What kind of shit *is* this, Smolka? Won't she even beat my *meat?*"

Me, with my refrain: "Ah, look, if she doesn't want to do it, let's go—"

Mandel: "Who the fuck is she that she won't even give a guy a hand-job? A measly hand-job. Is that the world to ask of her? I ain't leaving till she either sucks it or pulls it—one or the other! It's up to her, the fucking whore!"

So Smolka goes back in for a second conference, and returns nearly half an hour later with the news that the girl has changed her mind: she will jerk off one guy, but only with his pants on, and that's *all*. We flip a coin—and I win the right to get the syph! Mandel claims the coin grazed the ceiling, and is ready to murder me—he is still screaming foul play when I enter the living room to reap my reward.

She sits in her slip on the sofa at the other end of the linoleum floor, weighing a hundred and seventy pounds and growing a mustache. Anthony Peruta, that's my name for when she asks. But she doesn't. "Look," says Bubbles, "let's get it straight—you're the only one I'm doing it to. You, and that's it."

"It's entirely up to you," I say politely.

"All right, take it out of your pants, *but don't take them down.* You hear me, because I told him, I'm not doing anything to anybody's balls."

"Fine, fine. Whatever you say."

"And don't try to touch me either."

"Look, if you want me to, I'll go."

"Just take it out."

"Sure, if that's what you want, here . . . here," I say, but prematurely. "I-just-have-to-get-it—" Where *is* that thing? In the classroom I sometimes set myself consciously to thinking about DEATH and HOSPITALS and HORRIBLE AUTOMOBILE ACCIDENTS in the hope that such grave thoughts will cause my "boner" to recede before the bell rings and I have to stand. It seems that I can't go up to the blackboard in school, or try to get off a bus, without its jumping up and saying, "Hi! Look at me!" to everyone in sight—and now it is nowhere to be found.

"Here!" I finally cry.

"Is that it?"

"Well," I answer, turning colors, "it gets bigger when it gets harder . . ."

"Well, I ain't got all night, you know."

Nicely: "Oh, I don't think it'll be all *night*—"

"Laydown!"

Bubbles, not wholly content, lowers herself into a straight chair, while I stretch out beside her on the sofa—and suddenly she has hold of it, and it's as though my poor cock has got caught in some kind of machine. Vigorously, to put it mildly, the ordeal begins. But it is like trying to jerk off a jellyfish.

"What's a matter?" she finally says. "Can't you come?"

"Usually, yes, I can."

"Then stop holding it back on me."

"I'm not. I am trying, Bubbles—"

"Cause I'm going to count to fifty, and if you don't do it by then, that ain't my fault."

Fifty? I'll be lucky if it is still attached to my body by fifty. *Take it easy,* I want to scream. *Not so rough around the edges, please!*—"eleven, twelve, thirteen"—and I think to myself, *Thank God, soon it'll be over—hang on, only another forty seconds to go*—but simultaneous with the relief comes, of course, the disappointment, and it is keen: this only happens to be what I have been dreaming about night and day since I am thirteen. At long last, not a cored apple, not an empty milk bottle greased with vaseline, but a girl in a slip, with two tits and a cunt—and a mustache, but who am I to be picky? This is what I have been imagining for myself . . .

Which is how it occurs to me what to do. I will forget

that the fist tearing away at me belongs to Bubbles—I'll pretend it's my own! So, fixedly I stare at the dark ceiling, and instead of making believe that I am getting laid, as I ordinarily do while jerking off, I make believe that I am jerking off.

And it begins instantly to take effect. Unfortunately, however, I get just about where I want to be when Bubbles' workday comes to an end.

"Okay, that's it," she says, "fifty," *and stops!*

"No!" I cry. "More!"

"Look, I already ironed two hours, you know, before you guys even got here—"

"JUST ONE MORE! I BEG OF YOU! TWO MORE! PLEASE!"

"N-O!"

Whereupon, unable (as always!) to stand the frustration—the deprivation and disappointment—I reach down, I grab it, and POW!

Only right in my eye. With a single whiplike stroke of the master's own hand, the lather comes rising out of me. I ask you, who jerks me off as well as I do it myself? Only, reclining as I am, the jet leaves my joint on the horizontal, rides back the length of my torso, and lands with a thick wet burning splash right in my own eye.

"Son of a bitch kike!" Bubbles screams. "You got gissum all over the couch! And the walls! And the lamp!"

"I got it in my eye! And don't you say kike to me, you!"

"You *are* a kike, Kike! You got it all over everything, you mocky son of a bitch! Look at the doilies!"

It's just as my parents have warned me—comes the first

disagreement, no matter how small, and the only thing a *shikse* knows to call you is a dirty Jew. What an awful discovery—my parents who are always wrong . . . are right! And my eye—it's as though it's been dropped in fire —and now I remember why. On Devil's Island, Smolka has told us, the guards used to have fun with the prisoners by rubbing sperm in their eyes *and making them blind*. I'm going blind! A *shikse* has touched my dick with her bare hand, and now I'll be blind forever! Doctor, my psyche, it's about as difficult to understand as a grade-school primer! Who needs dreams, I ask you? Who needs *Freud?* Rose Franzblau of the *New York Post* has enough on the ball to come up with an analysis of somebody like me!

"Sheeny!" she is screaming. "Hebe! You can't even come off unless you pull your own pudding, cheap bastard fairy Jew!"

Hey, enough is enough, where is her sympathy? "But my eye!" and rush for the kitchen, where Smolka and Mandel are rolling around the walls in ecstasy. "—right in the"—erupts Mandel, and folds in half onto the floor, beating at the linoleum with his fists—"right in the fucking—"

"Water, you shits, I'm going blind! I'm on fire!" and flying full-speed over Mandel's body, stick my head beneath the faucet. Above the sink Jesus still ascends in his pink nightie. That useless son of a bitch! I thought he was supposed to make the Christians compassionate and kind. I thought other people's suffering is what he told them to feel *sorry* for. What bullshit! If I go blind, it's his fault! Yes, somehow he strikes me as the ultimate cause for all this pain and confusion. And oh God, as the cold water runs down my face, how am I going to explain my blindness to my parents! My mother virtually spends half her life up my ass as it is, checking on the manufacture of my stool—how am I possibly going to hide the fact that I no longer have my sight? "Tap, tap, tap, it's just me, Mother —this nice big dog brought me home, with my cane." "A *dog?* In my house? Get him out of here before he makes everything filthy! Jack, there's a dog in the house and I just washed the kitchen floor!" "But, Momma, he's here to stay, he has to stay—he's a seeing-eye dog. I'm blind." "Oh my God! Jack!" she calls into the bathroom. "Jack, Alex is home with a dog—he's gone blind!" "Him, blind?" my father replies. "How could he be blind, he doesn't even know what it means to turn off a light." "How?" screams my mother. *"How? Tell us how such a thing—"*

Mother, how? How else? Consorting with Christian girls.

Mandel the next day tells me that within half an hour after my frenetic departure, Bubbles was down on her fucking dago knees sucking his cock.

The top of my head comes off: "She *was?*"

"Right on her fucking dago knees," says Mandel. "Schmuck, what'd you go home for?"

"She called me a kike!" I answer self-righteously. "I thought I was blind. Look, she's anti-Semitic, Ba-ba-lu."

"Yeah, what do I give a shit?" says Mandel. Actually I don't think he knows what anti-Semitic means. "All I know is I got laid, *twice.*"

"You *did?* With a *rubber?*"

"Fuck, I didn't use nothing."

"But she'll get pregnant!" I cry, and in anguish, as though it's me who will be held accountable.

"What do I care?" replies Mandel.

Why do *I* worry then! Why do I alone spend hours testing Trojans in my basement? Why do I alone live in mortal terror of the syph? Why do I run home with my little bloodshot eye, imagining myself blinded forever, when half an hour later Bubbles will be down eating cock on her knees! Home—to my mommy! To my Tollhouse cookie and my glass of milk, home to my nice clean bed! *Oy*, civilization and its discontents! Ba-ba-lu, speak to me, talk to me, tell me what it was like when she did it! I have to know, and with details—exact details! What about her tits? What about her nipples? What about her thighs? What does she do with her thighs, Ba-ba-lu, does she wrap them around your ass like in the hot books, or does she squeeze them tight around your cock till you want to scream, like in my dreams? And what about her hair down there? Tell me everything there is to tell about pubic hairs and the way they smell, I don't care if I heard it all before. And did she really kneel, are you shitting me? Did she actually kneel on her *knees*? and what about her teeth, where do *they* go? And does she suck on it, or does she blow on it, or somehow is it that she does *both*? Oh God, Ba-ba-lu, did you shoot in her mouth? Oh my God! And did she swallow it right down, or spit it out, or get mad—tell me! what did she do with your hot come! Did you warn her you were going to shoot, or did you just come off and let *her* worry? And who put it in—

did she put it in or did you put it in, or does it just get *drawn* in by itself? And where were all your clothes?— on the couch? on the floor? exactly *where?* I want details! Details! Actual details! Who took off her brassiere, who took off her panties—her *panties*—did *you?* did *she?* When she was down there blowing, Ba-ba-lu, did she have anything on at all? And how about the pillow under her ass, did you stick a pillow under her ass like it says to do in my parents' marriage manual? What happened when you came inside her? Did she come too? Mandel, clarify something that I have to know—*do* they come? Stuff? Or do they just moan a lot—*or what?* How does she come! What is it like! Before I go out of my head, I have to know what it's like!

THE MOST PREVALENT FORM OF DEGRADATION IN EROTIC LIFE

I don't think I've spoken of the disproportionate effect The Monkey's handwriting used to have upon my psychic equilibrium. What hopeless calligraphy! It looked like the work of an eight-year-old—it nearly drove me crazy! Nothing capitalized, nothing punctuated—only those oversized irregular letters of hers slanting downward along the page, then dribbling off. And *printed*, as on the drawings the rest of us used to carry home in our little hands from *first grade!* And that spelling. A little word like "clean" comes out three different ways on the same sheet of paper. You know, as in "Mr. Clean"?—two out of three times it begins with the letter *k*. K! As in "Joseph K." Not to mention "dear" as in the salutation of a letter: d-e-r-e. Or d-e-i-r. And that very first time (this I love) d-i-r. On the evening we are scheduled for dinner at Gracie Mansion—D! I! R! I mean, I just have to ask myself—what am I doing having an affair with a woman nearly thirty years of age who thinks you spell "dear" with three letters!

Already two months had passed since the pickup on Lexington Avenue, and still, you see, the same currents of feeling carrying me along: desire, on the one hand, *delirious* desire (I'd never known such abandon in a woman in my life!), and something close to contempt on the other. Correction. Only a few days earlier there had been our trip to Vermont, that weekend when it had seemed that my wariness of her—the apprehension aroused by the model-y glamour, the brutish origins, above everything, the sexual recklessness—that all this fear and distrust had been displaced by a wild upward surge of tenderness and affection.

Now, I am under the influence at the moment of an essay entitled "The Most Prevalent Form of Degradation in Erotic Life"; as you may have guessed, I have bought a set of the *Collected Papers,* and since my return from Europe, have been putting myself to sleep each night in the solitary confinement of my womanless bed with a volume of Freud in my hand. Sometimes Freud in hand, sometimes Alex in hand, frequently both. Yes, there in my unbuttoned pajamas, all alone, I lie, fiddling with it like a little boy-child in a dopey reverie, tugging on it, twisting it, rubbing and kneading it, and meanwhile reading spellbound through "Contributions to the Psychology of Love," ever heedful of the sentence, the phrase, the *word* that will liberate me from what I understand are called my fantasies and fixations.

In the "Degradation" essay there is that phrase, "currents of feeling." For "a fully normal attitude in love" (deserving of semantic scrutiny, that "fully normal," but to go on—) for a fully normal attitude in love, says he, it is necessary that two currents of feeling be united: the tender, affectionate feelings, and the sensuous feelings. And in many instances this just doesn't happen, sad to say. "Where such men love they have no desire, and where they desire they cannot love."

Question: Am I to consider myself one of the fragmented multitude? In language plain and simple, are Alexander Portnoy's sensual feelings fixated to his incestuous fantasies? What do you think, Doc? Has a restriction so pathetic been laid upon my object choice? Is it true that only if the sexual object fulfills for me the condition of being degraded, that sensual feeling can have free play? Listen, does that explain the preoccupation with *shikses?*

Yes, but if so, if so, how then explain that weekend in Vermont? Because down went the dam of the incest-barrier, or so it seemed. And *swoosh,* there was sensual

feeling mingling with the purest, deepest streams of tenderness I've ever known! I'm telling you, the confluence
of the two currents was terrific! And in her as well! She
even said as much!

Or was it only the colorful leaves, do you think, the fire
burning in the dining room of the inn at Woodstock, that
softened up the two of us? Was it tenderness for one another that we experienced, or just the fall doing its work,
swelling the gourd (John Keats) and lathering the tourist
trade into ecstasies of nostalgia for the good and simple
life? Were we just two more rootless jungle-dwelling eroto-
maniacs creaming in their pre-faded jeans over Historical
New England, dreaming the old agrarian dream in their
rent-a-car convertible—or is a fully normal attitude in
love the possibility that it seemed for me during those
few sunny days I spent with The Monkey in Vermont?

What exactly transpired? Well, we drove mostly. And
looked: the valleys, the mountains, the light on the fields;
and the leaves of course, a lot of ooing and ahhing. Once
we stopped to watch somebody in the distance, high up
on a ladder, hammering away at the side of a barn—and
that was fun, too. Oh, and the rented car. We flew to
Rutland and rented a convertible. A convertible, can you
imagine? A third of a century as an American boy, and
this was the first convertible I had ever driven myself.
Know why? Because the son of an insurance man knows
better than others the chance you take riding around in
such a machine. He knows the awful actuarial details! All
you have to do is hit a bump in the road, and that's it,
where a convertible is concerned: up from the seat you go

flying (and not to be *too* graphic), out onto the highway cranium first, and if you're *lucky*, it's a wheelchair for life. And turn over in a convertible—well, you can just kiss your life goodbye. And this is statistics (I am told by my father), not some cockamaimy story he is making up for the fun of it. Insurance companies aren't in business to lose money—when they say something, Alex, it's true! And now, on the heels of my wise father, my wise mother: "Please, so I can sleep at night for four years, promise me one thing, grant your mother this one wish and then she'll never ask anything of you again: when you get to Ohio, promise you won't ride in an open convertible. So I can shut my eyes in bed at night, Alex, promise you won't take your life in your hands in any crazy way." My father again: "Because you're a plum, Alex!" he says, baffled and tearful over my imminent departure from home. "And we don't want a plum to fall off the tree before it's ripe!"

1. Promise, Plum, that you'll never ride in a convertible. Such a small thing, what will it hurt you to promise?

2. You'll look up Howard Sugarman, Sylvia's nephew. A lovely boy—*and president of the Hillel*. He'll show you around. *Please* look him up.

3. Plum, Darling, Light of the World, you remember your cousin Heshie, the torture he gave himself and his family with that girl. What Uncle Hymie had to go through, to save that boy from his craziness. You remember? Please, do we have to say any more? Is my meaning clear, Alex? Don't give yourself away cheap. Don't throw a brilliant future away on an absolute nothing. I don't think we have to say anything more. *Do* we? You're a

baby yet, sixteen years old and graduating high school. That's a baby, Alex. You don't know the hatred there is in the world. So I don't think we have to say any more, not to a boy as smart as you. ONLY YOU MUST BE CAREFUL WITH YOUR LIFE! YOU MUST NOT PLUNGE YOURSELF INTO A LIVING HELL! YOU MUST LISTEN TO WHAT WE ARE SAYING AND WITHOUT THE SCOWL, THANK YOU, AND THE BRILLIANT BACK TALK! WE KNOW! WE HAVE LIVED! WE HAVE SEEN! IT DOESN'T WORK, MY SON! THEY ARE ANOTHER BREED OF HUMAN BEING ENTIRELY! YOU WILL BE TORN ASUNDER! GO TO HOWARD, HE'LL INTRODUCE YOU AT THE HILLEL! DON'T RUN FIRST THING TO A BLON-DIE, *PLEASE!* BECAUSE SHE'LL TAKE YOU FOR ALL YOU'RE WORTH AND THEN LEAVE YOU BLEADING IN THE GUTTER! A BRILLIANT INNO-CENT BABY BOY LIKE YOU, SHE'LL EAT YOU UP ALIVE!

She'll eat me up alive?

Ah, but we have our revenge, we brilliant baby boys, us plums. You know the joke, of course—Milty, the G.I., telephones from Japan. "Momma," he says, "it's Milton, I have good news! I found a wonderful Japanese girl and we were married today. As soon as I get my discharge I want to bring her home, Momma, for you to meet each other." "So," says the mother, "bring her, of course." "Oh, wonderful, Momma," says Milty, "wonderful—only I was wondering, in your little apartment, where will me and Ming Toy sleep?" "Where?" says the mother. "Why, in the bed? Where else should you sleep with your bride?" "But then where will *you* sleep, if we sleep in the bed? Momma, are you sure there's room?" "Milty darling, please," says the mother, "everything is fine, don't you worry, there'll be all the room you want: as soon as I hang up, I'm killing myself."

What an innocent, our Milty! How stunned he must be over there in Yokohama to hear his mother come up with such a statement! Sweet, passive Milton, you wouldn't hurt a fly, would you, *tateleh?* You hate bloodshed, you wouldn't dreaming of *striking* another person, let along committing a murder on him. *So you let the geisha girl do it for you!* Smart, Milty, *smart!* From the geisha girl, believe me, she won't recover so fast. From the geisha girl, Milty, she'll *plotz!* Ha ha! You did it, Miltaleh, and without even lifting a finger! Of course! Let the *shikse* do the killing for you! You, you're just an innocent bystander! Caught in the crossfire! A victim, right, Milt?

Lovely, isn't it, the business of the bed?

When we arrive at the inn in Dorset, I remind her to slip one of her half-dozen rings onto the appropriate finger. "In public life one must be discreet," I say, and tell her that I have reserved a room in the name of Mr. and Mrs. Arnold Mandel. "A hero out of Newark's past," I explain.

While I register, The Monkey (looking in New England erotic in the extreme) roams around the lobby examining the little Vermont gifties for sale. "Arnold," she calls. I turn: "Yes, dear." "We simply must take back with us some maple syrup for Mother Mandel. She loves it so," and smiles her mysteriously enticing Sunday *Times* underwear-ad smile at the suspicious clerk.

What a night! I don't mean there was more than the usual body-thrashing and hair-tossing and empassioned vocalizing from The Monkey—no, the drama was at the same Wagnerian pitch I was beginning to become accustomed to: it was the flow of feeling that was new and terrific. "Oh, I can't get *enough* of you!" she cried. "Am I a nymphomaniac, or is it the wedding ring?" "I was thinking maybe it was the illicitness of an 'inn.'" "Oh, it's something! I feel, I feel so crazy . . . and so tender—so wildly tender with you! Oh baby. I keep thinking I'm going to cry, and I'm so *happy!*"

Saturday we drove up to Lake Champlain, stopping along the way for The Monkey to take pictures with her Minox; late in the day we cut across and down to Woodstock, gaping, exclaiming, sighing, The Monkey snuggling. Once in the morning (in an overgrown field near the lake shore) we had sexual congress, and then that afternoon, on a dirt road somewhere in the mountains of central Vermont, she said, "Oh, Alex, pull over, now—I want you to come in my mouth," and so she blew me, and with the top down!

What am I trying to communicate? Just that we began to feel something. Feel *feeling!* And without any diminishing of sexual appetite!

"I know a poem," I said, speaking somewhat as though I were drunk, as though I could lick any man in the house, "and I'm going to recite it."

She was nestled down in my lap, eyes still closed, my softening member up against her cheek like a little chick. "Ah come on," she groaned, "not now, I don't understand poems."

"You'll understand this one. It's about fucking. A swan fucks a beautiful girl."

She looked up, batting her false eyelashes. "Oh, goody."

"But it's a serious poem."

"Well," she said, licking my prick, "it's a serious offense."

"Oh, irresistible, witty Southern belles—especially when they're *long* the way you are."

"Don't bullshit me, Portnoy. Recite the dirty poem."

"Porte-noir," I said, and began:

> "A sudden blow: the great wings beating still
> Above the staggering girl, her thighs caressed
> By the dark webs, her nape caught in his bill,
> He holds her helpless breast upon his breast."

"Where," she asked, "did you learn something like *that?*"

"Shhh. There's more:

> "How can those terrified vague fingers push
> The feathered glory from her loosening thighs?"

"Hey!" she cried. "Thighs!"

> "And how can body, laid in that white rush,
> But feel the strange heart beating where it lies?
> A shudder in the loins engenders there
> The broken wall, the burning roof and tower
> And Agamemnon dead.

Being so caught up,
So mastered by the brute blood of the air,
Did she put on his knowledge with his power
Before the indifferent beak could let her drop?

"That's it," I said.

Pause. "Who wrote it?" Snide. "You?"

"William Butler Yeats wrote it," I said, realizing how tactless I had been, with what insensitivity I had drawn attention to the chasm: I am smart and you are dumb, that's what it had meant to recite to this woman one of the three poems I happen to have learned by heart in my thirty-three years. "An Irish poet," I said lamely.

"Yeah?" she said. "And where did you learn it, at his knee? I didn't know you was Irish."

"In college, baby." From a girl I knew in college. Also taught me "The Force That Through the Green Fuse Drives the Flower." But enough—why compare her to another? *Why not let her be what she is?* What an idea! *Love her as she is! In all her imperfection—which is, after all, maybe only human!*

"Well," said The Monkey, still playing Truck Driver, "I never been to college myself." Then, Dopey Southern, "And down home in Moundsville, honey, the only poem we had was 'I see London, I see France, I see Mary Jane's underpants.' 'Cept I didn't wear no underpants . . . Know what I did when I was fifteen? Sent a lock of my snatch-hair off in an envelope to Marlon Brando. Prick didn't even have the courtesy to acknowledge receipt."

Silence. While we try to figure out what two such unlikely people are doing together—in Vermont yet.

Then she says, "Okay, what's Agamemnon?"

So I explain, to the best of my ability. Zeus, Agamemnon, Clytemnestra, Helen, Paris, Troy . . . Oh, I feel like a shit—and a fake. Half of it I *know* I'm getting wrong.

But *she's* marvelous. "Okay—now say it all again."

"You serious?"

"I'm serious! Again! But, for Christ's sake, *slow.*"

So I recite again, and all this time my trousers are still down around the floorboard, and it's growing darker on the path where I have parked out of sight of the road, beneath the dramatic foliage. The leaves, in fact, are falling into the car. The Monkey looks like a child trying to master a multiplication problem, but not a dumb child— no, a quick and clever little girl! Not stupid at all! *This girl is really very special. Even if I did pick her up in the street!*

When I finish, you know what she does? Takes hold of my hand, draws my fingers up between her legs. Where Mary Jane *still* wears no underpants. "Feel. It made my pussy all wet."

"Sweetheart! You understood the poem!"

I s'pose I deed!" cries Scarlett O'Hara. Then, "Hey, I did! I understood a poem!"

"And with your cunt, no less."

"My Breakthrough-baby! You're turning this twat into a genius! Oh, Breakie, darling, eat me," she cries, thrusting a handful of fingers into my mouth—and she pulls me down upon her by my lower jaw, crying, "Oh, eat my educated cunt!"

Idyllic, no? Under the red and yellow leaves like that?

In the room at Woodstock, while I shave for dinner, she soaks herself in hot water and Sardo. What strength she has stored in that slender frame—the glorious acrobatics she can perform while dangling from the end of my dork! You'd think she'd snap a vertebra, hanging half her torso backward over the side of the bed—in ecstasy! Yi! Thank God for that gym class she goes to! What screwing I am getting! What a deal! And yet it turns out that she is also a human being—yes, she gives every indication that this may be so! *A human being! Who can be loved!*

But by *me?*

Why not?

Really?

Why not!

"You know something," she says to me from the tub, "my little hole's so sore it can hardly breathe."

"Poor hole."

"Hey, let's eat a big dinner, a lot of wine and chocolate mousse, and then come up here, and get into our two-hundred-year-old bed—and not screw!"

"How you doin', Arn?" she asked later, when the lights were out. "This is fun, isn't it? It's like being eighty."

"Or eight," I said. "I got something I want to show you."

"No. Arnold, *no.*"

During the night I awakened, and drew her toward me.

"Please," she moaned, "I'm saving myself for my husband."

"That doesn't mean shit to a swan, lady."

"Oh please, please, do fuck off—"

"Feel my feather."

"Ahhh," she gasped, as I stuffed it in her hand. "A *Jew-swan*! Hey!" she cried, and grabbed at my nose with the other hand. "The indifferent beak! I just understood more poem! . . . *Didn't* I?"

"Christ, you *are* a marvelous girl!"

That took her breath away. "Oh, *am* I?"

"Yes!"

"*Am I?*"

"Yes! Yes! Yes! *Now* can I fuck you?"

"Oh, sweetheart, darling," cried The Monkey, "pick a hole, any hole, I'm yours!"

After breakfast we walked around Woodstock with The Monkey's painted cheek glued to the arm of my jacket. "You know something," she said, "I don't think I hate you any more."

We started for home late in the afternoon, driving all the way to New York so that the weekend would last longer. Only an hour into the trip, she found WABC and began to move in her seat to the rock music. Then all at once she said, "Ah, fuck that noise," and switched the radio off.

Wouldn't it be nice, she said, not to have to go back?

Wouldn't it be nice someday to live in the country with somebody you really liked?

Wouldn't it be nice just to get up all full of energy when it got light and go to sleep dog-tired when it got dark?

Wouldn't it be nice to have a lot of responsibilities and

just go around doing them all day and not even realize they were responsibilities?

Wouldn't it be nice to just not think about yourself for whole days, whole weeks, whole months at a stretch? To wear old clothes and no make-up and not have to come on tough all the time?

Time passed. She whistled. "Wouldn't that be something?"

"What now?"

"To be grown-up. You know?"

"Amazing," I said.

"What is?"

"Almost three days, and I haven't heard the hillbilly routine, the Betty-Boop-dumb-cunt routine, the teeny-bopper bit—"

I was extending a compliment, she got insulted. "They're not 'bits,' man, they're not routines—they're *me!* And if how I act isn't good enough for you, then tough tittie, Commissioner. Don't put me down, okay, just because we're nearing that fucking city where you're so *important.*"

"I was only saying you're smarter than you let on when you act like a broad, that's all."

"Bull*shit.* It's just practically humanly im*possible* for anybody to be as stupid as you think I am!" Here she leaned forward to flip on "The Good Guys." And the weekend might as well not have happened. She knew all the words to all the songs. She was sure to let me know that. "Yeah yeah yeah, yeah yeah yeah." A remarkable performance, a tribute to the cerebellum.

At dark I pulled into a Howard Johnson's. "Like let's eat," I said. "Like food. Like nourishment, man."

"Look," she said, "maybe I don't know what I am, but you don't know what you want me to be, either! And don't forget that!"

"Groovy, man."

"Prick! Don't you see what my life is? You think I *like* being nobody? You think I'm crazy about my hollow life? I hate it! I hate *New York!* I don't ever want to go back to that sewer! I want to live in Vermont, Commissioner! I want to live in Vermont with you—and be an adult, whatever the hell that is! I want to be Mrs. Somebody-I-Can-Look-Up-To. And Admire! And Listen To!" She was crying. "Someone who won't try to fuck-up my head! Oh, I think I love you, Alex. I really think I do. Oh, but a lot of good that's going to do me!"

In other words: Did I think maybe I loved her? Answer: No. What I thought (this'll amuse you), what I thought wasn't Do I love her? or even Could I love her? Rather: *Should* I love her?

Inside the restaurant the best I could do was say that I wanted her to come with me to the Mayor's formal dinner party.

"Arnold, let's have an affair, okay?"

"—Meaning?"

"Oh, don't be *cautious*. Meaning what do you *think?* An *affair.* You bang just me and I bang just you."

"And that's it?"

"Well, sure, mostly. And also I telephone a lot during the day. It's a hang-up—can't I say 'hang-up' *either?* Okay

—it's a *compulsion*. Okay? All I mean is like I can't help it. I mean I'm going to call your office *a lot*. Because I like everybody to know I belong to somebody. That's what I've learned from the fifty thousand dollars I've handed over to that shrink. All I mean is whenever I get to a job, I like call you up—and say I love you. Is this coherent?"

"Sure."

"Because that's what I really want to be: *so* coherent. Oh, Breakie, I adore you. Now, anyway. Hey," she whispered, "want to smell something—something *staggering?*" She checked to see if the waitress was in the vicinity, then leaned forward, as though to reach beneath the table to straighten a stocking. A moment later she passed her fingertips over to me. I pressed them to my mouth. "My Sin, baby," said The Monkey, "straight from the pickle barrel . . . and for you! Only you!"

So go ahead, love her! Be brave! Here is fantasy begging you to make it real! So erotic! So wanton! So gorgeous! Glittery perhaps, but a beauty nonetheless! Where we walk together, people stare, men covet and women whisper. In a restaurant in town one night, I overhear someone say, "Isn't that what's-her-name? Who was in *La Dolce Vita?*" And when I turn to look—for whom, Anouk Aimée?—I find they are looking at us: at her who is with me! Vanity? Why not! Leave off with the blushing, bury the shame, you are no longer your mother's naughty little boy! Where appetite is concerned, a man in his thirties is responsible to no one but himself! That's what's so nice about growing up! You want to take? You take! Debauch

a little bit, for Christ's sake! STOP DENYING YOUR-
SELF! STOP DENYING THE TRUTH!

Ah, but there is (let us bow our heads), there is "my
dignity" to consider, my good name. What people will
think. What *I* will think. Doctor, this girl once did it *for
money*. Money! Yes! I believe they call that "prostitu-
tion"! One night, to praise her (I imagined, at any rate,
that that was my motive), I said, "You ought to market
this, it's too much for one man," just being chivalrous,
you see . . . or intuitive? Anyway, she answers, "I have."
I wouldn't let her alone until she explained what she'd
meant; at first she claimed she was only being clever, but
in the face of my cross-examination she finally came up
with this story, which struck me as the truth, or a portion
thereof. Just after Paris and her divorce, she had been
flown out to Hollywood (she says) to be tested for a
part in a movie (which she didn't get. I pressed for the
name of the movie, but she claims to have forgotten, says
it was never made). On the way back to New York from
California, she and the girl she was with ("Who's this
other girl?" "A girl. A girl friend." "Why were you traveling with another girl?" "I just was!"), she and this other
girl stopped off to see Las Vegas. There she went to bed
with some guy that she met, perfectly innocently she
maintains; however, to her complete surprise, in the
morning he asked, "How much?" She says it just came out
of her mouth—"Whatever it's worth, Sport." So he offered
her three hundred-dollar bills. "And you took it?" I asked.
"I was twenty years old. Sure, I took it. To see what it
felt like, that's all." "And what *did* it feel like, Mary Jane?"

"I don't remember. Nothing. It didn't feel like anything."

Well, what do *you* think? She claims it only happened that once, ten years ago, and even then only came about through some "accidental" joining of his misunderstanding with her whimsy. But do you buy that? Should I? Is it impossible to believe that this girl may have put in some time as a high-priced call girl? Oh Jesus! Take her, I think to myself, and I am no higher in the evolutionary scale than the mobsters and millionaires who choose their women from the line at the Copa. This is the kind of girl ordinarily seen hanging from the arm of a Mafiosa or a movie star, not the 1950 valedictorian of Weequahic High! Not the editor of the *Columbia Law Review!* Not the high-minded civil-libertarian! Let's face it, whore or no whore, this is a clear-cut tootsie, right? Who looks at her with me knows precisely what I am after in this life. This is what my father used to call "a chippy." Of course! And can I bring home a chippy, Doctor? "Momma, Poppa, this is my wife, the chippy. Isn't she a wild piece of ass?" Take her fully for my own, you see, and the whole neighborhood will know at last the truth about my dirty little mind. The so-called genius will be revealed in all his piggish proclivities and feelthy desires. The bathroom door will swing open (unlocked!), and behold, there sits the savior of mankind, drool running down his chin, absolutely gaa-gaa in the eyes, and his prick firing salvos at the light bulb! A laughingstock, at last! A bad boy! A *shande* to his family forever! Yes, yes, I see it all: for my abominations I awake one morning to find myself chained to a toilet in Hell, me and the other chippy-mongers of the world— "*Shtarkes,*" the Devil will say, as we are issued our fresh white-on-white shirts, our Sulka ties, as we are fitted in our nifty new silk suits, "*gantze k'nockers,* big shots with your long-legged women. Welcome. You really accomplished a lot in life, you fellows. You really distinguished yourselves, all right. And you in particular," he says, lifting a sardonic eyebrow in my direction, "who entered the high school at the age of *twelve,* who was an ambassador to the world from the Jewish community of Newark—" Ah-hah, I knew it. It's no Devil in the proper sense, it's Fat Warshaw, the Reb. My stout and pompous spiritual leader! He of the sumptuous enunciation and the Pall Mall breath! Rabbi Re-ver-ed! It is the occasion of my bar mitzvah, and I stand shyly at his side, sopping it up like gravy, getting quite a little kick out of being sanctified, I'll tell you. Alexander Portnoy-this and Alexander Portnoy-that, and to tell you the absolute truth, that he talks in syllables, and turns little words into big ones, and big ones into whole sentences by themselves, to be frank, it doesn't seem to bother me as much as it would ordinarily. Oh, the sunny Saturday morning meanders slowly along as he lists my virtues and accomplishments to the assembled relatives and friends, syllable by syllable. Lay it on them, Warshaw, blow my horn, don't hurry yourself on my account, please. I'm young, I can stand here all day, if that's what has to be. ". . . devoted son, loving brother, fantastic honor student, avid newspaper reader (up on every current event, knows the full names of each and every Supreme Court justice and Cabinet member, also the minority and majority leaders of both Houses of

Congress, also the chairmen of the important Congressional committees), entered Weequahic High School this boy at the age of *twelve*, an I.Q. on him of 158, *one hunder-ed and-a fif-a-ty eight-a,* and now," he tells the awed and beaming multitude, whose adoration I feel palpitating upward and enveloping me there on the altar— why, I wouldn't be at all surprised if when he's finished they don't pick me up and carry me around the synagogue like the Torah itself, bear me gravely up and down the aisles while the congregants struggle to touch their lips to some part of my new blue Ohrbach's suit, while the old men press forward to touch their tallises to my sparkling London Character shoes. "Let me through! Let me touch!" and when I am world-renowned, they will say to their grandchildren, "Yes, I was there, I was in attendance at the bar mitzvah of Chief Justice Portnoy" —"an ambassador," says Rabbi Warshaw, "now our ambassador extraordinary—" Only the tune has changed! And how! "Now," he says to me, "with the mentality of a pimp! With the human values of a race-horse jockey! What is to him the heights of human experience? Walking into a restaurant with a long-legged *kurveh* on his arm! An easy lay in a body stocking!" "Oh, please, Re-ver-ed, I'm a big boy now—so you can knock off the rabbinical righteousness. It turns out to be a little laughable at this stage of the game. I happened to prefer beautiful and sexy to ugly and icy, so what's the tragedy? Why dress me up like a Las Vegas hood? Why chain me to a toilet bowl for eternity? For loving a saucy girl?" "Loving? *You?* Too-ey on you! *Self*-loving, boychick, that's how I

spell it! With a capital self! Your heart is an empty refrigerator! Your blood flows in cubes! I'm surprised you don't
clink when you walk! The saucy girl, so-called—I'll bet
saucy!—was a big fat feather in your prick, *and that alone
is her total meaning, Alexander Portnoy!* What *you* did
with *your* promise! Disgusting! Love? Spelled l-u-s-t!
Spelled s-e-l-f!" "But I felt stirrings, in Howard Johnson's—" "In the prick! Sure!" "No!" "Yes! That's the only
part you *ever* felt a stirring in your *life!* You whiner! You
big bundle full of resentments! Why, you have been stuck
on yourself since the first grade, for Christ's sake!" "Have
not!" "Have! Have! This is the bottom truth, friend! Suffering mankind don't mean shit to you! That's a *blind*,
buddy, and don't you kid yourself otherwise! Look, you
call out to your brethren, look what I'm sticking my dicky
into—look who *I'm* fucking: a fifty-foot fashion model! I
get free what others pay upwards of three hundred dollars for! Oh boy, ain't *that* a human triumph, huh? Don't
think that three hundred bucks don't titillate you plenty
—cause it does! Only how about look what I'm loving,
Portnoy!" "Please, don't you read the *New York Times?*
I have spent my whole adult life protecting the rights of
the defenseless! Five years I was with the ACLU, fighting
the good fight for practically nothing. And before that a
Congressional committee! I could make twice, *three*
times the money in a practice of my own, but I don't! I
don't! Now I have been appointed—don't you read the
papers!—I am now Assistant Commissioner of Human Opportunity! Preparing a special report on bias in the building trades—" "Bull*shit.* Commissioner of Cunt, that's who

you are! Commissioner of Human Opportunists! Oh, you jerk-off artist! You case of arrested development! All is vanity, Portnoy, but you really take the cake! A hundred and fifty-eight points of I.Q. and all of it right down the drain! A lot of good it did to skip those two grades of grammar school, you dummy!" *"What?"* "And spending-money your father sent yet to Antioch College—that the man could hardly afford! All the faults come from the parents, right, Alex? What's wrong, they did—what's good, you accomplished all on your own! You ignoramus! You icebox heart! Why are you chained to a toilet? I'll tell you why: poetic justice! So you can pull your peter till the end of time! Jerk your precious little dum-dum ad infinitum! Go ahead, pull off, Commissioner, that's all you ever really gave your heart to anyway—your stinking putz!"

I arrive in my tuxedo while she is still in the shower. The door has been left unlocked, apparently so that I can come right in without disturbing her. She lives on the top floor of a big modern building in the East Eighties, and it irritates me to think that anybody who happened through the corridor could walk in just as I have. I warn her of this through the shower curtain. She touches my cheek with her small wet face. "Why would anyone want to do that?" she says. "All my money's in the bank."

"That's not a satisfactory reply," I answer, and retreat to the living room, trying not to be vexed. I notice the slip of paper on the coffee table. Has a child been here, I wonder. No, no, I am just face to face with my first speci-

men of The Monkey's handwriting. A note to the cleaning lady. Though at first glance I imagine it must be a
note *from* the cleaning lady.

Must? Why "must"? Because she's "mine"?

**dir willa polish the flor by bathrum *pleze* & dont
furget the insies of windose mary jane r**

Three times I read the sentence through, and as happens with certain texts, each reading reveals new sub-
tleties of meaning and implication, each reading augurs
tribulations yet to be visited upon my ass. Why allow this
"affair" to gather any more momentum? What was I
thinking about in Vermont! Oh that *z*, that *z* between the
two *e*'s of "pleze"—this is a mind with the depths of a
movie marquee! And "furget"! Exactly how a prostitute
would misspell that word! But it's something about the
mangling of "dear," that tender syllable of affection now
collapsed into three lower-case letters, that strikes me as
hopelessly pathetic. How unnatural can a relationship be!
This woman is ineducable and beyond reclamation. By
contrast to hers, my childhood took place in Brahmin
Boston. What kind of business can the two of us have
together? Monkey business! *No* business!

The phone calls, for instance, I cannot tolerate those
phone calls! Charmingly girlish she was when she warned
me about telephoning all the time—but surprise, she
meant it! I am in my office, the indigent parents of a
psychotic child are explaining to me that their offspring is
being systematically starved to death in a city hospital.

They have come to us bearing their complaint, rather than to the Department of Hospitals, because a brilliant lawyer in the Bronx has told them that their child is obviously the victim of discrimination. What I can gather from a call to the chief psychiatrist at the hospital is that the child refuses to ingest any food—takes it and holds it in his mouth for hours, but refuses to swallow. I have then to tell these people that neither their child nor they are being victimized in the way or for the reason they believe. My answer strikes them as duplicitous. It strikes *me* as duplicitous. I think to myself, "He'd swallow that food if he had *my* mother," and meanwhile express sympathy for their predicament. But now they refuse to leave my office until they see "the Mayor," as earlier they refused to leave the social worker's office until they had seen "the Commissioner." The father says that he will have me fired, along with all the others responsible for starving to death a defenseless little child just because he is a Puerto Rican! *"Es contrario a la ley discriminar contra cualquier persona—"* reading to me out of the bilingual CCHO handbook—that *I* wrote! At which point the phone rings. The Puerto Rican is shouting at me in Spanish, my mother is waving a knife at me back in my childhood, and my secretary announces that Miss Reed would like to speak to me on the telephone. For the third time that day.

"I miss you, Arnold," The Monkey whispers.

"I'm afraid I'm busy right now."

"I do do love you."

"Yes, fine, may I speak with you later about this?"

"How I want that long sleek cock inside me—"

"Bye now!"

What else is wrong with her, while we're at it? She moves her lips when she reads. Petty? You think so? Ever sit across the dinner table from a woman with whom you are supposedly having an affair—a twenty-nine-year-old person—and watch her lips move while she looks down the movie page for a picture the two of you can see? I know what's playing before she even tells me—from reading the lips! And the books I bring her, she carries them around from job to job in her tote bag—to read? No! So as to impress some fairy photographer, to impress passers-by in the street, *strangers,* with her many-sided character! Look at that girl with that smashing ass—carrying a book! With real words in it! The day after our return from Vermont, I bought a copy of *Let Us Now Praise Famous Men*—wrote on a card, "To the staggering girl," and had it gift-wrapped for presentation that night. "Tell me books to read, okay?"—this the touching plea she made the night we returned to the city: "Because why should I be dumb, if like you say, I'm so smart?" So, here was Agee to begin with, and with the Walker Evans' photographs to help her along: a book to speak to her of her own early life, to enlarge her perspective on her origins (origins, of course, holding far more fascination for the nice left-wing Jewish boy than for the proletarian girl herself). How earnest I was compiling that reading list! Boy, was I going to improve her mind! After Agee, Adamic's *Dynamite!*, my own yellowing copy from college; I imagined her benefiting from my undergraduate underlinings, coming to understand the distinction between the relevant

and the trivial, a generalization and an illustration, and
so on. Furthermore, it was a book so simply written, that
hopefully, without my pushing her, she might be encour-
aged to read not just the chapters I had suggested, those
touching directly upon her own past (as I imagined it)—
violence in the coal fields, beginning with the Molly Ma-
guires; the chapter on the Wobblies—but the entire
history of brutality and terror practiced by and upon the
American laboring class, from which she was descended.
Had she never read a book called *U.S.A.?* Mortimer
Snerd: "Duh, I never read nothing, Mr. Bergen." So I
bought her the Modern Library Dos Passos, a book with
a hard cover. Simple, I thought, keep it simple, but educational, elevating. Ah, you get the dreamy point, I'm sure.
The texts? W. E. B. Du Bois' *The Souls of Black Folk. The
Grapes of Wrath. An American Tragedy.* A book of Sher-
wood Anderson's I like, called *Poor White* (the title, I
thought, might stir her interest). Baldwin's *Notes of a
Native Son.* The name of the course? Oh, I don't know—
Professor Portnoy's "Humiliated Minorities, an Introduc-
tion." "The History and Function of Hatred in America."
The purpose? To save the stupid *shikse;* to rid her of her
race's ignorance; to make this daughter of the heartless
oppressor a student of suffering and oppression; to teach
her to be compassionate, to bleed a little for the world's
sorrows. Get it now? The perfect couple: she puts the id
back in Yid, I put the *oy* back in *goy.*

Where am I? Tuxedoed. All civilized-up in my evening
clothes, and "dir willa" still sizzling in my hand, as The

Monkey emerges wearing the frock she has bought specifically for the occasion. *What* occasion? Where does
she think we're going, to shoot a dirty movie? Doctor, it
barely reaches her ass! It is crocheted of some kind of
gold metallic yarn and covers nothing but a body stocking
the color of her skin! And to top this modest outfit off,
over her real head of hair she wears a wig inspired by
Little Orphan Annie, an oversized aureole of black cork-
screw curls, out of whose center pokes this dumb painted
face. What a mean little mouth it gives her! She really *is*
from West Virginia! The miner's daughter in the neon
city! "And this," I think, "is how she is going with me to
the Mayor's? Looking like a stripper? 'Dear,' and *she*
spells it with three letters! And hasn't read two pages of
the Agee book in an entire week! Has she even looked at
the pictures? Duh, I doubt it! Oh, wrong," I think, jam-
ming her note into my pocket for a keepsake—I can have
it laminated for a quarter the next day—"wrong! This is
somebody whom I picked up off the street! Who sucked
me off before she even knew my name! Who once ped-
dled her ass in Las Vegas, if not elsewhere! Just look at
her—a moll! The Assistant Human Opportunity Commissioner's moll! What kind of dream am I living in? Being
with such a person is for me *all wrong!* Mean-ing-less! A
waste of everybody's energy and character and time!"

"Okay," says The Monkey in the taxi, "what's bugging
you, Max?"

"Nothing."

"You hate the way I look."

"Ridiculous."

"Driver—Peck and Peck!"

"Shut up. Gracie Mansion, driver."

"I'm getting radiation poisoning, Alex, from what you're giving off."

"I'm not giving off shit! I've said *nothing*."

"You've got those black Hebe eyes, man, they say it for you. *Tutti!*"

"Relax, Monkey."

"*You* relax!"

"I am!" But my manly resolve lasts about a minute more. "Only for Christ's sake," I tell her, "don't say cunt to Mary Lindsay!"

"*What?*"

"You heard right. When we get there don't start talking about your wet pussy to whoever opens the door! Don't make a grab for Big John's *shlong* until we've been there at least half an hour, okay?"

With this, a hiss like the sound of air brakes rises from the driver—and The Monkey heaves herself in a rage against the rear door. "I'll say and do and wear anything I want! This is a free country, you uptight Jewish prick!"

You should have seen the look given us upon disembarking by Mr. Manny Schapiro, our driver. "Rich joik-offs!" he yells. "Nazi bitch!" and burns rubber pulling away.

From where we sit on a bench in Carl Schurz Park, we can see the lights in Gracie Mansion; I watch the other members of the new administration arriving, as I stroke her arm, kiss her forehead, tell her there is no reason to cry, the fault is mine, yes, yes, I am an uptight Jewish prick, and apologize, apologize, apologize.

"—picking on me all the time—in just the way you *look* at me you pick on me, Alex! I open the door at night, I'm so *dying* to see you, thinking all day long about nothing but you, and there are those fucking orbs already picking out every single thing that's *wrong* with me! As if I'm not insecure enough, as if insecurity isn't my whole hang-up, you get that expression all over your face the minute I open my mouth—I mean I can't even give you the time of the day without *the look:* oh shit, here comes another dumb and stupid remark out of that brainless twat. I say, 'It's five to seven,' and you think, 'How fucking dumb can she be!' Well, I'm not brainless, and I'm not a twat either, just because I didn't go to fucking Harvard! And don't give me any more of your shit about behaving in front of *The Lindsays.* Just who the fuck are *The Lindsays?* A God damn mayor, and his wife! A fucking *mayor!* In case you forget, I was married to one of the richest men in France *when I was still eighteen years old*—I was a guest at Aly Khan's for dinner, when you were still back in Newark, New Jersey, finger-fucking your little Jewish girl friends!"

Was this my idea of a love affair, she asked, sobbing miserably. To treat a woman like a leper?

I wanted to say, "Maybe then this isn't a love affair. Maybe it's what's called a mistake. Maybe we should just go our different ways, with no hard feelings." But I didn't! For fear she might commit suicide! Hadn't she five minutes earlier tried to throw herself out the rear door of the

taxi? So suppose I had said, "Look, Monkey, this is it"—
what was to stop her from rushing across the park, and
leaping to her death in the East River? Doctor, you must
believe me, this was a real possibility—this is why I said
nothing; but then her arms were around my neck, and oh,
she said plenty. "I love you, Alex! I worship and adore
you! So don't put me down, please! Because I couldn't
take it! Because you're the very best man, woman, or
child I've ever known! In the whole animal kingdom! Oh,
Breakie, you have a big brain and a big cock and I love
you!"

And then on a bench no more than two hundred feet
from *The Lindsays'* mansion, she buried her wig in my lap
and proceeded to suck me off. "Monkey, *no*," I pleaded,
"*no*," as she passionately zipped open my black trousers,
"there are plainclothesmen everywhere!"—referring to the
policing of Gracie Mansion and its environs. "They'll haul
us in, creating a public nuisance—*Monkey, the cops*—"
but turning her ambitious lips up from my open fly, she
whispered, "Only in your imagination" (a not unsubtle
retort, if meant subtly), and then down she burrowed,
some furry little animal in search of a home. And mastered me with her mouth.

At dinner I overheard her telling the Mayor that she
modeled during the day and took courses at Hunter at
night. Not a word about her cunt, as far as I could tell.
The next day she went off to Hunter, and that night,
for a surprise, showed me the application blank she had
gotten from the admissions office. Which I praised her

for. And which she never filled out, of course—except for her age: 29.

A fantasy of The Monkey's, dating from her high school years in Moundsville. The reverie she lived in, while others learned to read and write:

Around a big conference table, at rigid attention, sit all the boys in West Virginia who are seeking admission to West Point. Underneath the table, crawling on her hands and knees, and nude, is our gawky teen-age illiterate, Mary Jane Reed. A West Point colonel with a swagger stick tap-tapping behind his back, circles and circles the perimeter of the table, scrutinizing the faces of the young men, as out of sight Mary Jane proceeds to undo their trousers and to blow each of the candidates in his turn. The boy selected for admission to the military academy will be he who is most able to maintain a stern and dignified soldierly bearing while shooting off into Mary Jane's savage and knowing little weapon of a mouth.

Ten months. Incredible. For in that time not a day— very likely, not an hour—passed that I did not ask myself, "Why continue with this person? This brutalized woman! This coarse, tormented, self-loathing, bewildered, lost, identityless—" and so on. The list was inexhaustible, I reviewed it interminably. And to remember the ease with which I had plucked her off the street (the sexual triumph of my life!), well, that made me groan with disgust. How can I go on and on with someone whose reason and judgment and behavior I can't possibly respect? Who sets off

inside me daily explosions of disapproval, hourly thunder-
claps of admonition! And the sermonizing! Oh, what a
schoolmaster I became. When she bought me those Italian loafers for my birthday, for instance—such a lecture
I gave in return!

"Look," I said, once we were out of the store, "a little
shopping advice: when you go off to do something so
very simple as exchanging money for goods, it isn't necessary to flash your snatch at everyone this side of the
horizon. *Okay?*"

"Flash *what?* Who flashed anything?"

"You, Mary Jane! Your supposedly private parts!"

"I did not!"

"Please, every time you stood up, every time you sat
down, I thought you were going to get yourself hooked by
the pussy on the salesman's nose."

"Jee-zuz, I gotta sit, I gotta stand, don't I?"

"But not like you're climbing on and off a horse!"

"Well, I don't know what's bugging you—he was a fag-
got anyway."

"What's 'bugging' me is that the space between your
legs has now been seen by more people than watch Hunt-
ley and Brinkley! So why not bow out while you're still
champeen, *all right?*" Yet, even as I make my accusation,
I am saying to myself, "Oh, lay off, Little Boy Blue—if you
want a lady instead of a cunt, then get yourself one.
Who's holding you here?" Because this city, as we know,
is alive with girls wholly unlike Miss Mary Jane Reed,
promising, unbroken, uncontaminated young women—
healthy, in fact, as milkmaids. *I* know, because these were

her predecessors—only they didn't satisfy, either. They were wrong, *too*. Spielvogel, believe me, I've been there, I've tried: I've eaten their casseroles and shaved in their johns, I've been given duplicate keys to their police locks and shelves of my own in the medicine chest, I have even befriended those cats of theirs—named Spinoza and Clytemnestra and Candide and Cat—yes, yes, clever and erudite girls, fresh from successful adventures in sex and scholarship at wholesome Ivy League colleges, lively, intelligent, self-respecting, self-assured, and well-behaved young women—social workers and research assistants, schoolteachers and copy readers, girls in whose company I did not feel abject or ashamed, girls I did not have to father or mother or educate or redeem. And they didn't work out, either!

Kay Campbell, my girl friend at Antioch—could there have been a more exemplary person? Artless, sweet-tempered, without a trace of morbidity or egoism—a thoroughly commendable and worthy human being. And where is she now, that find! Hello, Pumpkin! Making some lucky *shaygets* a wonderful wife out there in middle America? How could she do otherwise? Edited the literary magazine, walked off with all the honors in English literature, picketed with me and my outraged friends outside of that barbershop in Yellow Springs where they wouldn't cut Negro hair—a robust, genial, large-hearted, large-assed girl with a sweet baby face, yellow hair, no tits, unfortunately (essentially titless women seem to be my destiny, by the way—now, why *is* that? is there an

essay somewhere I can read on that? is it of import? or
shall I go on?). Ah, and those peasant legs! And the blouse
always hanging loose from her skirt at the back. How
moved I was by that blithesome touch! And by the fact
that on high heels she looked like a cat stuck up a tree, in
trouble, out of her element, all wrong. Always the first of
the Antioch nymphs to go barefoot to classes in spring.
"The Pumpkin," is what I called her, in commemoration
of her pigmentation and the size of her can. Also her
solidity: hard as a gourd on matters of moral principle,
beautifully stubborn in a way I couldn't but envy and
adore.

She never raised her voice in an argument. Can you
imagine the impression this made on me at seventeen,
fresh from my engagement with The Jack and Sophie
Portnoy Debating Society? Who had ever heard of such
an approach to controversy? Never ridiculed her opponent! Or seemed to hate him for his ideas! Ah-hah, so *this*
is what it means to be a child of *goyim*, valedictorian of a
high school in Iowa instead of New Jersey; yes, this is
what the *goyim* who have got something have got! Authority without the temper. Virtue without the self-
congratulation. Confidence sans swagger or condescen-
sion. Come on, let's be fair and give the *goyim* their due,
Doctor: when they are impressive, they are very impressive. So *sound!* Yes, that's what hypnotized—the hearti-
ness, the sturdiness; in a word, her pumpkinness. My
wholesome, big-bottomed, lipstickless, barefooted *shikse*,
where are you now, Kay-Kay? Mother to how many? Did
you wind up really fat? Ah, so what! Suppose you're big

as a house—you *need* a showcase for that character of yours! The very best of the Middle West, *so why did I let her go?* Oh, I'll get to that, no worry, self-laceration is never more than a memory away, we know that by now. In the meantime, let me miss her substantiality a little. That buttery skin! That unattended streaming hair! And this is back in the early fifties, before streaming hair became the style! This was just *naturalness,* Doctor. Round and ample, sun-colored Kay! I'll bet that half a dozen kiddies are clinging to that girl's abundant behind (so unlike The Monkey's hard little handful of a model's ass!). I'll bet you bake your own bread, right? (The way you did that hot spring night in my Yellow Springs apartment, in your halfslip and brassiere, with flour in your ears and your hairline damp with perspiration—remember? showing me, despite the temperature, how real bread should taste? You could have used my heart for batter, that's how soft it felt!) I'll bet you live where the air is still unpoisoned and nobody locks his door—and still don't give two shits about money or possessions. Hey, I don't either, Pumpkin, still unbesmirched myself on those and related middle-class issues! Oh, perfectly ill-proportioned girl! No mile-long mannequin you! So she had no tits, so what? Slight as a butterfly through the rib cage and neck, but planted like a bear beneath! *Rooted,* that's what I'm getting at! Joined by those lineman's legs to this American ground!

You should have heard Kay Campbell when we went around Greene County ringing doorbells for Stevenson in our sophomore year. Confronted with the most awesome

Republican small-mindedness, a stinginess and bleakness
of spirit that could absolutely bend the mind, The Pumpkin never was anything but ladylike. I was a barbarian.
No matter how dispassionately I began (or condescendingly, because that's how it came out), I invariably wound
up in a sweat and a rage, sneering, insulting, condemning,
toe-to-toe with these terrible pinched people, calling
their beloved Ike an illiterate, a political and moral moron—probably I am as responsible as anyone for Adlai
losing as badly as he did in Ohio. The Pumpkin, however,
gave such unflawed and kindly attention to the opposition
point of view that I expected sometimes for her to turn
and say to me, "Why, Alex, I think Mr. Yokel is right—I
think maybe he *is* too soft on communism." But no, when
the last idiocy had been uttered about our candidate's
"socialistical" and/or "pinko" ideas, the final condemna-
tion made of his sense of humor, The Pumpkin proceeded,
ceremoniously and (awesome feat!) without a hint of
sarcasm—she might have been the judge at a pie-baking
contest, such a perfect blend was she of sobriety and good
humor—proceeded to correct Mr. Yokel's errors of fact
and logic, even to draw attention to his niggardly morality. Unencumbered by the garbled syntax of the apoca-
lypse or the ill-mannered vocabulary of desperation,
without the perspiring upper lip, the constricted and air-
hungry throat, the flush of loathing on the forehead, she
may even have swayed half a dozen people in the county.
Christ, yes, this was one of the great *shikses*. I might have
learned something spending the rest of my life with such
a person. Yes, I might—if I could learn something! If I

could be somehow sprung from this obsession with fellatio
and fornication, from romance and fantasy and revenge
—from the settling of scores! the pursuit of dreams! from
this hopeless, senseless loyalty to the long ago!

In 1950, just seventeen, and Newark two and a half
months behind me (well, not exactly "behind": in the
mornings I awake in the dormitory baffled by the un-
familiar blanket in my hand, and the disappearance of
one of "my" windows; oppressed and distraught for minutes on end by this unanticipated transformation given
my bedroom by my mother)—I perform the most openly
defiant act of my life: instead of going home for my first
college vacation, I travel by train to Iowa, to spend
Thanksgiving with The Pumpkin and her parents. Till
September I had never been farther west than Lake
Hopatcong in New Jersey—now I am off to Ioway! And
with a blondie! Of the Christian religion! Who is more
stunned by this desertion, my family or me? What daring!
Or was I no more daring than a sleepwalker?
   The white clapboard house in which The Pumpkin had
grown up might have been the Taj Mahal for the emotions it released in me. Balboa, maybe, knows what I felt
upon first glimpsing the swing tied up to the ceiling of the
front porch. *She was raised in this house. The girl who has
let me undo her brassiere and dry-hump her at the dormitory door, grew up in this white house. Behind those*
goyische *curtains! Look, shutters!*
   "Daddy, Mother," says The Pumpkin, when we disembark at the Davenport train station, "this is the weekend

guest, this is the friend from school whom I wrote you about—"

I am something called "a weekend guest"? I am something called "a friend from school"? What tongue is she speaking? I am "the *bonditt*," "the *vantz*," I am the insurance man's son. I am Warshaw's ambassador! "How do you do, Alex?" To which of course I reply, "Thank you." Whatever anybody says to me during my first twenty-four hours in Iowa, I answer, "Thank you." Even to inanimate objects. I walk into a chair, promptly I say to it, "Excuse me, thank you." I drop my napkin on the floor, lean down, flushing, to pick it up, "Thank you," I hear myself saying to the napkin—or is it the floor I'm addressing? Would my mother be proud of her little gentleman! Polite even to the furniture!

Then there's an expression in English, "Good morning," or so I have been told; the phrase has never been of any particular use to me. Why should it have been? At breakfast at home I am in fact known to the other boarders as "Mr. Sourball," and "The Crab." But suddenly, here in Iowa, in imitation of the local inhabitants, I am transformed into a veritable geyser of good mornings. That's all anybody around that place knows how to say—they feel the sunshine on their faces, and it just sets off some sort of chemical reaction: Good *morning!* *Good* morning! Good *morning!* sung to half a dozen different tunes! Next they all start asking each other if they had "a good night's sleep." And asking me! Did I have a good night's sleep? I don't really know, I have to think—the question comes as something of a surprise. Did I Have A Good

Night's Sleep? Why, yes! I think I did! Hey—did you? "Like a log," replies Mr. Campbell. And for the first time in my life I experience the full force of a simile. This man, who is a real estate broker and an alderman of the Davenport town council, says that he slept like a log, and I actually *see* a log. *I* get it! Motionless, heavy, *like a log!* "Good *morning*," he says, and now it occurs to me that the word "morning," as he uses it, refers specifically to the hours between eight A.M. and twelve noon. I'd never thought of it that way before. He wants the hours between eight and twelve to be *good*, which is to say, enjoyable, pleasurable, beneficial! We are all of us wishing each other four hours of pleasure and accomplishment. Why, that's terrific! Hey, that's very nice! Good morning! And the same applies to "Good afternoon"! And "Good evening"! And "Good night"! My God! The English language is *a form of communication!* Conversation isn't just crossfire where you shoot and get shot at! Where you've got to duck for your life and aim to kill! Words aren't only bombs and bullets—no, they're little gifts, containing *meanings!*

Wait, I'm not finished—as if the experience of being on the inside rather than the outside of these *goyische* curtains isn't overwhelming enough, as if the incredible experience of my wishing hour upon hour of pleasure to a houseful of *goyim* isn't sufficient source for bewilderment, there is, to compound the ecstasy of disorientation, the name of the street upon which the Campbell house stands, the street where *my* girl friend grew up! skipped!

skated! hop-scotched! sledded! all the while I dreamed of
her existence some fifteen hundred miles away, in what
they tell me is the same country. The street name? Not
Xanadu, no, better even than that, oh, more preposterous
by far: *Elm*. Elm! It is, you see, as though I have walked
right through the orange celluloid station band of our old
Zenith, directly into "One Man's Family." Elm. Where
trees grow—which must be elms!

To be truthful, I must admit that I am not able to draw
such a conclusion first thing upon alighting from the
Campbell car on Wednesday night: after all, it has taken
me seventeen years to recognize an oak, and even there
I am lost without the acorns. What I see first in a land-
scape isn't the flora, believe me—it's the fauna, the human
opposition, who is screwing and who is getting screwed.
Greenery I leave to the birds and the bees, they have
their worries, I have mine. At home who knows the name
of what grows from the pavement at the front of our
house? It's a tree—and that's it. The kind is of no consequence, who cares what kind, just as long as it doesn't
fall down on your head. In the autumn (or is it the spring?
Do you know this stuff? I'm pretty sure it's not the winter) there drop from its branches long crescent-shaped
pods containing hard little pellets. Okay. Here's a scien-
tific fact about our tree, comes by way of my mother,
Sophie Linnaeus: If you shoot those pellets through a
straw, you can take somebody's eye out and make him
blind for life. (SO NEVER DO IT! NOT EVEN IN JEST!
AND IF ANYBODY DOES IT TO YOU, YOU TELL ME
INSTANTLY!) And this, more or less, is the sort of botan-

ical knowledge I am equipped with, until that Sunday afternoon when we are leaving the Campbell house for the train station, and I have my Archimedean experience: Elm Street . . . . . then . . . . . elm *trees!* How simple! I mean, you don't *need* 158 points of I.Q., you don't *have* to be a genius to make sense of this world. It's really all so very simple!

A memorable weekend in my lifetime, equivalent in human history, I would say, to mankind's passage through the entire Stone Age. Every time Mr. Campbell called his wife "Mary," my body temperature shot into the hundreds. There I was, eating off dishes that had been touched by the hands of a woman named *Mary.* (Is there a clue here as to why I so resisted calling The Monkey by her name, except to chastise her? No?) Please, I pray on the train heading west, let there be no pictures of Jesus Christ in the Campbell house. Let me get through this weekend without having to see his pathetic *punim*—or deal with anyone wearing a cross! When the aunts and uncles come for the Thanksgiving dinner, please, let there be no anti-Semite among them! Because if someone starts in with "the pushy Jews," or says "kike" or "jewed him down"—Well, I'll jew them down all right, I'll jew their fucking teeth down their throat! No, no violence (as if I even had it in me), let *them* be violent, that's *their* way. No, I'll rise from my seat—and (*vuh den?*) make a speech! I will shame and humiliate them in their bigoted hearts! Quote the Declaration of Independence over their candied yams! Who the fuck are they, I'll ask, to think they own Thanksgiving!

Then at the railroad station her father says, "How do you do, young man?" and I of course answer, "Thank you." Why is *he* acting so nice? Because he has been forewarned (which I don't know whether to take as an insult or a blessing), or because he doesn't know yet? Shall I say it then, before we even get into the car? Yes, I must! I can't go on living a lie! "Well, it sure is nice being here in Davenport, Mr. and Mrs. Campbell, what with my being Jewish and all." Not quite ringing enough perhaps. "Well, as a friend of Kay's, Mr. and Mrs. Campbell, and a Jew, I do want to thank you for inviting me—" Stop pussyfooting! What then? Talk Yiddish? *How?* I've got twenty-five words to my name—half of them dirty, and the rest mispronounced! Shit, just shut up and get in the car. "Thank you, thank you," I say, picking up my own bag, and we all head for the station wagon.

Kay and I climb into the back seat, *with the dog.* Kay's dog! To whom she talks as though he's human! Wow, she really *is* a goy. What a stupid thing, to talk to a dog—except Kay isn't stupid! In fact, I think she's smarter really than I am. And yet talks to a dog? "As far as dogs are concerned, Mr. and Mrs. Campbell, we Jews by and large—" Oh, forget it. Not necessary. You are ignoring anyway (or trying awfully hard to) that eloquent appendage called your nose. Not to mention the Afro-Jewish hairpiece. Of course they know. Sorry, but there's no escaping destiny, *bubi,* a man's cartilage is his fate. *But I don't want to escape!* Well, that's nice too—because you can't. *Oh, but yes I can—if I should want to!* But you said you don't want to. *But if I did!*

As soon as I enter the house I begin (on the sly, and somewhat to my own surprise) to sniff: what will the odor be like? Mashed potatoes? An old lady's dress? Fresh cement? I sniff and I sniff, trying to catch the scent. There! is *that* it, is that Christianity I smell, or just the dog? Everything I see, taste, touch, I think, *"Goyish!"* My first morning I squeeze half an inch of Pepsodent down the drain rather than put my brush where Kay's mother or father may have touched the bristles with which they cleanse their own *goyische* molars. True! The soap on the sink is bubbly with foam from somebody's hands. Whose? *Mary's?* Should I just take hold of it and begin to wash, or should I maybe run a little water over it first, just to be safe. But safe from *what?* Schmuck, maybe you want to get a piece of soap to wash the soap with! I tiptoe to the toilet, I peer over into the bowl: "Well, there it is, boy, a real *goyische* toilet bowl. The genuine article. Where your girl friend's father drops his gentile turds. What do you think, huh? Pretty impressive." Obsessed? Spellbound!

Next I have to decide whether or not to line the seat. It isn't a matter of hygiene, I'm sure the place is clean, spotless in its own particular antiseptic *goy* way: the question is, what if it's warm yet from a Campbell behind—from her mother! *Mary!* Mother also of Jesus Christ! If only for the sake of my family, maybe I should put a little paper around the rim; it doesn't cost anything, and who will ever know?

I will! *I* will! So down I go—and it *is* warm! Yi, seventeen years old and I am rubbing asses with the enemy!

How far I have traveled since September! *By the waters of Babylon, there we sat down, yea, we wept when we remembered Zion!* And yea is right! On the can I am besieged by doubt and regret, I am suddenly languishing with all my heart for home . . . When my father drives out to buy "real apple cider" at the roadside farmer's market off in Union, I won't be with him! And how can Hannah and Morty go to the Weequahic-Hillside game Thanksgiving morning without me along to make them laugh? Jesus, I hope we win (which is to say, lose by less than 21 points). Beat Hillside, you bastards! Double U, Double E, Q U A, H I C! Bernie, Sidney, Leon, "Ushie," come on, backfield, FIGHT!

> Aye-aye ki-ike-us,
> Nobody likes us,
> We are the boys of Weequahic High—
> Aye-aye ki-ucch-us,
> *Kish mir in tuchis,*
> We are the boys of Weequahic High!

Come on—hold that line, make that point, kick 'em in the *kishkas,* go team go!

See, I'm missing my chance to be clever and quick-witted in the stands! To show off my sarcastic and mocking tongue! And after the game, missing the historical Thanksgiving meal prepared by my mother, that freckled and red-headed descendant of Polish Jews! Oh, how the blood will flow out of their faces, what a deathly silence will prevail, when she holds up the huge drumstick, and cries, "Here! For guess who!" and Guess-who is found to be AWOL! Why have I deserted my family? Maybe around the table we don't look like a painting by Norman Rockwell, but we have a good time, too, don't you worry! We don't go back to the Plymouth Rock, no Indian ever brought maize to any member of our family as far as we know—but just smell that stuffing! And look, cylinders of cranberry sauce at *either* end of the table! And the turkey's name, "Tom"! Why then can't I believe I am eating my dinner in America, that America is where *I* am, instead of some other place to which I will one day travel, as my father and I must travel every November out to that hayseed and his wife in Union, New Jersey (the *two* of them in overalls), for real Thanksgiving apple cider.

"I'm going to Iowa," I tell them from the phone booth on my floor. "To *where?*" "To Davenport, Iowa." "On your first college vacation?!" "—I know, but it's a great opportunity, and I can't turn it down—" "Oppor*tunity?* To do *what?*" "Yes, to spend Thanksgiving with this boy named Bill Campbell's family—" "*Who?*" "Campbell. Like the soup. He lives in my dorm—" But they are expecting me. Everybody is expecting me. Morty has the tickets to the game. What am I talking *opportunity?* "And who is this boy all of a sudden, Campbell?" "My friend! Bill!" "But," says my father, "the *cider.*" Oh my God, it's happened, what I swore I wouldn't permit!—I am in tears, and "cider" is the little word that does it. The man is a natural—he could go on Groucho Marx and win a fortune guessing the secret-woid. He guesses mine, every single time! And wins my jackpot of contrition! "I can't back out, I'm sorry, I've accepted—we're *going!*" "Going? And

how, Alex—I don't understand this plan at all," interrupts
my mother—*"how* are you going, if I may be so bold, and
where? and in a convertible too, *that too*—" "NO!" "And if
the highways are icy, Alex—" "We're going, Mother, *in a
Sherman tank!* Okay? *Okay?*" "Alex," she says sternly, "I
hear it in your voice, I know you're not telling me the
whole truth, you're going to hitchhike in a convertible or
some other crazy thing—two months away from home,
seventeen years old, and he's going wild!"

Sixteen years ago I made that phone call. A little more
than half the age I am now. November 1950—here, it's
tattooed on my wrist, the date of my Emancipation Proc-
lamation. Children unborn when I first telephoned my
parents to say I wasn't coming home from college are just
entering college, I suppose—only I'm still telephoning my
parents to say I'm not coming home! Fighting off my
family, still! What use to skip those two grades in grammar school and get such a jump on everybody else, when
the result is to wind up so far behind? My early promise is
legend: starring in all those grade-school plays! taking on
at the age of twelve the entire DAR! Why then do I live
by myself and have no children of my own? It's no *non
sequitur,* that question! Professionally I'm going somewhere, granted, but *privately*—what have I got to show
for myself? Children should be playing on this earth who
look like me! *Why not?* Why should every *shtunk* with a
picture window and a carport have offspring, and not me?
It don't make sense! Think of it, half the race is over, and
I still stand here at the starting line—me, the first one out
of his swaddling clothes and into his track suit! a hundred

and fifty-eight points of I.Q., and still arguing with the authorities about the rules and regulations! disputing the course to be run! calling into question the legitimacy of the track commission! Yes, "crab" is correct, Mother! "Sourball" is perfect, right on The Nose's nose! "Mr. Conniption-Fit"—*c'est moi!*

Another of these words I went through childhood thinking of as "Jewish." Conniption. "Go ahead, have a conniption-fit," my mother would advise. "See if it changes anything, my brilliant son." And how I tried! How I used to hurl myself against the walls of her kitchen! Mr. Hot-Under-The-Collar! Mr. Hit-The-Ceiling! Mr. Fly-Off-The-Handle! The names I earn for myself! God forbid somebody should look at you cockeyed, Alex, their life isn't worth two cents! Mr. Always-Right-And-Never-Wrong! Grumpy From The Seven Dwarfs Is Visiting Us, Daddy. Ah, Hannah, Your Brother Surly Has Honored Us With His Presence This Evening, It's A Pleasure To Have You, Surly. "Hi Ho Silver," she sighs, as I rush into my bedroom to sink my fangs into the bedspread, "The Temper Tantrum Kid Rides Again."

Near the end of our junior year Kay missed a period, and so we began, and with a certain eager delight—and wholly without panic, interestingly—to make plans to be married. We would offer ourselves as resident baby-sitters to a young faculty couple who were fond of us; in return they would give us their roomy attic to live in, and a shelf to use in their refrigerator. We would wear old clothes and eat spaghetti. Kay would write poetry about having a baby, and, she said, type term papers for extra money. We had our scholarships, what more did we need? (besides a mattress, some bricks and boards for bookshelves, Kay's Dylan Thomas record, and in time, a crib). We thought of ourselves as adventurers.

I said, "And you'll convert, right?"

I intended the question to be received as ironic, or thought I had. But Kay took it seriously. Not solemnly, mind you, just seriously.

Kay Campbell, Davenport, Iowa: "Why would I want to do a thing like that?"

Great girl! Marvelous, ingenuous, candid girl! Content, you see, as she was! What one *dies* for in a woman—I now realize! *Why would I want to do a thing like that?* And nothing blunt or defensive or arch or superior in her tone. Just common sense, plainly spoken.

Only it put our Portnoy into a rage, incensed The Temper Tantrum Kid. What do you mean *why* would you want to do a thing like that? Why do you think, you simpleton-*goy!* Go talk to your dog, ask *him.* Ask Spot what *he* thinks, that four-legged genius. "Want Kay-Kay to be a Jew, Spottie—huh, big fella, huh?" Just what the fuck makes you so self-satisfied, anyway? That you carry on conversations with dogs? that you know an elm when you see one? that your father drives a station wagon made out of wood? What's your hotsy-totsy accomplishment in life, baby, that Doris Day snout?

I was, fortunately, so astonished by my indignation that I couldn't begin to voice it. How could I be feeling a wound in a place where I was not even vulnerable? What did Kay and I care less about than one, money, and two, religion? Our favorite philosopher was Bertrand Russell. Our religion was Dylan Thomas' religion, Truth and Joy! Our children would be atheists. I had only been making a joke!

Nonetheless, it would seem that I never forgave her: in the weeks following our false alarm, she came to seem to me boringly predictable in conversation, and about as desirable as blubber in bed. And it surprised me that she should take it so badly when I finally had to tell her that I didn't seem to care for her any more. I was very honest, you see, as Bertrand Russell said I should be. "I just don't want to see you any more, Kay. I can't hide my feelings, I'm sorry." She wept pitifully: she carried around the campus terrible little pouches underneath her bloodshot blue eyes, she didn't show up for meals, she missed classes . . . And I was astonished. Because all along I'd thought it was I who had loved her, not she who had loved me. What a surprise to discover just the opposite to have been the case.

Ah, twenty and spurning one's mistress—that first unsullied thrill of sadism with a woman! And the dream of the women to come. I returned to New Jersey that June, buoyant with my own "strength," wondering how I could ever have been so captivated by someone so ordinary and so fat.

Another gentile heart broken by me belonged to The Pilgrim, Sarah Abbott Maulsby—New Canaan, Foxcroft, and Vassar (where she had as companion, stabled in

Poughkeepsie, that other flaxen beauty, her palomino). A tall, gentle, decorous twenty-two-year-old, fresh from college, and working as a receptionist in the office of the Senator from Connecticut when we two met and coupled in the fall of 1959.

I was on the staff of the House subcommittee investigating the television quiz scandals. Perfect for a closet socialist like myself: commercial deceit on a national scale, exploitation of the innocent public, elaborate corporate chicanery—in short, good old capitalist greed. And then of course that extra bonus, Charlatan Van Doren. Such character, such brains and breeding, that candor and schoolboyish charm—the ur-WASP, wouldn't you say? And turns out he's a fake. Well, what do you know about that, Gentile America? Supergoy, a *gonif!* Steals money. Covets money. Wants money, will do anything for it. Goodness gracious me, almost as bad as Jews—you sanctimonious WASPs!

Yes, I was one happy yiddel down there in Washington, a little Stern gang of my own, busily exploding Charlie's honor and integrity, while simultaneously becoming lover to that aristocratic Yankee beauty whose forebears arrived on these shores in the seventeenth century. Phenomenon known as Hating Your Goy And Eating One Too.

Why didn't I marry that beautiful and adoring girl? I remember her in the gallery, pale and enchanting in a navy blue suit with gold buttons, watching with such pride, with such love, as I took on one afternoon, in my first public cross-examination, a very slippery network

P.R. man . . . and I was impressive too, for my first time out: cool, lucid, persistent, just the faintest hammering of the heart—and only twenty-six years old. Oh yeah, when I am holding all the moral cards, watch out, you crooks you! I am nobody to futz around with when I know myself to be four hundred per cent in the right.

Why didn't I marry the girl? Well, there was her cutesy-wootsy boarding school argot, for one. Couldn't bear it. "Barf" for vomit, "ticked off" for angry, "a howl" for funny, "crackers" for crazy, "teeny" for tiny. Oh, and "divine." (What Mary Jane Reed means by "groovy"— I'm always telling these girls how to talk right, me with my five-hundred-word New Jersey vocabulary.) Then there were the nicknames of her friends; there were the friends themselves! Poody and Pip and Pebble, Shrimp and Brute and Tug, Squeek, Bumpo, Baba—it sounded, I said, as though she had gone to Vassar with Donald Duck's nephews . . . But then my argot caused her some pain too. The first time I said fuck in her presence (and the presence of friend Pebble, in her Peter Pan collar and her cablestitch cardigan, and tanned like an Indian from so much tennis at the Chevy Chase Club), such a look of agony passed over The Pilgrim's face, you would have thought I had just branded the four letters on her flesh. Why, she asked so plaintively once we were alone, why *had* I to be so "unattractive"? What possible pleasure had it given me to be so "ill-mannered"? What on earth had I "proved"? "Why did you have to be so pus-y like that? It was so un*called*-for." Pus-y being Debutante for disagreeable.

In bed? Nothing fancy, no acrobatics or feats of daring and skill; as we screwed our first time, so we continued— I assaulted and she surrendered, and the heat generated on her mahogany fourposter (a Maulsby family heirloom) was considerable. Our one peripheral delight was the full-length mirror on the back of the bathroom door. There, standing thigh to thigh, I would whisper, "Look, Sarah, look." At first she was shy, left the looking to me, at first she was modest and submitted only because I wished her to, but in time she developed something of a passion for the looking glass, too, and followed the reflection of our joining with a certain startled intensity in her gaze. Did she see what I saw? *In the black pubic hair, ladies and gentlemen, weighing one hundred and seventy pounds, at least half of which is still undigested halvah and hot pastrami, from Newark, NJ, The Shnoz, Alexander Portnoy! And his opponent, in the fair fuzz, with her elegant polished limbs and the gentle maidenly face of a Botticelli, that ever-popular purveyor of the social amenities here in the Garden, one hundred and fourteen pounds of Republican refinement, and the pertest pair of nipples in all New England, from New Canaan, Connecticut, Sarah Abbott Maulsby!*

What I'm saying, Doctor, is that I don't seem to stick my dick up these girls, as much as I stick it up their backgrounds—as though through fucking I will discover America. *Conquer* America—maybe that's more like it. Columbus, Captain Smith, Governor Winthrop, General Washington—now Portnoy. As though my manifest destiny is to seduce a girl from each of the forty-eight states.

As for Alaskan and Hawaiian women, I really have no feelings either way, no scores to settle, no coupons to cash in, no dreams to put to rest—who are they to me, a bunch of Eskimos and Orientals? No, I am a child of the forties, of network radio and World War Two, of eight teams to a league and forty-eight states to a country. I know all the words to "The Marine Hymn," and to "The Caissons Go Rolling Along"—and to "The Song of the Army Air Corps." I know the song of the *Navy* Air Corps: "Sky anchors aweigh/ We're sailors of the air/ We're sailing everywhere—" I can even sing you the song of the Seabees. Go ahead, name your branch of service, Spielvogel, I'll sing you your song! Please, allow me—it's my money. We used to sit on our coats, I remember, on the concrete floor, our backs against the sturdy walls of the basement corridors of my grade school, singing in unison to keep up our morale until the all-clear signal sounded— "Johnny Zero." "Praise the Lord and Pass the Ammunition." "The sky-pilot said it/ You've got to give him credit/ For a son of a gun of a gunner was he-e-e-e!" You name it, and if it was in praise of the Stars and Stripes, I know it word for word! Yes, I am a child of air raid drills, Doctor, I remember Corregidor and "The Cavalcade of America," and that flag, fluttering on its pole, being raised at that heartbreaking angle over bloody Iwo Jima. Colin Kelly went down in flames when I was eight, and Hiroshima and Nagasaki went up in a puff, one week when I was twelve, and that was the heart of my boyhood, four years of hating Tojo, Hitler, and Mussolini, and loving this brave determined republic! Rooting my little Jewish

heart out for our American democracy! Well, we won, the
enemy is dead in an alley back of the Wilhelmstrasse, and
dead because I *prayed* him dead—and now I want what's
coming to me. *My* G.I. bill—real American ass! The cunt
in country-'tis-of-thee! I pledge allegiance to the twat of
the United States of America—and to the republic for
which it stands: Davenport, Iowa! Dayton, Ohio! Sche-
nectady, New York, and neighboring Troy! Fort Myers,
Florida! New Canaan, Connecticut! Chicago, Illinois!
Albert Lea, Minnesota! Portland, Maine! Moundsville,
West Virginia! Sweet land of *shikse*-tail, of thee I sing!
    From the mountains,
    To the prairies,
    To the oceans, white-with-my-fooaahhh-mmm!
    God bless A-me-ri-cuuuuhhhh!
    My home, SWEET HOOOOOHHHH-M!

Imagine what it meant to me to know that generations
of Maulsbys were buried in the graveyard at Newbury-
port, Massachusetts, and generations of Abbotts in Salem.
Land where my fathers died, land of the Pilgrims' pride
. . . Exactly. Oh, and more. Here was a girl whose mother's flesh *crawled* at the sound of the words "Eleanor
Roosevelt." Who herself had been dandled on the knee
of Wendell Willkie at Hobe Sound, Florida, in 1942
(while my father was saying prayers for F.D.R. on the
High Holidays, and my mother blessing him over the
Friday night candles). The Senator from Connecticut had
been a roommate of her Daddy's at Harvard, and her
brother, "Paunch," a graduate of Yale, held a seat on the

New York Stock Exchange and (how lucky could I be?) played polo (yes, games from on top of a horse!) on Sunday afternoons someplace in Westchester County, as he had throughout college. She could have been a Lindabury, don't you see? A daughter of my father's boss! Here was a girl who knew how to sail a boat, knew how to eat her dessert using two pieces of silverware (a piece of cake you could pick up in your hands, and you should have seen her manipulate it with that fork and that spoon —like a Chinese with his chopsticks! What skills she had learned in far-off Connecticut!). Activities that partook of the exotic and even the taboo she performed so simply, as a matter of course: and I was as wowed (though that's not the whole story) as Desdemona, hearing of the Anthropapagi. I came across a newspaper clipping in her scrapbook, a column entitled "A Deb A Day," which began, "SARAH ABBOTT MAULSBY—'Ducks and quails and pheasants better scurry' around New Canaan this fall because Sally, daughter of Mr. and Mrs. Edward H. Maulsby of Greenley Road, is getting in practice for small game season. Shooting—" with a gun, Doctor—"shooting is just one of Sally's outdoor hobbies. She loves riding too, and this summer hopes to try a rod and reel—" and get this; I think this tale would win my son too—"hopes to try a rod and reel on some of those trout that swim by 'Windview' her family's summer home."

What Sally couldn't do was eat me. To shoot a gun at a little quack-quack is fine, to suck my cock is beyond her. She was sorry, she said, if I was going to take it so hard, but it was just something she didn't care to try. I mustn't

act as though it were a personal affront, she said, because
it had nothing at all to do with me as an individual . . .
Oh, didn't it? Bullshit, girlie! Yes, what made me so irate
was precisely my belief that I was being discriminated
against. My father couldn't rise at Boston & Northeastern
for the very same reason that Sally Maulsby wouldn't
deign to go down on me! Where was the justice in this
world? Where was the B'nai B'rith Anti-Defamation
League—! "I do it to you," I said. The Pilgrim shrugged;
kindly she said, "You don't have to, though. You know
that. If you don't want to . . ." "Ah, but I *do* want to—it
isn't a matter of 'have' to. *I want to.*" "Well," she answered, "I don't." "*But why not?*" "Because. I don't."
"Shit, that's the way a child answers, Sarah—'because'!
Give me a reason!" "I—I just don't do that, that's all." "But
that brings us back to why. *Why?*" "Alex, I can't. I just
can't." "Give me a single good reason!" "Please," she replied, knowing her rights, "I don't think I have to."

No, she didn't have to—because to me the answer was
clear enough anyway: *Because you don't know how to
hike out to windward or what a jib is, because you have
never owned evening clothes or been to a cotillion* . . .
Yes sir, if I were some big blond *goy* in a pink riding suit
and hundred-dollar hunting boots, don't worry, she'd be
down there eating me, of that I am sure!

I am wrong. Three months I spent applying pressure to
the back of her skull (pressure met by a surprising coun-
terforce, an impressive, even moving display of stubborn-
ness from such a mild and uncontentious person), for
three months I assaulted her in argument and tugged her

nightly by the ears. Then one night she invited me to hear the Budapest String Quartet playing Mozart at the Library of Congress; during the final movement of the Clarinet Quintet she took hold of my hand, her cheeks began to shine, and when we got back to her apartment and into bed, Sally said, "Alex . . . I will." "Will what?" But she was gone, down beneath the covers and out of sight: blowing me! That is to say, she took my prick in her mouth and held it there for a count of sixty, held the surprised little thing there, Doctor, like a thermometer. I threw back the blankets—this I had to see! Feel, there wasn't very much to feel, but oh the sight of it! Only Sally was already finished. Having moved it by now to the side of her face, as though it were the gear shift on her Hillman-Minx. And there were tears on her face.

"I did it," she announced.

"Sally, oh, Sarah, don't cry."

"But I did do it, Alex."

". . . You mean," I said, "that's all?"

"You mean," she gasped, *more?*"

"Well, to be frank, a little more—I mean to be truthful with you, it wouldn't go unappreciated—"

"But it's getting big. I'll suffocate."

JEW SMOTHERS DEB WITH COCK, *Vassar Grad Georgetown Strangulation Victim; Mocky Lawyer Held*

"Not if you breathe, you won't."

"I will, I'll choke—"

"Sarah, the best safeguard against asphyxiation is breathing. Just breathe, and that's all there is to it. More or less."

God bless her, she tried. But came up gagging. "I told
you," she moaned.

"But you weren't breathing."

"I can't with that in my mouth."

"Through your nose. Pretend you're swimming."

"But I'm *not*."

"PRETEND!" I suggested, and though she gave another
gallant try, surfaced only seconds later in an agony of
coughing and tears. I gathered her then in my arms (that
lovely willing girl! convinced by Mozart to go down on
Alex! oh, sweet as Natasha in *War and Peace!* a tender
young countess!). I rocked her, I teased her, I made her
laugh, for the first time I said, "I love you too, my baby,"
but of course it couldn't have been clearer to me that despite all her many qualities and charms—her devotion,
her beauty, her deerlike grace, her place in American history—there could never be any "love" in me for The Pilgrim. Intolerant of her frailties. Jealous of her accomplishments. Resentful of her family. No, not much room
there for love.

No, Sally Maulsby was just something nice a son once
did for his dad. A little vengeance on Mr. Lindabury for
all those nights and Sundays Jack Portnoy spent collecting down in the colored district. A little bonus extracted
from Boston & Northeastern, for all those years of service,
and exploitation.

IN EXILE

On Sunday mornings, when the weather is warm enough, twenty of the neighborhood men (this in the days of short center field) play a round of seven-inning softball games, starting at nine in the morning and ending about one in the afternoon, the stakes for each game a dollar a head. The umpire is our dentist, old Dr. Wolfenberg, the neighborhood college graduate—night school on High Street, but as good as Oxford to us. Among the players is our butcher, his twin brother our plumber, the grocer, the owner of the service station where my father buys his gasoline—all of them ranging in age from thirty to fifty, though I think of them not in terms of their years, but only as "the men." In the on-deck circle, even at the plate, they roll their jaws on the stumps of soggy cigars. Not boys, you see, but men. Belly! Muscle! Forearms black with hair! Bald domes! And then the voices they have on them—cannons you can hear go off from as far as our front stoop a block away. I imagine vocal cords inside them thick as clotheslines! lungs the size of zeppelins! Nobody has to tell them to stop mumbling and speak up, never! And the outrageous things they say! The chatter in the infield isn't chatter, it's kibitzing, and (to this small boy, just beginning to learn the art of ridicule)

hilarious, particularly the insults that emanate from the
man my father has labeled "The Mad Russian," Biderman,
owner of the corner candy store (and bookie joint) who
has a "hesitation" side-arm delivery, not only very funny
but very effective. "Abracadabra," he says, and pitches his
backbreaking drop. And he is always giving it to Dr.
Wolfenberg: "A blind ump, okay, but a blind dentist?"
The idea causes him to smote his forehead with his glove.
"Play ball, comedian," calls Dr. Wolfenberg, very Connie
Mack in his perforated two-tone shoes and Panama hat,
"start up the game, Biderman, unless you want to get
thrown out of here for insults—!" "But how do they teach
you in that dental school, Doc, by Braille?"

Meanwhile, all the way from the outfield comes the
badinage of one who in appearance is more cement-mixer
than Homo sapiens, the prince of the produce market,
Allie Sokolow. The *pisk* he opens on him! (as my mother
would put it). For half an inning the invective flows in
toward home plate from his position in deep center field,
and then when his team comes to bat, he stations himself
in the first-base coaching box and the invective flows un-
interruptedly out in the opposite direction—and none of
it has anything to do with any contretemps that may
actually be taking place on the field. Quite the opposite.
My father, when he is not out working on Sunday mornings, comes by to sit and watch a few innings with me; he
knows Allie Sokolow (as he knows many of the players),
since they were all boys together in the Central Ward,
before he met my mother and moved to Jersey City. He
says that Allie has always been like this, "a real show-

man." When Allie charges in toward second base, screaming his gibberish and double-talk in the direction of home
plate (where there isn't even a batter as yet—where Dr.
Wolfenberg is merely dusting the plate with the whisk
broom he brings to the game), the people in the stands
couldn't be more delighted: they laugh, they clap, they
call out, "You tell him, Allie! You give it to him, Sokolow!"
And invariably Dr. Wolfenberg, who takes himself a little
more seriously than your ordinary nonprofessional person
(and is a German Jew to boot), holds up his palm, halting
an already Sokolow-stopped game, and says to Biderman,
"Will you please get that *meshuggener* back in the outfield?"

I tell you, they are an endearing lot! I sit in the wooden
stands alongside first base, inhaling that sour springtime
bouquet in the pocket of my fielder's mitt—sweat, leather,
vaseline—and laughing my head off. I cannot imagine
myself living out my life any other place but here. Why
leave, why go, when there is everything here that I will
ever want? The ridiculing, the joking, the acting-up, the
pretending—anything for a laugh! I love it! And yet underneath it all, *they mean it, they are in dead earnest.* You
should see them at the end of the seven innings when
that dollar has to change hands. Don't tell *me* they don't
mean it! Losing and winning is not a joke . . . and yet it
is! And that's what charms me most of all. Fierce as the
competition is, they cannot resist clowning and kibitzing
around. Putting on a show! How I am going to love growing up to be a Jewish man! Living forever in the Weequahic section, and playing softball on Chancellor Avenue

from nine to one on Sundays, a perfect joining of clown and competitor, kibitzing wiseguy and dangerous long-ball hitter.

I remember all this where? when? While Captain Meyerson is making his last slow turn over the Tel Aviv airport. My face is against the window. *Yes, I could disappear, I think, change my name and never be heard from again*—then Meyerson banks the wing on my side, and I look down for the first time upon the continent of Asia, I look down from two thousand feet in the air upon the Land of Israel, where the Jewish people first came into being, and am impaled upon a memory of Sunday morning softball games in Newark.

The elderly couple seated beside me (the Solomons, Edna and Felix), who have told me in an hour's flight time all about their children and grandchildren in Cincinnati (with, of course, a walletful of visual aids), now nudge each other and nod together in silent satisfaction; they even poke some friends across the aisle, a couple from Mount Vernon they've just met (the Perls, Sylvia and Bernie), and these two *kvell* also to see a tall, good-looking, young Jewish lawyer (and single! a match for somebody's daughter!) suddenly begin to weep upon making contact with a Jewish airstrip. However, what has produced these tears is not, as the Solomons and Perls would have it, a first glimpse of the national homeland, the ingathering of an exile, but the sound in my ear of my own nine-year-old little boy's voice—*my* voice, I mean, at nine. Nine-year-old me! Sure a sourpuss, a face-maker, a little back-talker and *kvetch*, sure my piping is never

without its nice infuriating whiny edge of permanent dis-
gruntlement and grievance ("as though," my mother
says, "the world owes him a living—at nine years old"),
but a laugher and kidder too, don't forget that, an enthu-
siast! a romantic! a mimic! a nine-year-old lover of life!
fiery with such simple, neighborhoody dreams!—"I'm going up the field," I call into the kitchen, fibers of pink lox
lodged like sour dental floss in the gaps between my
teeth, "I'm going up the field, Ma," pounding my mitt
with my carpy-smelling little fist, "I'll be back around
one—" "*Wait* a minute. What time? Where?" "*Up the
field,*" I holler—I'm very high on hollering to be heard, it's
like being angry, except without the consequences, "*—to
watch the men!*"

And that's the phrase that does me in as we touch down
upon *Eretz Yisroel:* to watch the men.

Because I love those men! I want to grow up to *be* one
of those men! To be going home to Sunday dinner at one
o'clock, sweat socks pungent from twenty-one innings of
softball, underwear athletically gamy, and in the muscle
of my throwing arm, a faint throbbing from the low and
beautiful pegs I have been unleashing all morning long to
hold down the opposition on the base paths; yes, hair
disheveled, teeth gritty, feet beat and *kishkas* sore from
laughing, in other words, feeling great, a robust Jewish
man now gloriously pooped—yes, home I head for resusci-
tation . . . and to whom? To *my* wife and *my* children,
to a family of my own, and right there in the Weequahic
section! I shave and shower—rivulets of water stream off
my scalp a filthy brown, ah, it's good, ah yes, it's a regular

pleasure standing there nearly scalding myself to death with hot water. It strikes me as so *manly*, converting pain to pleasure. Then into a pair of snappy slacks and a freshly dry-cleaned "gaucho" shirt—perfecto! I whistle a popular song, I admire my biceps, I shoot a rag across my shoes, making it *pop*, and meanwhile my kids are riffling through the Sunday papers (reading with eyes the exact color of my own), giggling away on the living-room rug; and my wife, Mrs. Alexander Portnoy, is setting the table in the dining room—we will be having my mother and father as guests, they will be walking over any minute, as they do every Sunday. A future, see! A simple and satisfying future! Exhausting, exhilarating softball in which to spend my body's force—that for the morning—then in the afternoon, the brimming, hearty stew of family life, and at night three solid hours of the best line-up of radio entertainment in the world: yes, as I delighted in Jack Benny's trips down to his vault in the company of *my* father, and Fred Allen's conversations with Mrs. Nussbaum, and Phil Harris' with Frankie Remley, also shall my children delight in them with me, and so unto the hundredth generation. And then after Kenny Baker, I double-lock the front and back doors, turn off all the lights (check and—as my father does—double-check the pilot on the gas range so that our lives will not be stolen from us in the night). I kiss good night my pretty sleepy daughter and my clever sleepy son, and in the arms of Mrs. A. Portnoy, that kind and gentle (and in my sugary but modest fantasy, faceless) woman, I bank the fires of my abounding pleasure. In the morning I am off to downtown Newark, to the

Essex County Court House, where I spend my workdays seeking justice for the poor and the oppressed.

Our eighth-grade class visits the courthouse to observe the architecture. Home and in my room that night, I write in my fresh new graduation autograph album, under YOUR FAVORITE MOTTO, "Don't Step on the Underdog." MY FAVORITE PROFESSION? "Lawyer." MY FAVORITE HERO? "Tom Paine and Abraham Lincoln." Lincoln sits outside the courthouse (in Gutzon Borglum's bronze), looking tragic and fatherly: you just know how much he cares. A statue of Washington, standing erect and authoritarian in front of his horse, overlooks Broad Street; it is the work of J. Massey Rhind (we write this second unname-like name of a sculptor in our notebooks); our art teacher says that the two statues are "the city's pride," and we head off in pairs for the paintings at the Newark Museum. Washington, I must confess, leaves me cold. Maybe it's the horse, that he's leaning on a horse. At any rate, he is so obviously a *goy*. But Lincoln! I could cry. Look at him sitting there, so *oysgemitchet*. How he labored for the downtrodden—as will I!

A nice little Jewish boy? Please, I am the nicest little Jewish boy who ever lived! Only look at the fantasies, how sweet and savior-like they are! Gratitude to my parents, loyalty to my tribe, devotion to the cause of justice!

And? What's so wrong? Hard work in an idealistic profession; games played without fanaticism or violence, games played among like-minded people, and with laughter; and family forgiveness and love. What was so wrong with believing in all that? What happened to the good sense I had at nine, ten, eleven years of age? How have I come to be such an enemy and flayer of myself? And so alone! *Oh,* so alone! Nothing but *self!* Locked up in *me!* Yes, I have to ask myself (as the airplane carries me—I believe—away from my tormentor), what has become of my purposes, those decent and worthwhile goals? Home? I have none. Family? No! Things I could own just by snapping my fingers . . . so why not snap them then, and get on with my life? No, instead of tucking in my children and lying down beside a loyal wife (to whom I am loyal too), I have, on two different evenings, taken to bed with me—coinstantaneously, as they say in the whorehouses— a fat little Italian whore and an illiterate, unbalanced American mannequin. And that isn't even my idea of a good time, damn it! What is? I told you! And meant it— sitting at home listening to Jack Benny with my kids! Raising intelligent, loving, sturdy children! Protecting some good woman! Dignity! Health! Love! Industry! Intelligence! Trust! Decency! High Spirits! Compassion! What the hell do I care about sensational sex? How can I be floundering like this over something so simple, so *silly,* as pussy! How absurd that I should have finally come down with VD! At my age! Because I'm sure of it: I have contracted something from that Lina! It is just a matter of waiting for the chancre to appear. But I won't wait, I can't: In Tel Aviv a doctor, first thing, before the chancre *or* the blindness sets in!

Only what about the dead girl back at the hotel? For she will have accomplished it by now, I'm sure. Thrown herself off the balcony in her underpants. Walked into the sea and drowned herself, wearing the world's tiniest bikini. No, she will take hemlock in the moonlit shadows of the Acropolis—in her Balenciaga evening gown! That empty-headed, exhibitionistic, suicidal twat! Don't worry, when she does it, it'll be photographable—it'll come out looking like an ad for ladies' lingerie! There she'll be, as usual, in the Sunday magazine section—only dead! I must turn back before I have this ridiculous suicide forever on my conscience! I should have telephoned Harpo! I didn't even think of it—just ran for *my* life. Gotten her to a phone to talk to her doctor. But would he have talked? I doubt it! That mute bastard, he *has* to, before she takes her unreversible revenge! MODEL SLITS THROAT IN AMPHITHEATRE; Medea *Interrupted by Suicide* . . . and they'll publish the note they find, more than likely in a bottle stuffed up her snatch. "Alexander Portnoy is responsible. He forced me to sleep with a whore and then wouldn't make me an honest woman. Mary Jane Reed." Thank God the moron can't spell! It'll all be Greek to those Greeks! *Hope*fully.

Running away! In flight, escaping again—and from what? From someone else who would have me a saint! Which I ain't! And do not want or intend to be! No, any guilt on my part is *comical!* I will not *hear* of it! If she kills herself—But that's not what she's about to do. No, it'll be more ghastly than that: she's going to telephone the Mayor! And that's why I'm running! But she wouldn't. But she *would.* She *will!* More than likely already has. Remember? *I'll expose you, Alex. I'll call long-distance to John Lindsay. I'll telephone Jimmy Breslin.* And she is crazy enough to do it! Breslin, that cop! That precinct station genius! Oh Jesus, *let* her be dead then! Jump, you ignorant destructive bitch—better you than me! Sure, all I need is she should start telephoning around to the wire services: I can see my father going out to the corner after dinner, picking up the *Newark News*—and at long last, the word SCANDAL printed in bold type above a picture of his darling son! Or turning on the seven o'clock news to watch the CBS correspondent in Athens interviewing The Monkey from her hospital bed. "Portnoy, that's right. Capital P. Then O. Then I think R. Oh, I can't remember the rest, but I swear on my wet pussy, Mr. Rudd, he made me sleep with a whore!" No, no, I am *not* exaggerating: think a moment about the character, or absence of same. Remember Las Vegas? Remember her desperation? Then you see that this wasn't just my conscience punishing me; no, whatever revenge I might imagine, she could imagine too. And will yet! Believe me, we have not heard the last of Mary Jane Reed. I was supposed to save her life—*and didn't*. Made her sleep with whores instead! So don't think we have heard the last word from her!

And there, to cause me to kick my ass even more, there all blue below me, the Aegean Sea. The Pumpkin's Aegean! My poetic American girl! Sophocles! Long ago! Oh, Pumpkin—baby, say it again, *Why would I want to do a thing like that?* Someone who knew who she was! Psychologically so intact as not to be in need of salvation or redemption by me! Not in need of conversion to my glorious faith! The poetry she used to read to me at Antioch, the education she was giving me in literature, a whole new perspective, an understanding of art and the artistic way . . . oh, why did I ever let her go! I can't believe it—because she wouldn't be *Jewish?* "The eternal note of sadness—" "The turbid ebb and flow of human misery—"

Only, is *this* human misery? I thought it was going to be loftier! *Dignified* suffering! *Meaningful* suffering— something perhaps along the line of Abraham Lincoln. Tragedy, not farce! Something a little more Sophoclean was what I had in mind. The Great Emancipator, and so on. It surely never crossed my mind that I would wind up trying to free from bondage nothing more than my own prick. LET MY PETER GO! There, that's Portnoy's slo- gan. That's the story of my life, all summed up in four heroic dirty words. A travesty! My politics, descended entirely to my putz! JERK-OFF ARTISTS OF THE WORLD UNITE! YOU HAVE NOTHING TO LOSE BUT YOUR BRAINS! The *freak* I am! Lover of no one and nothing! Unloved and unloving! And on the brink of becoming John Lindsay's Profumo!

So it seemed, an hour out of Athens.

Tel Aviv, Jaffa, Jerusalem, Beer-She'va, the Dead Sea, Sedom, 'Ein Gedi, then north to Caesarea, Haifa, Akko, Tiberias, Safed, the upper Galilee . . . and always it is more dreamy than real. Not that I courted the sensation either. I'd had enough of the improbable with my com- panion in Greece and Rome. No, to make some *sense* out of the impulse that had sent me running aboard the El Al flight to begin with, to convert myself from this bewildered runaway into a man once again—in control of my will, conscious of my intentions, doing as I wished, not as I must—I set off traveling about the country as though the trip had been undertaken deliberately, with forethought, desire, and for praiseworthy, if conventional, reasons. Yes, I would have (now that I was unaccountably here) what is called an educational experience. I would improve myself, which is my way, after all. Or was, wasn't it? Isn't that why I still read with a pencil in my hand? To *learn?* To become *better?* (than whom?) So, I studied maps in my bed, bought historical and archeological texts and read them with my meals, hired guides, rented cars—doggedly in that sweltering heat, I searched out and saw everything I could: tombs, synagogues, fortresses, mosques, shrines, harbors, ruins, the new ones, the old. I visited the Carmel Caves, the Chagall windows (me and a hundred ladies from the Detroit Hadassah), the Hebrew University, the Bet She'an excavations— toured the green kibbutzim, the baked wastelands, the rugged border outposts in the mountains; I even climbed a little ways up Masada under the full artillery fire of the sun. And everything I saw, I found I could assimilate and understand. It was history, it was nature, it was art. Even the Negev, that hallucination, I experienced as real and of this world. A desert. No, what was incredible and strange to me, more novel than the Dead Sea, or even the dramatic wilderness of Tsin, where for an eerie hour I wandered in the light of the bleaching sun, between white rocks where (I learn from my guidebook) the tribes of

Israel wandered for so long (where I picked up as a souvenir—and have in fact right here in my pocket—such a stone as my guide informed me Zipporah used to circumcise the son of Moses—) what gave my entire sojourn the air of the preposterous was one simple but wholly (to me) implausible fact: I am in a Jewish country. In this country, everybody is Jewish.

My dream begins as soon as I disembark. *I am in an airport where I have never been before and all the people I see—passengers, stewardesses, ticket sellers, porters, pilots, taxi drivers—are Jews.* Is that so unlike the dreams that your dreaming patients recount? Is that so unlike the kind of experience one has while asleep? But awake, who ever heard of such a thing? The writing on the walls is Jewish—Jewish graffiti! The *flag* is Jewish. The faces are the faces you see on Chancellor Avenue! The faces of my neighbors, my uncles, my teachers, the parents of my boyhood friends. Faces like my own face! only moving before a backdrop of white wall and blazing sun and spikey tropical foliage. And it ain't Miami Beach, either. No, the faces of Eastern Europe, but only a stone's throw from Africa! In their short pants the men remind me of the head counselors at the Jewish summer camps I worked at during college vacations—only this isn't summer camp, either. It's home! These aren't Newark high school teachers off for two months with a clipboard and a whistle in the Hopatcong mountains of New Jersey. These are (there's no other word!) the natives. Returned! This is where it all began! Just been away on a long vacation,

that's all! Hey, here *we're* the WASPs! *My taxi passes
through a big square surrounded by sidewalk cafés such
as one might see in Paris or Rome. Only the cafés are
crowded with Jews. The taxi overtakes a bus. I look inside
its windows. More Jews. Including the driver. Including
the policemen up ahead directing traffic! At the hotel I
ask the clerk for a room. He has a thin mustache and
speaks English as though he were Ronald Colman. Yet he
is Jewish too.*

And now the drama thickens:

*It is after midnight. Earlier in the evening, the prome-
nade beside the sea was a gay and lively crush of Jews—
Jews eating ices, Jews drinking soda pop, Jews convers-
ing, laughing, walking together arm-in-arm. But now as I
start back to my hotel, I find myself virtually alone. At
the end of the promenade, which I must pass beyond to
reach my hotel, I see five youths smoking cigarettes and
talking. Jewish youths, of course. As I approach them, it
becomes clear to me that they have been anticipating my
arrival. One of them steps forward and addresses me in
English. "What time is it?" I look at my watch and realize
that they are not going to permit me to pass. They are
going to assault me! But how can that be? If they are
Jewish and I am Jewish, what motive can there be for
them to do me any harm?*

*I must tell them that they are making a mistake. Surely
they do not really want to treat me as a gang of anti-
Semites would. "Pardon me," I say, and edge my body
between them, wearing a stern expression on my pale
face. One of them calls, "Mister, what time—?" where-*

*upon I quicken my pace and continue rapidly to the ho-
tel, unable to understand why they should have wished
to frighten me so, when we are all Jews.*

Hardly defies interpretation, wouldn't you say?

*In my room I quickly remove my trousers and shorts
and under a reading lamp examine my penis. I find the
organ to be unblemished and without any apparent signs
of disease, and yet I am not relieved. It may be that in
certain cases (perhaps those that are actually most se-
vere) there is never any outward manifestation of infection. Rather, the debilitating effects take place within the
body, unseen and unchecked, until at last the progress of
the disorder is irreversible, and the patient is doomed.*

*In the morning I am awakened by the noise from be-
yond my window. It is just seven o'clock, yet when I look
outside I see the beach already swarming with people. It
is a startling sight at such an early hour, particularly as
the day is Saturday and I was anticipating a sabbath
mood of piety and solemnity to pervade the city. But the
crowd of Jews—yet again!—is gay. I examine my member in the strong morning light and am—yet again—overcome with apprehension to discover that it appears to be
in a perfectly healthy condition.*

*I leave my room to go and splash in the sea with the
happy Jews. I bathe where the crowd is most dense. I am
playing in a sea full of Jews! Frolicking, gamboling Jews!
Look at their Jewish limbs moving through the Jewish
water! Look at the Jewish children laughing, acting as if
they own the place . . . Which they do! And the lifeguard,
yet another Jew! Up and down the beach, so far as I can*

see, Jews—and more pouring in throughout the beautiful morning, as from a cornucopia. I stretch out on the beach, I close my eyes. Overhead I hear an engine: no fear, a Jewish plane. Under me the sand is warm: Jewish sand. I buy a Jewish ice cream from a Jewish vendor. "Isn't this something?" I say to myself. "A Jewish country!" But the idea is more easily expressed than understood; I cannot really grasp hold of it. Alex in Wonderland.

In the afternoon I befriend a young woman with green eyes and tawny skin who is a lieutenant in the Jewish Army. The Lieutenant takes me at night to a bar in the harbor area. The customers, she says, are mostly longshoremen. Jewish longshoremen? Yes. I laugh, and she asks me what's so funny. I am excited by her small, voluptuous figure nipped at the middle by the wide webbing of her khaki belt. But what a determined humorless self-possessed little thing! I don't know if she would allow me to order for her even if I spoke the language. "Which do you like better?" she asks me, after each of us has downed a bottle of Jewish beer, "tractors, or bulldozers, or tanks?" I laugh again.

I ask her back to my hotel. In the room we struggle, we kiss, we begin to undress, and promptly I lose my erection. "See," says The Lieutenant, as though confirmed now in her suspicion, "you don't like me. Not at all." "Yes, oh yes," I answer, "since I saw you in the sea, I do, I do, you are sleek as a little seal—" but then, in my shame, baffled and undone by my detumescence, I burst out—"but I may have a disease, you see. It wouldn't be fair." "Do you think

that is funny too?" she hisses, and angrily puts her uni-
form back on and leaves.

Dreams? If only they had been! But I don't need
dreams, Doctor, that's why I hardly have them—because I
have this life instead. With me it all happens in broad
daylight! The disproportionate and the melodramatic, this
is my daily bread! The coincidences of dreams, the sym-
bols, the terrifyingly laughable situations, the oddly omi-
nous banalities, the accidents and humiliations, the
bizarrely appropriate strokes of luck or misfortune that
other people experience with their eyes shut, I get with
mine open! Who else do you know whose mother actually
threatened him with the dreaded knife? Who else was
so lucky as to have the threat of castration so straight-
forwardly put by his momma? Who else, on top of this
mother, had a testicle that wouldn't descend? A nut that
had to be coaxed and coddled, *persuaded,* drugged! to
get it to come down and live in the scrotum like a man!
Who else do you know broke a leg chasing *shikses?* Or
came in his eye first time out? Or found a real live monkey
right in the streets of New York, a girl with a passion for
The Banana? Doctor, maybe other patients dream—with
me, *everything happens.* I have a life *without* latent content. The dream thing *happens!* Doctor: *I couldn't get it
up in the State of Israel!* How's *that* for symbolism, *bubi?*
Let's see somebody beat that, for acting-out! Could not
maintain an erection in The Promised Land! At least not
when I needed it, not when I wanted it, not when there
was something more desirable than my own hand to stick

it into. But, as it turns out, you can't stick tapioca pudding into anything. Tapioca pudding I am offering this girl. Wet sponge cake! A thimbleful of something melted. And all the while that self-assured little lieutenant, so proudly flying those Israeli tits, prepared to be mounted by some tank commander!

And then again, only worse. My final downfall and humiliation—Naomi, The Jewish Pumpkin, The Heroine, that hardy, red-headed, freckled, ideological hunk of a girl! I picked her up hitchhiking down to Haifa from a kibbutz near the Lebanese border, where she had been visiting her parents. She was twenty-one years old, nearly six feet tall, and gave the impression that she was still growing. Her parents were Zionists from Philadelphia who had come to Palestine just before the outbreak of World War Two. After completing her Army service, Naomi had decided not to return to the kibbutz where she had been born and raised, but instead to join a commune of young native-born Israelis clearing boulders of black volcanic rock from a barren settlement in the mountains overlooking the boundary with Syria. The work was rugged, the living conditions were primitive, and there was always the danger of Syrian infiltrators slipping into the encampment at night, with hand grenades and land mines. And she loved it. An admirable and brave girl! Yes, a Jewish Pumpkin! *I am being given a second chance.*

Interesting. I associate her instantly with my lost Pumpkin, when in physical type she is, of course, my mother. Coloring, size, even temperament, it turned out

—a real fault-finder, a professional critic of me. Must have perfection in her men. But all this I am blind to: the resemblance between this girl and the picture of my mother in her high school yearbook is something I do not even see.

Here's how unhinged and hysterical I was in Israel. Within minutes of picking her up on the road, I was seriously asking myself, "Why don't I marry her and stay? Why don't I go up to that mountain and start a new life?"

Right off we began making serious talk about mankind. Her conversation was replete with passionate slogans not unlike those of my adolescence. *A just society. The common struggle. Individual freedom. A socially productive life.* But how naturally she wore her idealism, I thought. Yes, this was my kind of girl, all right—innocent, good-hearted, *zaftig*, unsophisticated and unfucked-up. Of course! I don't want movie stars and mannequins and whores, or any combination thereof. I don't want a sexual extravaganza for a life, or a continuation of this masochistic extravaganza I've been living, either. No, I want simplicity, I want health, I want her!

She spoke English perfectly, if a little bookishly—just a hint of some kind of general European accent. I kept looking at her for signs of the American girl she would have been had her parents never left Philadelphia. *This might have been my sister*, I think, another big girl with high ideals. I can even imagine Hannah having emigrated to Israel, had she not found Morty to rescue her. But who was there to rescue me? My *shikses?* No, no, I rescue *them.* No, my salvation is clearly in this Naomi! Her hair is worn like a child's, in two long braids—a ploy, of course, a dream-technique if ever there was one, designed to keep me from remembering outright that high school picture of Sophie Ginsky, who the boys called "Red," who would go so far with her big brown eyes and her clever head. In the evening, after spending the day (at my request) showing me around the ancient Arab city of Akko, Naomi pinned her braids up in a double coil around her head, like a *grand*mother, I remember thinking. "How unlike my model friend," I think, "with the wigs and the hairpieces, and the hours spent at Kenneth's. How my life would change! A new man!—with this woman!"

Her plan for herself was to camp out at night in a sleeping bag. She was on her week's vacation away from the settlement, traveling on the few pounds that her family had been able to give her for a birthday present. The more fanatical of her fellows, she told me, would never have accepted such a gift, and would probably disapprove of her for failing to do so. She re-created for me a discussion that had raged in her parents' kibbutz when she was still a little girl, over the fact that some people owned watches and others didn't. It was settled, after several impassioned meetings of the kibbutz membership, by deciding to rotate the watches every three months.

During the day, at dinner, then as we walked along the romantic harbor wall at Akko that night, I told her about my life. I asked if she would come back with me and have a drink at my hotel in Haifa. She said she would, she had much to say about my story. I wanted to kiss her then, but thought, "What if I *do* have some kind of venereal infection?" I still hadn't been to see a doctor, partly because of a reluctance to tell some stranger that I had had contact with a whore, but largely because I had no symptoms of any kind. Clearly nothing was wrong with me, and I didn't *need* a doctor. Nevertheless, when I turned to ask her back to the hotel, I resisted an impulse to press my lips against her pure socialistical mouth.

"American society," she said, dropping her knapsack and bedroll on the floor, and continuing the lecture she had begun as we drove around the bay to Haifa, "not only sanctions gross and unfair relations among men, but it encourages them. Now, can that be denied? No. Rivalry, competition, envy, jealousy, all that is malignant in human character is nourished by the system. Possessions, money, property—on such corrupt standards as these do you people measure happines and success. Meanwhile," she said, perching herself cross-legged upon the bed, "great segments of your population are deprived of the minimal prerequisites for a decent life. Is that not true, too? Because your system is basically exploitive, inherently debasing and unjust. Consequently, Alex"—she used my name as a stern teacher would, there was the thrust of admonition in it—"there can never be anything resembling genuine equality in such an environment. And that is indisputable, you cannot help but agree, if you are at all honest.

"For instance, what did you accomplish with your quizscandal hearings? Anything? Nothing, if I may say so. You exposed the corruption of certain weak individuals. But as for the system that trained them in corruption, on that you had not the slightest effect. The system was unshaken. The system was untouched. And why? Because, Alex"— uh-oh, here it comes—"you are yourself as corrupted by the system as Mr. Charles Van Horn." (By gum, still imperfect! Dang!) "You are not the enemy of the system. You are not even a challenge to the system, as you seem to think. You are only one of its policemen, a paid employee, an accomplice. Pardon me, but I must speak the truth: you think you serve justice, but you are only a lackey of the bourgeoisie. You have a system inherently exploitive and unjust, inherently cruel and inhumane, heedless of human values, and your job is to make such a system appear legitimate and moral by acting as though justice, as though human rights and human dignity could actually exist in that society—when obviously no such thing is possible.

"You know, Alex"—what now?—"you know why I don't worry about who wears a watch, or about accepting five pounds as a gift from my 'prosperous' parents? You know why such arguments are silly and I have no patience with them? Because I know that inherently—do you understand, inherently!"—yes, I understand! English happens, oddly enough, to be *my* mother tongue!—"inherently the system in which I participate (and voluntarily, that is crucial too—voluntarily!), that the system is humane and just. As long as the community owns the means of production, as long as all needs are provided by the community, as long as no man has the opportunity to accumulate wealth or to live off the surplus value of another man's labor, then the essential character of the kibbutz is being maintained. No man is without dignity. In the broadest sense, there is equality. And that is what matters most."

"Naomi, I love you."

She narrowed those wide idealistic brown eyes. "How can you 'love' me? What are you saying?"

"I want to marry you."

Boom, she jumped to her feet. Pity the Syrian terrorist who tried to take her by surprise! "What is the *matter* with you? Is this supposed to be humorous?"

"Be my wife. Mother my children. Every *shtunk* with a picture window has children. *Why not me?* I carry the family name!"

"You drank too much beer at dinner. Yes, I think I should go."

"Don't!" And again told this girl I hardly knew, and didn't even like, how deeply in love with her I was. "Love"—oh, it makes me shudder!—"loooove," as though I could summon forth the feeling with the word.

And when she tried to leave I blocked the door. I pleaded with her not go out and lie down on a clammy beach somewhere, when there was this big comfortable Hilton bed for the two of us to share. "I'm not trying to turn you into a bourgeois, Naomi, If the bed is too luxurious, we can do it on the floor."

"Sexual intercourse?" she replied. "With *you?*"

"Yes! With me! Fresh from my inherently unjust system! Me, the accomplice! Yes! Imperfect Portnoy!"

"Mr. Portnoy, excuse me, but between your silly jokes, if that is even what they are—"

Here a little struggle took place as I rushed her at the

side of the bed. I reached for a breast, and with a sharp upward snap of the skull, she butted me on the underside of the jaw.

"Where the hell did you learn that," I cried out, "in the Army?"

"Yes."

I collapsed into my chair. "That's some training to give to girls."

"Do you know," she said, and without a trace of charity, "there is something very wrong with you."

"My tongue is bleeding, for one—!"

"You are the most unhappy person I have ever known. You are like a baby."

"No! Not so," but she waved aside any explanation I may have had to offer, and began to lecture me on my shortcomings as she had observed them that day.

"The way you disapprove of your life! Why do you do that? It is of no value for a man to disapprove of his life the way that you do. You seem to take some special pleasure, some pride, in making yourself the butt of your own peculiar sense of humor. I don't believe you actually want to improve your life. Everything you say is somehow always twisted, some way or another, to come out 'funny.' All day long the same thing. In some little way or other, everything is ironical, or self-depreciating. Self-depreciating?"

"Self-deprecating. Self-mocking."

"Exactly! And you are a highly intelligent man—that is what makes it even more disagreeable. The contribution you could make! Such stupid self-deprecation! How disagreeable!"

"Oh, I don't know," I said, "self-deprecation is, after all, a classic form of Jewish humor."

"Not Jewish humor! No! *Ghetto* humor."

Not much love in that remark, I'll tell you. By dawn I had been made to understand that I was the epitome of what was most shameful in "the culture of the Diaspora." Those centuries and centuries of homelessness had produced just such disagreeable men as myself—frightened, defensive, self-deprecating, unmanned and corrupted by life in the gentile world. It was Diaspora Jews just like myself who had gone by the millions to the gas chambers without ever raising a hand against their persecutors, who did not know enough to defend their lives with their blood. The Diaspora! The very word made her furious.

When she finished I said, "Wonderful. Now let's fuck."

"You *are* disgusting!"

"Right! You begin to get the point, gallant Sabra! *You* go be righteous in the mountains, okay? *You* go be a model for mankind! Fucking Hebrew saint!"

"Mr. Portnoy," she said, raising her knapsack from the floor, "you are nothing but a self-hating Jew."

"Ah, but Naomi, maybe that's the best kind."

"Coward!"

"Tomboy."

"*Shlemiel!*"

And made for the door. Only I leaped from behind, and with a flying tackle brought this big red-headed didactic dish down with me onto the floor. I'll show her

who's a *shlemiel!* And baby! And if I have VD? Fine!
Terrific! All the better! Let her carry it secretly back in
her bloodstream to the mountains! Let it spread forth from
her unto all those brave and virtuous Jewish boys and
girls! A dose of clap will do them all good! This is what
it's like in the Diaspora, you saintly kiddies, this is what
it's like in the exile! Temptation and disgrace! Corruption and self-mockery! Self-deprecation—and self-defeca-
tion too! Whining, hysteria, compromise, confusion, disease! Yes, Naomi, I am soiled, oh, I am impure—and also
pretty fucking tired, my dear, of never being quite good
enough for The Chosen People!

But what a battle she gave me, this big farm cunt! this
ex-G.I.! This mother-substitute! Look, can that be so? Oh
please, it can't be as simplistic as that! Not *me!* Or with a
case like mine, is it actually that you can't be simplistic
enough! Because she wore red hair and freckles, this makes
her, according to my unconscious one-track mind, my
mother? Just because she and the lady of my past are offspring of the same pale Polish strain of Jews? This then is
the culmination of the Oedipal drama, Doctor? More
farce, my friend! Too much to swallow, I'm afraid! *Oedi-
pus Rex* is a famous tragedy, schmuck, not another joke!
You're a sadist, you're a quack and a lousy comedian! I
mean this is maybe going too far for a laugh, Doctor
Spielvogel, Doctor Freud, Doctor Kronkite! How about a
little homage, you bastards, to The Dignity of Man! *Oedi-
pus Rex* is the most horrendous and *serious* play in the
history of literature—it is not a gag!

Thank God, at any rate, for Heshie's weights. They became mine after he died. I would carry them into the backyard, and out in the sunshine I would lift and lift and lift, back when I was fourteen and fifteen years old. "You're going to give yourself a *tsura* yet with those things," my mother would warn me from her bedroom window. "You're going to get a cold out there in that bathing suit." I sent away for booklets from Charles Atlas and Joe Bonomo. I lived for the sight of my torso swelling up in my bedroom mirror. I flexed under my clothes in school. I examined my forearms on the street corner for bulge. I admired my veins on the bus. Somebody someday would take a swing at me and my deltoids, and they would live to regret it! But nobody swung, thank God.

Till Naomi! For her, then, I had done all that puffing and quivering under the disapproving gaze of my mother. That isn't to say that she still didn't have it over me in the calves and the thighs—but in the shoulders and chest I had the edge, and forced her body down beneath me— and shot my tongue into her ear, tasting there the grit of our day's journey, all that holy soil. "Oh, I am going to fuck you, Jew girl," I whispered evilly.

"You are crazy!" and heaved up against me with all her considerable strength. "You are a lunatic on the loose!"

"No, oh no," I told her, growling from my throat, "oh no, you have got a lesson to learn, Naomi," and pressed, pressed hard, to teach my lesson: O you virtuous Jewess, the tables are turned, *tsatskeleh! You* on the defensive now, Naomi—explaining your vaginal discharge to the entire kibbutz! You think they got worked up over those watches! Wait'll they get a whiff of this! What I wouldn't

give to be at that meeting when you get arraigned on
the charge of contaminating the pride and future of
Zion! Then perhaps you'll come to have the proper awe
for us fallen psychoneurotic Jewish men! Socialism exists,
but so too do spirochetes, my love! So here's your intro-
duction, dear, to the slimier side of things. Down, down
with these patriotic khaki shorts, spread your chops, blood
of my blood, unlock your fortressy thighs, open wide that
messianic Jewish hole! Make ready, Naomi, I am about to
poison your organs of reproduction! I am about to change
the future of the race!

But of course I couldn't. Licked her earholes, sucked at
her unwashed neck, sank my teeth into the coiled braids
of hair . . . and then, even as resistance may actually have
begun to recede under my assault, I rolled off of her
and came to rest, defeated, against the wall—on my back.
"It's no good," I said, "I can't get a hard-on in this place."

She stood up. Stood over me. Got her wind. Looked
down. It occurred to me that she was going to plant the
sole of her sandal on my chest. Or maybe proceed to kick
the shit out of me. I remembered myself as a little school-
boy pasting all those reinforcements into my notebook.
How has it come to this?

"'Im-po-tent in Is-rael, da da daaah,'" to the tune of
"Lullaby in Birdland."

"Another joke?" she asked.

"And another. And another. Why disclaim my life?"

Then she said a kind thing. She could afford to, of
course, way up there. "You should go home."

"Sure, that's what I need, back into the exile."

And way way up there, she grinned. That healthy, monumental Sabra! The work-molded legs, the utilitarian shorts, the battle-scarred buttonless blouse—the beneficent, victorious smile! And at her crusty, sandaled feet, this . . . this what? This *son!* This *boy!* This *baby!* Alexander Portnoise! Portnose! Portnoy-oy-oy-oy-oy!

"Look at you," I said, "way up there. How big big women are! Look at you—how patriotic! You really *like* victory, don't you, honey? Know how to take it in your stride! Wow, are you guiltless! Terrific, really—an honor to have met you. Look, take me with you, Heroine! Up to the mountain. I'll clear boulders till I drop, if that's what it takes to be good. Because why not be good, and good and good and good—right? Live only according to principle! Without compromise! Let the other guy be the villain, right? Let the *goyim* make a shambles, let the blame fall solely on them. If I was born to be austere about myself, so be it! A grueling and gratifying ethical life, opulent with self-sacrifice, voluptuous with restraint! Ah, sounds good. Ah, I can just taste those rocks! What do you say, take me back with you—into the pure Portnovian existence!"

"You should go home."

"On the contrary! I should stay. Yes, stay! Buy a pair of those khaki short pants—become a man!"

"Do as you wish," she said. "I am leaving you."

"No, Heroine, no," I cried—for I was actually beginning to like her a little. "Oh, what a waste."

She liked that. She looked at me very victoriously, as though I had finally confessed to the truth about myself.

Screw her. "I mean, not being able to fuck away at a big healthy girl like you."

She shivered with loathing. "Tell me, please, *why* must you use that word all the time?"

"Don't the boys say 'fuck' up in the mountains?"

"No," she answered, condescendingly, "not the way that you do."

"Well," I said, "I suppose they're not as rich with rage as I am. With contempt." And I lunged for her leg. Because never enough. NEVER! I have TO HAVE.

But have *what?*

"No!" she screamed down at me.

"Yes!"

"*No!*"

"Then," I pleaded, as she began to drag me by her powerful leg across toward the door, "at least let me eat your pussy. I know I can still do that."

"Pig!"

And kicked. And landed! Full force with that pioneer's leg, just below the heart. The blow I had been angling for? Who knows what I was up to? Maybe I was up to nothing. Maybe I was just being myself. Maybe that's all I really am, a lapper of cunt, the slavish mouth for some woman's hole. Eat! And so be it! Maybe the wisest solution for me is to live on all fours! Crawl through life feasting on pussy, and leave the righting of wrongs and the fathering of families to the upright creatures! Who needs monuments erected in his name, when there is this banquet walking the streets?

Crawl through life then—if I have a life left! My head

went spinning, the vilest juices rose in my throat. Ow, my heart! And in Israel! Where other Jews find refuge, sanctuary and peace, Portnoy now perishes! Where other Jews flourish, I now expire! And all I wanted was to give a little pleasure—and make a little for myself. Why, why can I not have some pleasure without the retribution following behind like a caboose! Pig? Who, *me?* And all at once it happens again, I am impaled again upon the long ago, what was, what will never be! The door slams, she is gone—my salvation! my kin!—and I am whimpering on the floor with MY MEMORIES! My endless childhood! Which I won't relinquish—or which won't relinquish me! Which is it! Remembering radishes—the ones I raised so lovingly in my Victory Garden. In that patch of yard beside our cellar door. *My* kibbutz. Radishes, parsley, carrots—yes, I am a patriot too, you, only in another place! (Where I *also* don't feel at home!) But the silver foil I collected, how *about* that? The newspapers I carted to school! My booklet of defense stamps, all neatly pasted in rows so as to smash the Axis! My model airplanes—my Piper Cub, my Hawker Hurricane, my Spitfire! How can this be happening to that good kid I was, with my love for the R.A.F. and the Four Freedoms! My hope for Yalta and Dumbarton Oaks! My prayers for the U.N.O.! Die? *Why?* Punishment? *For what?* Impotent? *For what good reason?*

The Monkey's Revenge. Of course.

"ALEXANDER PORTNOY, FOR DEGRADING THE HUMANITY OF MARY JANE REED TWO NIGHTS RUNNING IN ROME, AND FOR OTHER CRIMES

TOO NUMEROUS TO MENTION INVOLVING THE
EXPLOITATION OF HER CUNT, YOU ARE SEN-
TENCED TO A TERRIBLE CASE OF IMPOTENCE.
ENJOY YOURSELF." "But, Your Honor, she is of age,
after all, a consenting adult—" "DON'T BULLSHIT ME
WITH LEGALISMS, PORTNOY. YOU KNEW RIGHT
FROM WRONG. YOU KNEW YOU WERE DEGRAD-
ING ANOTHER HUMAN BEING. AND FOR THAT,
WHAT YOU DID AND HOW YOU DID IT, YOU ARE
JUSTLY SENTENCED TO A LIMP DICK. GO FIND
ANOTHER WAY TO HURT A PERSON." "But if I may,
Your Honor, she was perhaps somewhat degraded before
I met her. Need I say more than 'Las Vegas'?" "OH,
WONDERFUL   DEFENSE,   JUST   WONDERFUL.
GUARANTEED TO SOFTEN THE COURT'S JUDG-
MENT. THAT'S HOW WE TREAT UNFORTUNATES,
EH, COMMISSIONER? THAT'S GIVING A PERSON
THE OPPORTUNITY TO BE DIGNIFIED AND HU-
MAN ACCORDING TO YOUR DEFINITION? SON OF
A BITCH!" "Your Honor, please, if I may approach the
bench—what after all was I doing but just trying to have
. . . well, what? . . . a little fun, that's all." "OH, YOU
SON OF A BITCH!" Well, why, damn it, can't I have
some *fun!* Why is the smallest thing I do for pleasure immediately illicit—while the rest of the world rolls laughing in the mud! *Pig?* She ought to see the charges and
complaints that are filed in my office in a single morning:
what people do to one another, out of greed and hatred!
For dough! For power! For spite! For *nothing!* What they
put a *shvartze* through to get a mortgage on a home!

A man wants what my father used to call an umbrella for a rainy day—and you ought to see those pigs go to work on him! And I mean the real pigs, the pros! Who do you think got the banks to begin to recruit Negroes and Puerto Ricans for jobs in this city, to send personnel people to interview applicants in Harlem? To do that simple thing? This *pig*, lady—Portnoy! You want to talk pigs, come down to the office, take a look through my In basket any morning of the week, I'll show you pigs! The things that other men do—and get away with! And with never a second thought! To inflict a wound upon a defenseless person makes them *smile*, for Christ's sake, gives a little *lift* to their day! The lying, the scheming, the bribing, the thieving—the larceny, Doctor, conducted without batting an eye. The indifference! The total moral indifference! They don't come down from the crimes they commit with so much as a case of indigestion! But me, I dare to steal a slightly unusual kind of a hump, and while away on my *vacation*—and now I can't get it up! I mean, God forbid I should tear the tag from my mattress that says, "Do Not Remove Under Penalty of Law"—what would they give me for that, the chair? It makes me want to *scream*, the ridiculous disproportion of the guilt! May I? Will that shake them up too much out in the waiting room? Because that's maybe what I need most of all, to howl. A pure howl, without any more words between me and it! "This is the police speaking. You're surrounded, Portnoy. You better come on out and pay your debt to society." "Up society's ass, Copper!" "Three to come out with those hands of yours up in the air, Mad Dog, or else we come in after you, guns blazing. One." "Blaze, you bastard cop, what do I give a shit? I tore the tag off my mattress—" "Two." "—But at least while I lived, *I lived big!*"

Aaaaaaaaaaaaaaaaaaaaaaaaaaaaaaaaaaaaaaaaaaaaaaaaaaa-
aaaaaaaaaaaaaaaaaaaaaaaaaaaaaaaaaaaaaaaaaaaaaaaaaaaa-
aaaaaaaaaaaaaaaaaaaaaaaaaaaaaaaaaaaaaaaaaaaaaaaaaaaa-
aaaaaaaaaaaaaaaaaaaaaaaaaaaaaaaaaaaaaaaaaaaaaaaaaaaa-
aaaaaaaaaaaaaaaaaaaaaaaaaaaaaahhhh!!!!!

PUNCH LINE

So [*said the doctor*]. Now vee may perhaps to begin. Yes?

ABOUT THE AUTHOR

PHILIP ROTH's first book, the novella and five stories entitled *Goodbye, Columbus,* was published in March 1959, and the following year received the National Book Award for Fiction. Mr. Roth was also honored in 1960 with an award from the National Institute of Arts and Letters. A long novel, *Letting Go,* was published in 1962, and his novel *When She Was Good* appeared in 1967. His short stories have been widely reprinted in anthologies of fiction in both this country and abroad, and have appeared in Martha Foley's annual collections, *The Best American Short Stories,* and in the *O Henry Prize Story* annuals.

In the ten years since the publication of *Goodbye, Columbus,* Mr. Roth has received grants from the Guggenheim, Rockefeller, and Ford foundations; and as a visiting writer, has served on the faculties of several American universities, most recently Princeton, the State University of New York at Stony Brook, and the University of Pennsylvania. He is thirty-five years old and lives in New York City.

February 1969